A MCKENZIE RIDGE NOVEL

HIDDEN

USA TODAY BESTSELLING AUTHOR

STEPHANIE ST. KLAIRE

HIDDEN

A MCKENZIE RIDGE NOVEL

STEPHANIE ST. KLAIRE

BOOKS BY STEPHANIE ST. KLAIRE

McKenzie Ridge Series

Rescued

Hidden

Forgotten

Fearless

Redemption

Brother's Keeper Series

The Fall of Declan

The Rise of Declan

Reclaiming Liam

Redeeming Luke

Pursuing Dace

Hunting Wylie

Love, Cass (a series companion novel)

The Keeper's Series

Final Deception

Familiar Threat

Deadly Pursuit

Fatal Diversion

Royal Reckoning

Forced Enemy

Trivial Deceit

Lethal Jeopardy

Dangerous Chaos

Corrupt Justice

Stand Alone

Chameleon Effect

ALSO READ

Don't forget to check out Stephanie St. Klaire's alter ego,
USA Today Bestselling Romantic Comedy and
Contemporary Author of Clean & Wholesome Romance,
Stephie Klaire.
Get started FREE…
www.stephieklaire.com

ACKNOWLEDGMENTS

Wow, another book published…
First and foremost, all glory to God for seeing me through
this journey, providing a way, and turning my trials to
triumphs. I am blessed.
To my hubby and our fave fab five (yes, five kids), this is all
for you…
To my parents for their endless support and encouragement,
thank you.
Special thanks to my dad for creating the star of this book,
Ruthie. She is the glue that holds this story together. HAHA!

My biggest thanks goes to all of my readers who took a
chance on a new author! You loved me, loved my book, raved
about it, and here we are with book two already. I hope you
love Hidden as much or more as you love Rescued. I will
keep bringing you the reads, as long as you'll have me!

I love you all more than bean dip…

HIGH-PITCHED SCREAMING HAD COLTON'S UNDIVIDED attention instantly. A brief stall allowed him to determine that it was coming from behind his home. Colton rushed through the back door, quickly making his way to the slight embankment that drifted down to the lakeshore, which rested just beyond his property. It was a woman screaming, and he only knew of one woman who would have access to the semi-private beach.

Worry and an anxious vibe rolled through him while he prepared for the worst. Something must have happened to *her,* and he was prepared to rescue her from her desperate cries. Wild thoughts of coyotes and wolves, or perhaps an ill-tempered bear, crossed his mind. Pulse racing, he made it to the edge of the beach where he quickly halted at the sight before him.

Laughter overcame him with such dramatic force that he bent at the waist, resting his hands on his knees in order to catch his breath. Megan Johnson was dancing and jumping around in the midst of a flock of rowdy...geese. She ran in a small circle, spinning around, trying to escape her attackers, all while holding a toddler over her head and out of reach from the vicious beasts. It looked like an awkward, spiritual, tribal dance with the baby as her offering to the Gods. The toddler giggled his way through the fearful event while yelling "duck" and clapping his hands.

Graceful wasn't a word he would use to describe Megan's dance of shame with the animals. She was awkward and clumsy, tripping and stumbling backwards, ready to fall to her brutal demise, taking the boy with her – but not before Colton swooped in to save the boy from falling, too. He also managed to grab the bag of day old bread that was dangling from Megan's pocket, right before she fell flat on her ass…in the chilly lake.

Colton was an animal lover, had many pets of his own and was known to care for the geese and lone duck that lived in their lake. The ferocious beasts were all too familiar with the old plastic-bag-full-of-bread and were after a treat, not so much the beautiful woman. They were easily corralled away from a dripping wet Megan, still sitting in the lake.

He noticed the two of them many times down the beach, feeding the geese and duck. He hoped his feathery friends would lure her closer, and it seemed today was his lucky day. She was a mess. He would be right here when she was ready to get cleaned up. If today worked out in his favor, he would bring his fowl friends a nice treat tomorrow.

* * *

STILL FLAILING HER ARMS ABOUT, SHE FINALLY REALIZED THE angry birds had moved on and were no longer out for blood. She watched as the "goose whisperer" himself, handsome fire fighter, Colton Sparks, rallied the fowl around him while he sat perched on an old weathered log…feeding them. She had been certain that this was a scene straight out of the Hitchcock movie, *The Birds,* so she knew what those monsters were capable of. But, there they sat, perfectly calm and patient, waiting for their turn to get a treat. They even took gentle bites from her nephew's hand.

How the hell did he do that? She answered her own question when she recalled their first meeting, just months prior at Dawson and Sam Tayler's wedding. She was the florist and new friend of the bride – he was one of the best men to the groom. They had spent that evening dancing close and sharing stories. Colton Sparks was easy on the eyes—tall, well-built, blonde hair, who had that sexy almost unkempt thing working and beautiful golden eyes. He was a hunky firefighter, who was a true, chivalrous, gentleman at heart. She didn't think they made men like him anymore.

His genuine heart and kind soul left her feeling like Cinderella. So, in true Cinderella fashion, she took off at midnight and didn't turn back. She knew better than to pursue a relationship – it was just better for everyone if she kept her distance. He was the kind of guy who wanted a white picket fence and a relationship, full of forevers. He already had the white picket fence, but she couldn't be his forever, no matter how tempting he was.

As luck would have it, she bought a house right next door to him. Fortunately, with his work hours and the acre or two between them, he had been pretty easy to avoid…until today when she and her nephew wandered a little farther than she would have liked. Damn birds.

A chilling shiver traced her spine, reminding her that she was still ass flat in the cold lake. Mortified by the show she must have provided, and the fact that she was still resting in the ice-cold water, she quickly found her feet and made her way out of the water to reclaim what was left of her dignity. A stinging sensation drew her attention to a nicely carved gap in her forearm, compliments of an embedded branch of sorts with a knife-sharp end. Of course, she was bleeding everywhere because dripping in muddy, cold water wasn't humiliating enough.

She made her way up the beach to where Colton and Jax, her nephew, were sharing a story, clean out of bread, and what appeared to be completely entranced sleeping geese snuggling in for affection. She rolled her eyes and shook her head ever so slightly, wondering again how he did it. Only moments ago, they were blood thirsty maniacs. Apparently, he had the same effect on birds as he did women.

Calm as they were, she still stood a safe distance so as to not *ruffle any feathers*. She did have a subtle sense of guilt over abandoning a two-year-old in the middle of those blood sucking animals. She watched as Colton stood and made his way to her. She kept a watchful eye on the geese, taking a step back when they began to get up and move. They waddled their way back down to the water and drifted off across the lake on their way to terrorize someone else, she thought.

"Hey, thanks for…uh…well, saving us. They've never done that before," she said with a sheepish smile, her embarrassment still evident by her rosy cheeks, while reaching for Jax.

Colton lifted the tot from his hip to hand him over. "You've probably never had a bag of bread dangling from your backside then…" He quickly pulled the little guy back noticing her bloody arm. "Whoa, that's a nasty cut. Why don't you come up to the house? I'll fix it up."

"It's okay, really. I have some Band-Aids and ointment. I'll be fine." She shrugged. She knew going into his house was the beginning of the end, and she wasn't one to tempt fate.

"What's with the just the one duck in a flock of geese?" she asked, trying to distract him from her gaping wound.

He playfully rolled his eyes at her and said, "Band-Aids, really? This is more than a Band-Aid job. I've got a first aid kit up at the house. C'mon."

He turned to walk up the path to his house and noticed she wasn't following. She stood with a bewildered look on her face as if she was debating whether or not this was a safe idea. "I'm a fire fighter, remember? I'm trained in this stuff. Helping people is my job. And the duck – her name is Ruthie – the geese took her in when the ducks wouldn't…strangest thing."

She took a moment, looked at her dripping arm, then took in the greater distance to her own house and gave in. "Okay, you're probably right. It's pretty gross."

He smiled at her with a wink and reached a hand out to her. She accepted it, and he pulled her up the small trail so she could walk in front of him. Again, the gentleman. He put Jax up on his shoulders and made a ride of it, earning himself giggles from the little guy and an endearing smile from the lady.

Smiling at the memory of their last meeting, he couldn't help the sense of optimism that consumed him. She may not think they were a good idea, but he thought otherwise. An odd circumstance to earn a second chance, but beggars can't be choosers.

He recalled how intrigued he was by her when they first met. He still was, and he wanted to get to know her better. There was something about her that had his attention from hello, something other than her beauty and the genuine nature about her that made his heart palpitate and his breaths catch. Despite their hours together, talking and dancing like old friends, he knew little about her, and he knew she wanted it that way. What was the mystery surrounding Megan Johnson? He couldn't wait to solve it.

2

____

MEGAN WAS WARMED BY THE GESTURE AND HOW GREAT Colton was with Jax. She shouldn't be surprised. She remembered his playfulness with Sam and Dawson's children, Ellie and Gavin. He was one of *those* guys – the kind you write about in your love-struck teen diary. The kind fairy tales are made of, and the kind that got sexier with a baby on his shoulders. That warmth was turning to tingles, and she scolded herself for responding to all of his adorable man-charm. *This* wasn't going to happen.

Colton abruptly stopped her at the gate. Megan gave him an odd look, not sure what to think when he called out for "Rambo." She was unsure what to think of a dog named Rambo but appreciated his consideration rather than surprising her with another random animal attack for the day. Or was she?

Megan quickly jumped behind Colton when Rambo came into view, and he was anything but a four-legged K9. When she saw what was headed directly for them, she thought a dog would be a more welcomed sight. Rambo approached with his head lowered and at full speed, charging them, forcing Megan to grab onto Colton in fear.

"Hey, it's okay. Rambo is a good guy!" Colton defended.

"What the hell is it?" She panicked.

"He's a rooster! Tell me you've seen a rooster before," he joked.

"What's wrong with him, where are his feathers?"

"He has feathers. He's just missing some...gives him character," Colton replied with confidence, clearly a fan of Rambo's.

Rambo began to circle them, focusing on Megan, smelling and pecking at her feet and ankles, getting to know his new friends. He was rather large, in her opinion, for a rooster. He had copper feathers, what were left of them, a black ring around his neck, and a disgusting red fleshy thing flopping over one eye. The only thing he was missing was a few tattoos to fill in those bald spots. Rambo looked like a hard ass. He also looked hungry.

What the hell was with this man and his birds, she wondered. Violent, bordering lethal, eat you for lunch birds.

She closed her eyes and buried her face in Colton's arm and asked, "Oh, my God, what is he doing. What is he..."

She looked down to see that her pecking friend was now perched on her feet and rubbing his head on her shins. Confused by his behavior, she gave Colton a bewildered look of shock before looking back to the rooster who had her cemented in place while he cuddled her legs.

"He's harmless if he knows you. I think he feels pretty good about you now," Colton laughed.

"And if he didn't *know* me?" she replied, tossing up air quotes with the word *know*.

"Well, he would be chasing you."

"Chasing me? Does he think he's a dog or something?"

she asked, her question more of a joke but closer to the truth than she could have ever imagined.

"Something like that. He was rescued from some kind of dog and cock fighting ring that was busted in the back woods a few years back. Pretty sure he was the smartest one there," Colton shared, remembering how he came across his guard rooster.

"Smart how? He's a rooster."

A look of offense and question traced the lines of his face. She had obviously hit a sore spot by questioning the intelligence of his pet...rooster. She had heard of his love for animals and should have known better. "He survived a cock fighting ring and apparently was bait in the dog ring. He plays dead."

"Plays...dead. Like a dog?" she asked in confusion.

"Exactly. He plays dead. Probably learned it from being around the dogs or something. When he was found, he was presumed dead. They picked him up to dispose of him with the rest of the deceased animals, and he took off running."

She began laughing hysterically at the thought of some poor man or woman charged with the duty of disposing of dead animal carcasses and one getting up and running off. "That's the funniest thing I've heard in a long time!"

"It is pretty funny. But yeah, he's smart. Sometimes, I think he thinks he's a dog. He follows commands and patrols the yard all day. Anyone comes by...he lets everyone know. If he doesn't know you...look out."

She bent down to gently pet Rambo, feeling a connection of sorts. He was a fighter, like her. She liked that. "Well, Rambo, I'm impressed."

"Hear that boy? The lady is impressed," Colton said, patting his rooster's head.

If Rambo could impress her, Colton had a fighting chance to impress her, too. Or so he hoped.

* * *

THEY MADE THEIR WAY TO THE REAR DOOR THAT ENTERED into a well-planned, tidy mudroom. There were various dog beds along one side and several perched on shelves above, making it evident that he had a few more pets. Of course he did. She looked around carefully, trying to avoid a surprise from one or more of the bed owners.

Colton reached for a small stack of clothing sitting on the tidy built-in folding table next to his washer and dryer. "Here, why don't you throw these on and toss your clothes in the wash real quick?"

She looked at him with an uneasy expression, stuttering over her words, unable to come up with a quick excuse.

"Relax. They're clean and much warmer than what you have on. It'll take a little bit to clean that wound up right anyway. You can change in here." Not giving her an opportunity to protest, he nodded to the small powder room to her left and closed the mudroom door behind him, bouncing Jax on his hip as he left.

Megan quickly changed and tossed her soiled clothes in the fastest cycle his washing machine had. This was an in and out job, no hanging out longer than necessary. Colton was tempting, which was why it was a quick one-time visit.

She made her way out of the mudroom to a kitchen and dining room that caused her jaw to drop. The large expansive space boasted a chef's kitchen with all of the modern amenities, giving away one of Colton's passions. The kitchen merged with the dining room and opened to the living space to the left.

Megan was impressed with how thoughtfully laid out each space was, appreciating the well-kept details. It wasn't the bachelor pad she had assumed it would be. He even had a glass-covered plate of cookies as his table centerpiece. It was comfortable, warm…homey. Reeling her thoughts back in from where they were headed, she took a seat at the dining room table and waited for Colton.

As if on cue, Colton walked in with what looked like an oversized tackle box. That was some first aid kit. She looked around him, unable to find Jax. She stood in a panic, calling his name. Colton intercepted her with his large hands on her shoulders to calm her.

"Hey, it's okay! He's in the other room, playing ball with Nancy. I thought she could distract him while we patch up that arm," he said, feeling guilty for drawing such emotion so quickly. He noticed how on edge she was with Jax and made a note to be more considerate of that hot button. Something must have happened. It wasn't typical *mom fear* – it was something greater. He was determined to figure out what that was.

Surprise crossed Megan's face at the mention of a woman's name. Of course, there was a woman there. Why wouldn't there be? Look at him. It made sense now. The home décor, tidiness…Colton had a live-in girlfriend. That thought should have offered relief and a really good excuse to keep her distance, but it didn't. It wrangled up something more like jealousy, which pissed her off. There wasn't any reason to be jealous. Even if he was available, she couldn't explore any kind of relationship with him.

"So, how long have you been dating?" She asked nonchalantly.

"Dating who? I don't have a girlfriend." He gave her a funny look of amusement while he began to clean her wound.

Squinting at the sting, she offered an assuming statement rather than a question, "Oh, you have a roommate."

"Nnnno, no roommate." His smug grin stung as much as the wound on her arm.

Megan was annoyed by the relief his two admissions granted. Shit, she was in trouble, she thought. She sat in silence for a moment, trying to decide how to gage just who Nancy was to him.

"No girlfriend, no roommate, no family to speak of. Just me and my pets. They're my family."

He finished bandaging her up in silence, enjoying the direction her inquiry was leaning. If he didn't know better, she had been jealous at the thought of a woman living there and relieved that he was as available as the air she breathed. This day may end in his favor after all.

As if she knew her presence was needed to solve the mystery at hand, in walked Nancy, Jax in tow, just as Colton applied the final strip of tape to the bandage. "Good timing… Nancy! I want you to meet Megan."

The snorting, one eyed, white English bulldog walked over to Megan for a hello sniff that earned her a timid pet from their guest. Megan began to giggle, eventually erupting into a tear jerking laugh. "That's Nancy?"

"Dog!" Jax said, firm grip on Nancy's collar.

"Yep, buddy, that's a dog alright! Nancy…is a dog!" More laughter poured out as Meg felt the overall silliness of the past several minutes.

"I thought she was like…a…live innnn…" she paused to choose her words carefully, "girl."

"A live in girl?" Boom, he was right. She *had* assumed the worst and had been jealous. A new wave of confidence rolled through him.

"Yeah, I mean look at your place. Look at *you*…you're…"

she paused with an *oh shit* look on her face. She was about to show her hand, "a nice guy."

Pleased with her quick save, she was hopeful he didn't catch on to her blushing cheeks and heavier breathing. This man was oh so bad for her, and he was single. There was that tingle again.

Jax joined in on the laughter, and his excitement had him tugging on Nancy's collar and yelling, "Dog!" over and over again.

"Honey, don't pull on her like that. You'll hurt her… gentle buddy," she said, moving her hand over his to show him how to handle his new friend.

"Nancy's okay. She's as gentle as they come. If she doesn't like something, she just leaves, but that rarely happens. She's a nurturer, very motherly."

"Motherly?"

"Yeah, she was left behind by a family who had left her locked in the house. She lost her eye trying to find a way out. Lost a whole litter of pups. Now, she takes care of everyone. She's our little mama around here," he said, giving her a praise worthy scratch of the ears.

"That's a horrible story! Just horrible!" Megan said in shock.

"It is, people do really dumb shit, but she is here now, and happy! She has a…gas…issue. But we overlook it – don't we Nance?"

Megan began to laugh at the odd, yet warming afternoon she was spending with her new friend and his critters, stinky as they were. He was making it hard to keep him in the friend zone with all of his charming ways, but she would fight the temptation he offered. Nancy may have fallen under his spell, but Megan was a step ahead of him and in full armor.

Colton recognized that he had been holding Megan's arm,

and now hand, for some time. The realization spread quickly, and they both found themselves speechless and unable to let go. The silence between them was deafening, and their locked eyes were creating a sweat worthy heat that was laced in undeniable desire. The spell was broken when a large German Shepherd entered the room and sat in front of Megan, holding a mewing kitten, by the nape of its neck, in his mouth.

She jumped, startled by yet another animal, and stated the obvious, "That's not Nancy! Oh, my God, it's eating a kitten!! Do something!!! Oh no, where's his other leg?" she shouted as she leaned back in her chair, attempting to distance herself from the cat-eating monster.

Colton laughed again, finding her antics amusing. She clearly had little to no experience with animals. "That's Duke. He only has three legs, but it doesn't slow him down."

Duke laid the tiny kitten in her lap while he sat at her feet. She scooped up the tiny ball of fur and held it close, inspecting it for any sign of harm. The small sounds and rooting nose promptly flooded her heart with warm fluttery feelings that were unfamiliar to her.

"That means it's feeding time again. If Nancy isn't around when they begin to cry, this ol' boy panics and brings them to me, one by one," Colton said, nodding to the nuzzling kitten.

"Aww, that is very sweet. Why does he need Nancy?"

"Oh, they're a stray litter. Found them on a hike a few days back. Coyote probably got mom."

"Oh, my God. That is awful. What is it with you and animals with a devastating back-story? Rambo, Nancy, and Duke…now this poor sweet kitten?" Her eyes began to water at the thought of what happened to its mother. What on earth was happening to her? They were animals, for crap's sake!

"Can you carry Whiskers there, and I'll grab these." He

went to get the large stack of bowls from the mudroom counter, but Megan took off at a dead run when she heard the front screen door open and close, followed by far away giggles.

"Jax!"

3

———

BEFORE COLTON COULD CALM OR WARN HER, SHE MADE HER way through the front screen door to the expansive wraparound porch. She found Jax sitting smack dab in front of the biggest behemoth of an animal with dark, serious eyes pinned on her tiny nephew. She rushed to him, putting herself between the beast and Jax. Now she was the focus of the dark eyed, pointy eared, gray monstrosity of a dog, so steely it almost made her wet her pants.

She looked adorable and maybe a little ridiculous in his oversized sweatpants and shirt. She guarded Jax, one arm straight out in front of her, legs planted firmly but apart, kitten in her other hand, raised above her head. Baby boys and kittens were not on the appetizer menu today if she could help it.

Colton had a few endearing thoughts, followed by a few that were naughty, before her words brought him back to present.

"What the hell is it? What do I do? What do I do?" she hollered as if in battle.

She heard the cries of the tiny kitten again, only in unison this time. She scanned the expansive porch that reached either end of the house, each end flanked with a porch swing. Then she saw the dark stained rocking chairs with a basket placed between them, tucked under a small table. More kittens. Megan ducked her head, confusion crossing her furrowed brow, and saw Nancy in the basket of kittens, nuzzling them. Duke was perched to her far right, then a black and white dog, and finally Rambo.

Her gaze reverted to the black and white dog. It wasn't a dog at all – it was a one-horned goat with crossed eyes. "Baaaaahaha."

Relaxing in her battle stance, she eased back from her oversized nemesis and looked to Colton with a wide-eyed *what the hell* look. At second glance, she could see each of the animals had the same tilt to their head and the same *what the hell* look pinned on her.

"So you met big boy Boss! He's our gentle giant."

"Boss? Of course…Boss." Her tone full of snark. Anything that big deserved the name Boss.

Colton lined the bowls up against the front porch railing in order of size, largest to smallest. His pets sat patiently, waiting for the magic words. When he said *eat up*, they each made their way to their designated bowl, also in size order. The largest bowl was vacant, and big ol' Boss was still front and center, watching her every move.

"What's going on here? Wha-what is he doing? Why isn't he eating?" She stuttered.

"He hasn't been told to yet." Colton walked to where Megan was standing and made a quick hand gesture that prompted Boss to find his vacant bowl and eat.

"Hasn't been…he's deaf? Of course you have a deaf dog. What's the goat's story?" She was really intrigued now. This guy was a real friggin' Dr. Doolittle. The row of furry, feathery fannies was now complete.

"Oh, Doug? Their stories are similar to each other's. I take the animals nobody wants. The animals they think are damaged."

"Wow, that's very admirable." As if he couldn't get any more perfect, he nailed her with his own heart-wrenching story.

"I don't know about admirable. I just understand them. I grew up in the system, the kid nobody wanted, so I give them all a home."

And there it was, the final nail in the coffin where her resistance to his charm and sexy rested. This man was incredible. Tears welled, and her heart pinched at the thought of a lonely orphaned Colton. How could anyone not want him? He wasn't like anyone she had ever met. She wanted him, even if she couldn't have him.

He motioned for her to take a seat on one of the rocking chairs, which she did. He set down the plate of cookies from the dining room table, giving one to Jax with her permission. Then he pulled two tiny bottles from his pocket and handed one to her, keeping one for himself. She gave him a puzzled look before watching him pick up a kitten and begin to feed it. Picking up on his cue, she followed his lead and fed her little furry friend.

They sat long beyond the kitten feeding, sharing stories and enjoying each other's company. Colton filled her in on Boss being their deaf, gentle giant that had seizures, and Doug the goat's special affections for his partner in crime, Nancy. Boss had found the kittens on their hike, no more than a few hours old.

They made sandwiches and talked about her limited experience with animals. It began and ended with purse-sized pups that her friends toted around as accessories. Amused by his brood, she joked that they were like a really small gang, all looking out for and taking care of each other. She loved their closeness, despite their varying differences. She had a feeling that was because of him.

The conversation was light and pleasant before it turned a bit more serious, having shared his every detail from his orphan status to orphaned, animal whisperer status. He wanted to know more about Megan. After hours of conversation, he knew very little about her.

"So, tell me your story, Megan Johnson. We've been talking about me all night. I'm starting to think you like me," he teased with a wiggle of his brow.

Her relaxed body language tensed at his question. She didn't like talking about her past, or the story she wanted people to know, anyway. She also didn't like that he was on to something – she *did* like him. But, both issues needed to remain vague for everyone's sake.

"Well, you know where I live," she joked, nodding to her house in the distance.

She winked at him, remembering how they met. "You also know I own Blooming Grounds, the perfect mix of florist and barista!"

"I'm from New York, originally. My sister passed away in a car accident with her husband last year. That's how that sweet boy ended up with me." She paused, carefully considering how much or little to tell so as not to raise suspicion. "I wanted a different life for us, a fresh start, simplicity. We ended up here in McKenzie Ridge."

She stalled before saying, "A friend told me about it. It sounded perfect, the simple life I was looking for."

She smiled, remembering her sister and the life she had before devastation struck. Her life took a dramatic turn the night her sister had left them. Her heart ached, thinking about Jax growing up without her and all that Lydia was missing.

"I'm sorry. It sounds like you two were close," he said with a soft voice, sympathetic.

She smiled and snorted a laugh. "We were. Very close. I see her in him every day, so I suppose it could be worse. I could have none of her at all."

"You're very good with him, and he obviously adores you."

"Oh, it wasn't always like this. I didn't grow up around kids, never babysat. One day, without warning, I have this baby, who I'm putting diapers on backward and learning the hard way that babies don't drink chocolate milk. Oh, and with boys, you better get that new diaper over him fast and hope there isn't a draft." She laughed again at how far they had really come. She had so many nights flooded in tears trying to figure out how to be a mom overnight and without a single person to call for help.

"Now who's admirable?" he replied, sincerity in every word.

"I don't know about admirable," she said, turning his words back on him. "It's all worth it. He's worth it."

"Well, I think you're both pretty terrific," he said, looking down at the small boy sleeping in his arms.

They sat for a while longer, watching the sun set behind the hills and peaks in the west. Animals were scattered about their feet, with the exception of Rambo, who kept watch over the compound. Colton appreciated her opening up to him but sensed a sadness about her beyond the loss of her sister. There was a mystery there, and he wanted to solve it and find his way into her heart. She was special.

4

———

The following morning, Megan started her day at the shop she had purchased shortly after finding her way to McKenzie Ridge. Blooming Grounds sat in the heart of Main Street, on the North side, and it was well known for its quirky combination. It provided the town's only florist but also served as a coffee shop, full of morning pastries and light afternoon lunches. Nothing made flower shopping more pleasant than the aroma of freshly brewed, local coffee or having a cup of Joe amongst fragrant, fresh blooms.

Fairly new to McKenzie, she was in love. It was a small mountain town nestled in the Pacific Cascade Mountains of Oregon. It's breathtaking Pacific Northwest beauty and ample outdoor activities made it an appealing tourist attraction year round. McKenzie's Main Street had a rustic charm, lined with unique shops, delicious eateries, and an array of other things to explore.

It was the perfect place to settle down, for now, different from the glamorous, high society, socialite life she abruptly abandoned nine months prior.

The simple life of small-town living was anything but

simple. It was *damn* hard! Although its charm was appealing to her, it didn't boast the amenities she was accustomed to— her idea of a spa and what resided in Lumberjack nation were two completely different things.

Shopping was plentiful in McKenzie, if you were looking for antler chandeliers, coonskin hats, and, of course, flannel. There was zero purpose for Christian Louboutin and Jimmy Choo in her new world, and you wouldn't find Louis or Jimmy for miles and miles. She settled for blue-collar jeans that actually did wonders for her ass – not bad for forty dollars – Ugg-style boots, and, of course, the occasional fur vest and flannel.

She was trying to blend in, even bought drug store makeup and wore her hair in a messy bun. Gone were her days of Mac, Prada, and Barneys. Here were the days of simplicity and becoming Megan Johnson.

She was lost in thought, recalling the previous night with Colton and his furry and feathered clan. He walked her home after sunset, carrying a sleeping Jax. The dogs and goat followed while Rambo manned the fort until their return.

He was so good with Jax, such a kind soul and easy on the eyes. Electricity sparked when his arms brushed hers, handing her the tiny tot. He gave her goose bumps and made her warm in all the right places. Unfortunately, they couldn't explore those feelings. She could leave at any time…today or 10 years from now—there was no way to know. It wouldn't be fair to drag Colton into her mess.

She could dream about it, though, and welcomed those dreams each night. Colton was on shift at the House the next several days, which was probably a good thing. The House, as it was called, held Police, Fire, and Emergency Medical. She was the only one from the tight group of friends who didn't work at the House or hospital. They all tended to work the same shifts, allowing them to work together as well as play together. She was happy to be a part of the family-like group, even if it meant seeing a lot of Colton.

Megan had struggled for months to keep Colton out of her mind, a mighty feat with him living within view. After last evening, the task of maintaining the "no sparks for Sparks" campaign was bordering impossible. If he were home, it would be far too easy to wander down to those rowdy geese and one duck with a bag of bread hanging from her back pocket again. He invited her back, anytime, to "help with the kittens." He was too tempting, and she wasn't above using orphaned kittens as an excuse to visit.

* * *

MEG SPENT THE NEXT FEW DAYS PREPPING FOR BLOOMING Grounds' first wine tasting. She loved Blooming Grounds. It was sweet, charming even. It had a uniqueness that set it apart from other shops in town with the coffee shop included. She wanted to put her mark on it, however, as the new owner, to offer sophistication and something new, a taste of the old her.

Breweries and distilleries were a popular culture in the area – it was part of the tourist attraction. The wine industry was beginning to feel Oregon's mark on it as well. There was something about the cool mountain weather and mineral bearing spring water that provided a harvest unlike any other.

She wanted to fit in here, wanted to be successful in McKenzie Ridge and create something this town wouldn't come up with on its own. Hosting wine and specialty beer tastings from local makers was her new mission. A win for area businesses and a win for the new business owner in town. This was the first time she had to depend on herself completely, and it felt good.

Megan invited her new friends, as few as they were, and opened the wine tasting invite to the town and its tourists. Sam Tayler and her handsome husband, Dawson, arrived first. They were like a brunette Ken and Barbie with two darling kids and a romance to die for. Their recent wedding was where she met Colton.

She appreciated the gang filing in a little early to take the edge of her nerves down a notch. Having their support was priceless. They really made the party a party. The adoration amongst them and strong bond were something she had never witnessed before and hoped she would have the chance to be a part of indefinitely.

Next to arrive was Sam's best "sister friend," Everly Shaw, and her Granny Lou. Lou was a kick-in-the-pants, old gal who seriously lacked a filter. That's why Megan liked her so much. She made a mental note to keep an eye on her drinking, though, as this was a professional event. She didn't expect Granny Lou to drink a drop of *fussy juice*. She had her *big purse*, which meant she was packin'…liquor.

The rest filed in shortly after…Morgan Jameson, Jessie Clarke, Carigan O'Reilly, and, of course, the dashing Blake Cooper. There was something to be said about the town and its hunky men. The shenanigans were off to a racing start as they all noticed hard ass, combat boot wearing Jessie, wearing a dress. Jessie was as tiny as they came but badass to the core. She kept up with every man and ran circles around a few as a Firefighter. She was tough as nails but, apparently, owned a pair of sexy heels.

Blake, of McKenzie's finest, seemed especially intrigued by Jessie. Distracted even. If one didn't know better, it would appear that the looks they were exchanging were about more than the little black dress Jessie was wearing. Morgan, Blake's partner, and Carigan, Dawson's partner in the ambulance, might have caught the same vibe based on their snickers, which earned them a middle finger hello from Jessie.

One person was missing. The only one who flooded her every thought for days and consumed her dreams each night. She was happy to see everyone else, but he was the one she was counting down the hours for.

The ground beneath her feet quaked, and her breath caught when the door swung open in what felt like slow motion. He was finally there and looking hot as hell in a black, perfectly tailored suit and a crisp white dress shirt, unbuttoned just enough to make her drool. Her body hummed in places it shouldn't, especially in public.

She shifted her stance from one foot to the other, trying to relieve the wakeup call he was sending. For a cool crisp fall evening, it was getting hot. She adjusted her skirt, straightened her posture, shoulders back, and approached him with her best smile. She was met first by his enticing scent—cool and fresh with a hint of citrus and sandalwood. When he hugged her hello, it was nearly her undoing.

* * *

THE ONLY THING COLTON SAW WHEN HE ENTERED BLOOMING Grounds was the sexy muse who owned it. She stood amongst a group of patrons, swirling a wine glass in her hand, her body language making it obvious she was describing what they were all tasting. She had a regal quality, which boasted a sense of class and charm that screamed of money and culture. She was easy on the eyes with her petite yet curvy figure, long auburn hair, and glassy golden eyes with her slightly turned up nose but hard on the heart. He needed a way in.

She made simplicity reek of elegance and ordinary look stunning and effortless to pull off. Megan wore a black, body contouring, pencil skirt that started high on her waist and hugged her body clear to mid-calf. To be that skirt, holding those curves, would be to have lived and died in the same moment. She looked of glamour with her glassy gem necklace that rested just above her ample gifts that were on display, compliments of the shape hugging, white, deep v-top.

The tall, shiny, red, peek-a-boo, fuck-me heels that she floated around in did things to him that he was almost ashamed of. He was glad he wore the jacket that he debated earlier in the evening. It now rested on his arm, camouflaging the sudden reason for his really tight pants.

5

———

THE INAUGURAL TASTING EVENT WAS OFF TO A GOOD START and quite the success. Patrons had been in and out of Blooming Grounds coffee shop – turned – tasting room, all evening. Finally catching her breath, Megan was able to stop and visit with her friends as things began to die down for the evening.

She interrupted a conversation that had her name written all over it – a set up. Sam and Evie were discussing the annual Holiday Fair with the group, explaining its possible demise. The committee had been formed, made up of the usual – the friends from the gang and a handful of retired locals. They lacked, however, a leader.

The Holiday Fair was a kick off to the holiday season. It gave local crafters, hobby bakers, and those with various wares, a place to peddle their goods. It also provided a unique shopping experience with typically one-of-a-kind items for patrons to scoop up.

The proceeds from McKenzie's event-of-the-year bene-fited the local children's charity that the Fire, Police, and

Emergency Medical ran. They assisted the area youth throughout the year with various needs, from scholarships to participate on the local sports team to a new set of clothes for someone in need. Christmas was, by far, their biggest challenge. The fair funded their holiday toy and coat drive, which ensured every child, who normally goes without at Christmas, had something special and a warm winter jacket.

The more the women talked, the more the men engaged with heartwarming stories of children they were able to help in surrounding communities. They were a small mountain town but part of a larger reach that spread for miles, which they enveloped into their community as well. Megan took in their ideas, past successes, and the stories of those in need. The wheels started turning.

Megan wasn't immune to charity work. It had been her primary focus until becoming who she was in McKenzie. She had spent her days on various fundraising committees for different charities, and nights hosting and attending the events she adored most. This Holiday Fair sounded nothing short of an event she could get behind, more so, take to the next level. Party planner extraordinaire, this was how she would make her mark on the town at epic proportions.

"So, are you in?" Sam asked, full of excitement.

"Before you say yes and we quit twisting your arms, you know this is a lot of work, free work...as in no pay, no free time...work!" Evie joked.

"Good! I love this kind of stuff! It will be fun! I need to keep busy," Megan replied with a subtle look to Colton. She most definitely did need to keep busy, or he would be her next big event.

"I used to do stuff like this all of the time. Really, I already have a ton of ideas and ways I think we can make it bigger and better than ever!" she finished.

"Why does that not surprise me, Fancy Pants?"

Jessie questioned, giving her an endearing nickname that most would be offended by. If Jessie called you anything at all crude, vulgar, or unsavory, it meant she liked you. Megan loved her nickname, or nicknames rather. Jessie had several for her.

Megan was flattered that they had asked her to lead the mission, even if it was only because she was the newbie sucker in town and none of them wanted the job. They were still going to be helping, and that meant a lot of fun girl time while they planned the party of the year. This was her chance to really show her colors, make her mark, without showing who she really was.

* * *

THE NIGHT WAS GOING SO WELL, AND MEGAN WAS overwhelmed with enthusiasm. The turnout was a fair share of locals and tourists alike, each complimenting her event and promising to come again. Her goal for the evening had been realized. She was developing a new, regular, local crowd and padding her business with returning visitors to their small town. Mission accomplished.

Her new friends were in part to thank as their influence and extended invites contributed to the list of attendees. It had been so long since she had this kind of camaraderie, friends who she could count on. Maybe one day, she could even confide in them, but for now, it worked just as it was. She wasn't yet ready to show her cards.

Colton's eyes had been on her all night – she hadn't noticed it as much as she had *felt* it. As the evening expired and the festivities wore down to a dull roar, it was harder not to notice. It was hot in Blooming Grounds, but Megan and Colton were the only two sweating.

The atmosphere died down to an intimate crowd, consisting of just the friends. Even Granny Lou said, "good night," off to relieve the babysitter caring for Sam and Dawson's children as well as Jax. Since the little ones would be sleeping, she offered to keep them all until morning, giving the adults a night to themselves. Even more reason to break out the good stuff.

Megan excused herself to the back to pull out a special bottle or two of wine she kept off the sales floor, just for the gang. It was time to celebrate a successful evening and to thank them for their help when the last customers found their way out of her shop. She began shifting crates, when heat poured down her spine, waking her libidinous desires. She didn't have to see him to know he had followed her.

"You are completely in your element tonight," he said.

She turned and smiled. "You think so? I love this, hosting events, doing something different."

"I can tell. You know how to work a room. I think you could have sold them all cases of soap just as well as wine," he joked, pinning her against the crates with just a look.

"Can I grab that?" he asked, reaching a hand out to her.

Her eyes widened at his question. She looked down at her chest and back to him with his hands extended. "Uh…um… uhhh…"

She choked on her words, stuttered and slurred. Perfectly sexy, she thought. Not sure how to answer him, her eyes glanced back and forth watching the door then him. As she mulled over what was happening, she knew one thing for sure – she didn't want anyone to walk in on what she thought was about to happen.

Just as she started to lean his direction, closing the gap

between them, a sly grin crossed his face as his brow raised in question, sounding alarms in her head. Mission aborted, she saw the flashing neon signs and red flags waving, realizing he wasn't asking to grab any part of her. She backed away, cleared her throat and raised her own eyebrows as if she was the one silently questioning him.

Colton pointed to the case of wine behind her and said, "I meant…the wine, but I am totally open to other offers."

"Oh…I know, I mean, of course you were. What else would you have meant by that?" She shrugged it off as if he was the one reading the situation wrong.

"Of course," he nodded, his charming grin still in place. "Can I help? Which one are you looking for?"

Megan turned to the racks behind her and pointed out which case she was aiming for. It had been placed in a precarious spot behind a few others to avoid mixing it into the evening's offering. When she turned to step away and allow him access, she hit a large wall of hot, hard muscle—Colton.

Narrowing the space between them, he closed in, hoping to finish what she had started moments before. When she bumped into him and lost her footing, he caught her in his arms, pulling her close. So close he could feel her racing pulse and her hot heavy breath against his neck.

"Thank…you," she muttered with her hands flat against his chest.

"You look amazing tonight."

"You clean up pretty well for a hunky firefighter. Nice… suit," she said with heavy, hooded eyes and a breathy, tone-trickling desire.

"Breathtaking." He leaned in to kiss her, full of passion and desire. The anticipation was almost too much after all of these months, hoping he would get his chance, wondering what she tasted like.

Megan relaxed into his embrace and took everything he had to offer. She slid her hands up his chest, taking note of every rock hard muscle she skimmed, finally resting her arms around his neck. His hands drifted further south, wrapping around her just below her waist at the curve of her perfect ass where he pulled her into his excitement, showing her just what she was doing to him. Fireworks. It was true what they said about *the one*…there would be *fireworks*.

"Hey, Meg can we grab more of that chee… Never mind. Carry on. You don't even hear me anyway… I'll just head back out…so, yeah." Evie joked, backing out of the room, giving them privacy.

* * *

"Hey!" Jessie scolded, "Where's the cheese?"

"Umm, probably melting!" she replied with a laugh. "Sparks and Meg are back there. Decided to give them… some quiet time."

"Sparks and Priss Pants? Aww, shit! I knew it!" Jessie said excitedly with an eye roll. "So what does that have to do with the cheese?"

Laughing at Jessie's disgust, Evie asked, "Where are you going?"

She stood from the table they had all migrated to and found her way to the back, apparently hungry, leaving the chuckles and giggles behind at the table. She stood in the doorway and scanned the room. Finding her target, she brushed passed the canoodling couple with an eye roll and heavy, meant to be heard, sigh of disgust. She grabbed the platter she was looking for from the cooler, taking a platter of chocolate-dipped everything while she was there.

Making her way back past Megan and Colton, she made

sure to bump in to them and holler, "Not near the food…get a room!" before heading back to the store front to rejoin the waiting group.

Breaking the kiss at the brash interruption, Megan rested her forehead on Colton's chest while she caught her breath. "Wow…" was all she could say.

"Yeah, wow. Sometimes I forget Jessie's a girl, and I want to kick her ass. This being one of those times," he chuckled.

"Colton, we shouldn't have…" She was quickly interrupted by another small kiss.

"No, we should have, and we did. I liked it. *You* liked it. Nothing more to it. Just don't over think it," he reasoned.

She hesitated for a moment, collecting her thoughts. She tried to come up with an appropriate response that wouldn't encourage him any more than she already had, but wouldn't hurt his feelings either. "I'm just not a relationship girl, not right now. I don't want to give you the wrong idea."

He smiled again, resting his forehead on hers, stroking her cheek with his thumb. "Honey, you didn't give me the wrong anything. We are just two people enjoying each other's company and sharing a little kiss. Nothing more, nothing less."

She grinned at his admission and warmed at his sincerity. He was letting her off the hook, even though she knew he wanted more. She just couldn't give it, not now, and maybe, not ever. He really was the perfect guy, and as her luck would have it, she met him at the worst possible time ever.

"Okay," she said with a nod. "I guess we should get back out there. Are we good?"

"We're great. Go ahead. I'll grab this case and be right behind you."

She kissed his cheek, leaving her hand on his chest a little longer than she intended before walking back to the front of her shop.

He watched her leave, enjoying the extra sway to her step, knowing it was for him. "It's okay, darlin'," he said quietly to himself, "I'll wait for you."

6

———

The wine was nearly gone, Blooming Grounds put back together, and plenty of laughter shared. The night was creeping to end, as much as Megan didn't want it to. The brewing friendships and camaraderie between this family-like group of friends had her hooked. Even if one of them was making it hard for her to sit comfortably.

Colton and Megan had been seated next to one another, compliments of meddling matchmakers in the group, and she was pretty sure it began and ended with Sam and Evie, likely assisted by Carigan and Morgan.

She adored them for their thoughtfulness, but they were making it increasingly hard to keep things in the friend zone with the handsome firefighter next to her.

It wasn't lost on the crowd that they laughed a little harder at each other's jokes and had a few more lingering looks than the rest. All it took was one kiss. One kiss branded forever in her mind as the quick beginning and end to anything that could transpire. Colton may be half way to dating already, but Megan was stuck in the past and not ready or able to move forward, no matter how hot and tempting the muse.

Thoughts of their brief escapade danced around in her head, blushing her cheeks. His grin and knowing-wink let her know that he knew exactly what she was recounting in her mind. If he read her that well already, she was in trouble.

The shifting in her seat, from the fury of heat he was causing her in all of her unmentionable places, earned her a chuckle. Damn, he was good.

* * *

A LOUD HONKING SOUND BROKE THE SPELL AND DREW everyone's attention to the street just outside. Megan was sitting, facing the window, and immediately spotted the cause for alarm just before he was hit by a car. A well-dressed man had been staring back at her while crossing the street from the opposite side and stepped right in front of a vehicle traveling down Main Street.

Screams scattered from the late-night crowd that had been out enjoying the warm fall evening. One scream in particular caught her by surprise…her own. The friends vacated their table and rushed outdoors to assess the scene. All off duty emergency and rescue personnel, they jumped into action and did what came as second nature to them.

Carigan grabbed Dawson's oversized professional first aid kit that he kept in his truck, a few cars away. Megan stood there completely in shock as Dawson and Colton assisted Carigan in an impressive attempt to save the stranger laying in the street before them. Blake set out flares and redirected the evening traffic and "looky-loos," making a path for the ambulance and fire truck that could be heard in the distance.

The upset driver that hit the mystery man was tended to

by Morgan while Jessie cleared the sidewalk of gawkers. Evie stood above the scene, phone to ear, directing and updating dispatch, and Sam stood at Meg's side, consoling her, wiping the tears she hadn't even realized were there. It was like a sobering scene straight out of a movie. The only thing missing was the eerie music, full of dramatic highs and lows to match the events as they unfolded.

Megan stared at the man lying on the pavement, eyes locked on his gaze. He was staring back with a smile that sent chills down her spine. A strange sense of fear filtered through her. There was something familiar about him, something dark and icy. The swarming sensation filled her with dread and the need to run.

Why did he have such a familiar look about him in a small town where she only knew a handful of people? He had been watching her from across the street. She noticed him just before he had moved her direction. He let out a brief chuckle that reeked of depravity as his eyes glazed over and he went blank. Tears stained her cheeks while her secret past began to haunt her where she stood.

How could anyone have found her? She had been so careful. No, he must have been a tourist, late to the party. She was safe here. She was impossible to find – all of her tracks were covered. This was just wine and a little paranoia.

Blake noticed Megan's reaction to the man and the man's focus on her before he took his final breath. Was this a case of shock on her part and his final moments being at the feet of a pretty girl, or was there more? Something was nudging him toward the latter. He would find out. He always did when there was malice of any kind, and this left an uneasy stench.

The on-duty paramedics continued where Dawson and Carigan had left off, giving every effort they had to save the stranger on their way to the hospital, even if it didn't look good for the man. The street had been cleared and reopened to traffic as if nothing had transpired. Sitting inside Blooming Grounds, Megan couldn't take her eyes off the street from where she sat.

They tossed the last bottle of wine and cleared the table that had been the host of their joyful evening until the past hour. Shaken to her core, Megan was at a loss for words when she was startled by the eyes pinned on her by the group of friends standing in front of her.

"You okay, Princess?" Jessie showed sincere concern, even with the princess dig tossed in.

"Oh, yeah. Just…wow, that was something else. Right?" She shook her head as if it would clear the images of the man and all that the past hour had held.

"Honey, it's okay to feel stunned. We are used to things like this in our lines of work," Carigan offered with sympathy for her friend.

"Yeah, this isn't something we see every day, but we see it. If you need to talk about it, we're here. Okay?" Evie offered.

"No, thank you, but I'm fine. It was just…a little shocking. That's all," she finished with a synthetic smile. She stood to hug them all goodbye and thank them for their help in her night's success.

Blake gave Colton a nod while hugging her goodbye, as if understanding why he was the last to leave. It was clear she was still shaken, and Blake, being Blake, didn't miss a thing. Colton nodded back before giving the standard "bro" goodbye handshake as he made his way out the door. Colton appreciated his friend's intuition and concern but had already decided that he was taking her home, whether she wanted him to or not.

Megan turned, startled by Colton still standing there. She

quickly wiped at the tears that had finally won and made their way down her cheeks.

"Oh, sorry! I thought you walked out with Blake. I don't know why I am crying. I didn't know the man. Too much wine and tired, I suppose." She laughed off the emotions and gave a simple shrug and eye roll, annoyed with her own behavior.

"Let me drive you home, Meg. We are practically going to the same place."

"Oh, Colton, I appreciate it, but…"

He cut her off before she could deliver any excuses. He moved in closer, placing his hands on either side of her waist, bending down so he was at eye level. "I'm not taking no for an answer, sweetheart. What you saw tonight…was awful. You're clearly shaken up and in no condition to drive. I'll drive you home, and I'll bring you back to town tomorrow morning for your car. We've had enough excitement for one night. We don't need another accident."

As the man from the street's face wandered through her mind, taunting her, provoking a reaction she didn't quite recognize, she finally caved. She nodded her head just as the tears started again, and she hiccuped a quiet sob. He pulled her in and held her tight, comforting her while she let out what had been stirring for the past hour.

He rubbed her back, kissed the top of her head, and whispered sweet words of encouragement. "It's okay, honey. It's over. I've got you," he said. "You're okay, darlin'. You're safe."

He was right in one regard – he *did* have her. He had her good and tight, and she didn't want him to let go. His arms were strong and packed with something she had never experienced—comfort, concern, and something else that she couldn't quite put a finger on. He felt like home on a dark and stormy night, and she wanted to stay there forever.

What he didn't have right was that she was okay. Sure, the sense of distress would pass when the wine completely wore off and she had a chance to reconcile the feelings provoked by watching a man possibly die at her feet. Her gut said *safe* was a term to be used loosely – that perhaps that man was there for *her*, and this might just be the beginning of something she thought couldn't find her.

* * *

THE DRIVE HOME WAS QUIET. SHE HADN'T SAID A WORD SINCE shedding her mountain of tears. Glancing at her sitting beside him with her arms wrapped around herself and her head leaning against the window, he could see the emotions streaming through her.

She began to rub her hands nervously across her lap as they pulled into her driveway. She lived alone with her nephew, and it hadn't bothered her until now. Paranoia had settled in as ghosts of her past taunted her with a single incident that likely had nothing to do with her. She sat staring at the front of her house long beyond parking in the driveway.

Colton had cut the engine, but she remained where she was, rubbing her hands as if building up the nerve to go inside. A shocking event will cause people to act anything other than their level of normal, but something about her sense of anxiety left him unsettled. She was nervous, maybe afraid, but why?

"You okay?" he asked, unsuccessful in gaining her attention. "I'll walk you in, get you settled."

Colton jumped out of the truck and made his way around to her side to help her out. When he opened her door, she was anything but focused, still lost in thought. He put a hand on her leg, startling her back to present.

"Whoa, you're okay! It's just me, honey. Where were you just now? You have me a little worried." His expression confirmed his words as he spoke softly to her, hoping not to further upset her.

Megan looked around, suddenly embarrassed by her behavior. "Oh geez, Colton, I am so sorry. I guess I'm just a little spent. Long day…lots of emotions." She chuckled as if acknowledging her odd behavior as silly, hoping to move on and not shed her secret fears.

"Okay, let's get you inside. I can stay a while if you'd like?" He paused, reading her expression before defining his intentions to put her at ease. "Just until you're settled in, promise. No agenda here…just a concerned friend."

Normally, Megan would stop the conversation before it reached this point. An adamant *no* would be easy to deliver, but tonight, she couldn't. He was hard to say no to, harder to resist, but his sincerity and kindness gave her the comfort she desperately needed. Just this once, she would break her own rules. She smiled a sweet smile and nodded as he held her hand, helping her down from his sky-high truck.

Making their way inside, she gestured to the couch, handing him the remote, expecting him to put on some form of sports news or movie centered around blowing crap up. To her surprise, he turned it to something sweet, a movie that most men probably hadn't heard of. He really was different from the rest, an amazing catch if she were fishing.

"Can I get you anything?" she asked with a shyness that he found cute.

"No, thank you. I'm good. A good ol' love story sounds like the perfect thing to wrap an odd evening," he replied with a wink.

"Sounds like a plan. I'll be right back." She excused herself to her bedroom for a quick change into something more comfortable so she could truly relax and try to shake the ominous cloud that seemed to be hovering over her.

She returned in a semi-fitted t-shirt and yoga pants that earned her an endearing grin of approval from her guest. She hadn't intended to dress for him but found satisfaction in knowing he had a thing for her in yoga pants. She grabbed her favorite movie-watching, throw blanket and sat on the couch beside him.

He was sitting at one end of the sofa with an arm stretched along the back. Not sure what motivated her to do so, she scooted in and leaned into him, resting her head against his shoulder. Before long, his arm found its way around her, it was strong and comforting and all she could do was melt into his embrace, finally feeling free of the stress the night had conjured up.

He could feel her body start to relax into him as he held her close. He kissed the top of her head when her breathing started to slow and deepen. Having her fall asleep in his arms wasn't what he had planned or even expected, but he wasn't going to complain. It felt *good* – it felt *right*.

Recalling the night's events like a highlight reel, he became more and more intrigued by the woman in his arms. She was lovely and kind. Her energy throughout the night was contagious – she was completely in her element.

Her enthusiasm over the Holiday Fair warmed Colton's heart. He could see the wheels turning and found it incredibly adorable. Nobody wanted that job, but she was damn near giddy with excitement. She seemed to be fitting in and feeling comfortable – that was encouraging to him.

He wanted to get through those walls of hers but was unsure how. He assumed there was something, or things, he still didn't know about her that were going to be his largest obstacles yet. Something dramatic, something hurtful perhaps, he didn't know, but he would find a way through it, straight to her heart.

Satisfied with his plan and commitment to explore who Megan Johnson was and claim her heart, he kissed the top of her head. She took in a deep relaxing breath in response, drawing a smile to his handsome face. He could get used to this.

He clicked off the TV and stood, scooping her up as he went. Finding his way down the hallway, through process of elimination, he located her room and gently placed her on her bed, sitting at the edge.

He kissed her temple and whispered, "Good night, darlin'."

He stood to leave, but she caught his hand and with eyes still closed, pulled him closer and whispered, "Stay? Please?"

Her plea was so soft, so innocent, laced with a hint of insecurity. He knew she wasn't asking for anything more than comfort and companionship. She was afraid to be alone for whatever reason. He was happy to be her chosen protector, the one to make her feel safe.

He crawled into her bed behind her and pulled her close. Still half asleep, she cozied her way into him as he draped his arm over her. A perfect fit, he found pleasure in knowing she wanted him, needed him, in such an emotional way. That far outweighed the physical in his mind.

Dropping one more sweet kiss to her temple, he said, "Always, sweetheart, always…"

He could get used to this…

7

____

THE BRIGHT SUNNY MORNING, FLOODING THROUGH THE lightly shaded windows, woke Megan with a smile on her face. Her morning stretch reached to the other side of the bed, which was empty. Thoughts of *him* flooded her mind as she remembered the night before. He had been so sweet, kind, and caring. Something she had come to expect from her hunky neighborhood firefighter.

When she turned to her right to read the time on her clock, she noticed a note propped on her nightstand.

> M-
> Went to feed my small gang. I put my number
>   in your phone under "Hunky Firefighter"
>   (your words, not mine). Call or come over
>   if I'm not back by the time you are ready.
> See you soon…
> -C

SHE LAUGHED AT THE *SMALL GANG* COMMENT — HE remembered. She blushed at the humiliating reminder of her lust-induced lack of filter, admitting he was a hunky fire-fighter. Her mind was flooded with thoughts of him, how fun he was at the shop the night before, how heroic he was when tragedy struck, and finally, how tender and compassionate he was with her when she felt weak. A regular Prince Charming.

Physical attraction between the two of them had been undeniable. There was blistering heat every time they were within close proximity. He flooded her thoughts by day and consumed her dreams by night. She had never met a man she wanted to explore more, until now. Tangled in her thoughts, she decided that it just might be a risk worth taking.

GETTING READY FOR THE DAY WAS MUCH EASIER AS *SMALL-town Megan Johnson.* Less makeup, less hair spray, Lycra leggings instead of silk. She really liked the relaxed elements of her life in McKenzie. Ready for the day and with Colton still gone, she decided to trek down the beach and meet him at his house.

Day old bread in hand, she cautiously approached the geese that seemed to be giving her less trouble of late, and handed them their broken up treat. Making her way up the small hill to Colton's yard, she was greeted by Rambo, who announced her presence to the world before giving her a quick nuzzle and running off to work, inspecting the perimeter for intruders. She shook her head and giggled at the idea of Rambo, the watch-Rooster. Who would have thought such a thing existed?

At Rambo's call, Doug rambled his way to Megan and offered his own greeting while escorting her to the porch where Duke and Boss guarded their family. Thoughts of a missing Nancy had her giggling again as the reality of Colton's zoo settled in.

"Where's Nancy?" she nervously asked the squad of furry friends. "Am I really talking to you like you are going to answer? You guys must be rubbing off on me," she admitted.

"I bet Nancy is with the kittens, huh? Was it time for breakfast? Who names a dog Nancy, and a goat Doug?" she asked, laughing at herself once again.

Thinking back to her first meeting, she stepped out of her comfort zone and cautiously approached the pair eyeing her. She had been speaking to them like people, not sure how else to address an animal, and felt absolutely ridiculous. Colton was kind, so his animals were kind. She recalled how gentle they were—one carried a tiny kitten in his mouth, for heaven sake.

She slowly extended her hand to Duke first. She remembered seeing that on TV once, so figured she would give it a whirl and see how he received her. Surely he would remember her. The German Shepherd replied with a quick sniff and a long slobbery lick as his greeting, followed by a shake from his lone front paw.

"How do you do that?" She questioned, looking under him, trying to determine how he managed to shake her hand and balance as he did on only his two back legs and bottom.

Next was Boss. She took a deep breath while mustering up the nerves to greet him as well. It didn't help that he had those dark piercing eyes pinned on her every move or that his head was as big as her torso, and sitting, he still came to her chest. Being deaf, she figured he would be easily spooked if she moved too quickly or just the wrong way.

Not interested in losing a hand to a startled beast of a dog, she moved directly in front of him, ensuring that locked gaze was truly on her. She ducked down slightly, eye-to-eye, trying to decipher the intention of his look.

"Shit. Is that a *what the fuck are you looking at* stare or a *how can I help you* stare?" she negotiated. "Shit, okay, you can do this Meg," she encouraged herself.

Closing her eyes tight, she slowly put her hand out in front of her and turned her head to the side so she wouldn't have to see whatever was about to happen, should her eyes betray her and open. She was saying a silent little prayer when she felt a gentle nudge. Opening one eye, she peeked out of the corner to see if it was a run like hell nudge or a stay a while nudge.

She found a tilted head looking back at her. The dog was confused.

"You and me both, buddy," she laughed. "Are we friends now?"

He offered another nudge with his head, followed by a large sandpaper tongue slopping drool all over her fist. Overcome with a sense of pride and joy, she reached for both dogs, giving them loving ear scratches while bouncing in place and squealing.

"Look at me, bonding with friggin' nature! Go me!" She cheered. "Did you see that Doug? Me and the dogs, buddy. You want a scratch too?"

* * *

Colton heard a voice and followed it to the porch where he found Megan, sitting in a rocker, surrounded by his dogs, with a goat head resting on her lap. Even Rambo was perched on the table next to her, watching the world from his new post while listening to her talk. The voices were all from

Megan. It seemed she had a different one for each animal she addressed.

"Hey! Sorry, I was in the shower and didn't hear you. It's just me here. Next time, just come in. No need to knock," he said, announcing his presence with a delighted smile.

She smiled back at him, happy to see him and for him to see her new pack. "Yep, just makin' friends over here!" she said radiating excitement. "Where's Nancy though – haven't seen her yet?"

"Oh, she's inside with the kittens. They just ate."

"Ahh, that's what I thought," she said in a sing song voice, scratching Rambo's neck. "She's such a good mama, huh, Rambo?"

Colton was impressed by the dissipation of her previous apprehension where the animals were concerned. She seemed perfectly comfortable, even enjoying them as much as they were enjoying her. He understood exactly why they were so mesmerized by the lady petting them and talking sweet to them. He was completely smitten too.

* * *

MEGAN FOUND HERSELF SPENDING MORE AND MORE TIME with Colton as the days passed. They spent their time taking walks along the trails that trace the property, leading to the mountains that surround them. Jax was much too heavy for Megan on that type of walk and that type of terrain, so Colton carried him in the hiking pack without hesitation. At night, they would eat easy dinners and watch the sun set before Colton would walk them home.

It was becoming a regular routine that both were enjoying immensely. Jax had become cranky on their hike to the waterfall the day before, so they had scrapped the plan until his playdate with Sam's kids. There was something special about the falls that Colton was excited to share with her.

They made their way through the increasingly rugged terrain, something she wasn't used to. An obvious city girl, she was starting to find her way through the hiking experience, swatting at fewer bugs and finding different elements less disgusting. She didn't even need to set out a blanket to sit on a rock or log anymore.

The views were stunning, the nature breath taking, and the hike rigorous. As the ascent became more challenging, Colton slowed the pace and helped her through the tougher spots…even a gentleman hiking. She hesitated slightly as a loud rushing sound seemed to intensify to a windy roar. Colton smiled and encouraged her to continue, boosting her up one last step before the thunderous sound came into view.

"Wow, this looks like heaven on earth, Colton," she said in a near whisper.

They had made it to the falls. It was stunning. The water rushed from the brim above in a rapid fall, landing in a beautiful pool of bright mossy rocks and boulders, surrounded by old fallen trees scattered about. The water gently rushed beyond, leaving the soothing sounds of a tranquil creek in its path through the forest.

"It's amazing, right?" he asked, knocking her from her water chasing trance.

"It's more than that. I've not seen anything like it before," she admitted.

"Take off your boots and socks," he stated rather than asked.

"Excuse me?" she questioned with a puzzled look about her.

He removed his boots and socks and began to roll his jean cuffs when he said, "Trust me – you need to try it."

"Colton, its fall. The snow is already falling at higher elevations. That water has got to be *freezing*. It's beautiful, but I'm not interested in frost bite," she lectured in shock.

He picked her up and effortlessly put her on a boulder nearly as tall as he was and pulled at her boots and socks. "Colton, seriously, I don't do cold water. I'm not one of those exhibitionist, polar plunge types. I like warm feet."

"Do you trust me?" He asked with a hopeful look, her bare feet in his hands after sliding her leggings up to her knees.

She sat in silence, eyes wide, and pondered his question, considering the look of anticipation on his face which was as innocent as a small child. His question was more than a quick, *can I throw you in the water* inquiry but more of a *where do we stand*? She smiled a sweet smile and nodded her head at his question. She really did trust him…with everything. That idea frightened her as much as it exhilarated her.

"Good!" he said with excitement and grabbed her off the rock, carrying her to the water.

She squealed in delight at the prospect of potentially being tossed in the frigid water. "Don't throw me in, *please*. Just don't put me down!" she begged.

"Oh, you're going in!" he announced, sloshing through the water, headed to the pool just below the falls.

"No! Please, no!" she managed to get out between her deep belly rolling laughs.

He stopped just below the falls, in front of a tall boulder that slowed the flow to the creek, making it passable. Slowly, he slid her down the front of him while holding her tight. She held her feet up as long as she could before he finally dunked her legs in the water. Her anticipatory screech was quickly dulled to a breathy 'wow.'

"It's warm. Oh, gosh…its sooo warm! How?" Her playfulness continued as she sloshed around, splashing water on each of them.

"The hot springs are up above. The overflow runs into the water above, warming it. Be careful, the moss is..."

He didn't finish his warning before she lost her footing on the slippery, moss covered rocks below the water and began to fall. He quickly swept in and scooped her into his arms and held her against him. Her breath caught with the shock of it all but more so at the feel of his rock-hard body against hers. The warmth she felt flowing through her was not from the water. It was *all* Colton.

"...slippery," was all he got out before leaning in and kissing her.

She wrapped her arms around his neck, not wanting to lose the closeness as his long, hard kiss sent a shiver through her heated core. She gave as much as she received, letting go of every doubt and giving in to every fantasy. He was hot – sex on a stick – whatever you want to call it...it was Colton.

He slowly shifted them back, leaning her against the large boulder behind her, pinning her with one of his arms on either side of her, never losing their connection. Slow, unrushed, and full of pleasure, he continued to have his way with her mouth while his right hand drifted down her body, feeling her as he went. He leaned her back, arching her over the round boulder, moving his lips down her neck to her collarbone and to her breasts while he unbuttoned her shirt. Leaving it open, he reached for the clasp that stood between him and tasting more than her mouth. He pulled away for only a moment when he freed her breasts to take in her beauty.

"You're beautiful," he said, running his hand from her neck, slowly to her breasts, before pleasuring one with his mouth the other with his hand.

His free hand continued the descent, breaking past the

elastic band of her pants, where he found her bare and more than ready for him. No panties. He was hard as hell. He stroked her core while she rocked her hips against him, trying to find a quicker pace to her greedy climax. She felt him everywhere. The sensations were so overwhelming she could hardly stand the touches she was craving more of.

The sound of nature's rushing waterfall, the warm water at her feet, and Colton's gift of pleasure, stole her breath as her body convulsed in pure ecstasy while she cried out his name. Kissing him deeply, she reached for his belt, but his hands intercepted as he slowly pulled away. She looked at him, confused by his actions, suddenly insecure.

"No. Not like this," he said, holding her head in his hands, looking into her eyes so deeply she could feel him in her soul. "You deserve better than this. Not *wild* in the woods."

She gave him a sweet smile, appreciating his sincere gesture, but she wasn't one to just take. She liked to give just as much. "But you didn't get to…" She paused, waving her arms in front, indicating something to do with his groin area, flustered and rosy cheeked.

"And I don't need to. Today is all about you, sweetheart. As much as I want to have you right here, hot, heavy, and hard on this rock…" He took a deep breath and gathered his wits before he completely came undone just thinking about her. "I'd rather it be special, sweet, so I can show you what you mean to me."

Her mouth opened and closed, but her words were absent. Completely flattered by his chivalrous gesture, even if it left her a little pent up, she couldn't believe that this was the man who wanted her heart. She wondered how he made it this long unattached. He was perfect.

"What if I want it…long…hard…and hot against this

rock?" she asked in a breathy voice, arching her back so her chest was proudly displayed, trying to seduce him.

He tossed his head back, let out a deep sigh, followed by a chuckle. "You're killing me! You are so tempting," he said in between small sweet kisses, "But, no…this isn't the way it's supposed to be."

She put on her best pouty face, bottom lip protruding and all, while he buttoned her shirt back up. He picked her up and wrapped her around his waist, giving her one more lasting kiss to remind her of what was to come. He set her down and said, "Besides, now we have something to look forward to, and this…this we'll revisit another time!"

He turned her around and smacked her ass, encouraging her to make her way back across the water so they could find their way back down the trail. Hand in hand, a lot of laughs, and plenty of kissing along the way, the heat never quite dissolved. It likely wouldn't until they finished what they had started. Hopefully, sooner rather than later.

8

SAM HELD THE NEXT HOLIDAY FAIR MEETING AT HER HOUSE on their regular "girl get together" day. The children played, and the ladies ate Granny's highly sought after baked goods while gossiping and catching up on town happenings. All of the ladies were there from their group with questions for their newest addition. That group was so tight. Without saying a word, they all had eyes on Megan, waiting for the juicy details of her budding relationship with their favorite firefighter.

Megan's mind wandered to thoughts of Colton when the kittens were mentioned during conversation. Colton was on a 48-hour shift, and Ellie was the appointed kitten care taker, supervised by Sam when he was working. Ellie was Sam and Dawson's five-year-old daughter. Being a new big sister, she retired her tomboy in a tutu getup for princess tomboy in a tutu. Her jeans and ratty shirt with Converse were still a staple, covered with a tutu, of course, but baseball caps were replaced by pretty hairdos and tiaras.

Ellie was a precocious riot, so adorable and the perfect caretaker of the kittens. Megan thought it was sweet that

Colton had let Ellie not only name them, but pick which one she wanted to keep. That was just like him—kind, caring, and thoughtful.

Whiskers, Mittens, Mr. Snuggles, and Bob were well taken care of and going to be a tough group to choose from. Kitten number five wasn't talked about as much or up for grabs. He was the runt and a total menace. He had already been claimed, based on that sole characteristic. "Flea Bag" belonged to Jessie, just as soon as he was old enough.

"Well, I love the idea of adding a Gala event to the end of the fair. How fun to dress up and bring a little elegance to McKenzie for a change!" Evie offered.

"I'm seriously not wearing a fucking dress again…especially not that kind of dress!" Jessie complained.

"Looks like you're on babysitting duty then," Carigan tossed on the table.

"Oh good, Jessie-girl. We can babysit together, play some drinkin' games after the tots head to bed!" Gran returned excitedly.

"Hmmm. As much as that sounds…fun, I think I'll pass on diaper duty, Lou. That's worse than the dress issue," Jessie said.

"Wait, you aren't going Gran?" Evie asked in surprise.

"Nahhh, honey. That's young folk stuff. Besides, it sounds a little too swanky for an old broad like me. I bet they won't even have a good bean dip, just some of that raw fish egg stuff and fancy mystery meat on a stick," Gran said.

"You and your bean dip," Evie said with an eye roll.

"Sounds like we are on the right track. Great plan, Meg!" Sam interrupted. "Now, let's get on with it…spill the beans, girl."

"What do you mean? Spill what beans?" She asked, innocently, despite her embarrassment shading her face.

"Oh, c'mon, Priss Pants! You, Sparks, and all these dreamy smiles between the two of you?" Jessie bluntly questioned.

"Oh, Colton. Nothing much. Just friends, neighbors… nothing major." Megan played it off, not ready to open up and bring more people into her private life than she already had.

Morgan chimed in, "Well, maybe you need to reevaluate your position, hon. You seem to be the only thing he likes to talk about down at the House."

"Well, we do see a lot of each other, so…"

Jessie cut her off with a dramatic eye roll and bluntly called her out. "Oh, come on! Seriously, the only one close to blind here is the old woman," she said, motioning toward Granny Lou. "Even she sees it. You aren't fooling anyone. Own it, Princess!"

"Such a sweet boy – I've always loved that boy like my own. He has such a good heart. Easy on the eyes, too…I'm not as old and blind as that one would like you to think," Granny half whispered, gesturing toward Everly.

Megan desperately wanted to tell her friends why she couldn't be with Colton…or anyone. They were becoming more and more like family. They would understand. Knowing, however, would put them in the same danger she was tempting fate with by seeing Colton. She didn't want to share her burdens with them. They didn't deserve it any more than she did.

"I don't know. I do like him, but it's just not a good time. I mean, I have the shop, Jax, still settling in here. It's just too much too fast," she offered as her truth, which really was an honest response.

"Oh, honey. You're young, your shop is lookin' mighty fine, and Jax is welcome at Granny's anytime you need to sneak away with that handsome boy, Colton. You are young.

You only live once. Chase that sexy boy around a few laps, if ya know what I mean!" Granny said with a wicked grin and obnoxious whistle.

She sat and thought for a moment, giggling at Granny's antics. Lou was right. She really had nothing to lose, but Colton did. She would need to be very careful. He was too special to gamble with.

"Well…I do like him. A lot! He is so sweet and thoughtful. Great with Jax. He's like one of those characters right out of one of those fairy tale, happily ever after, sexy books. Oh, and the animals! I didn't think they made men like that," she recited.

"What, like Dr. Doolittle?" Jessie snorted.

"No, not like Dr. Doolittle!" she defended with a laugh. "It's sweet. They all have a special story…*he's* special."

"Sounds like you're already half-way dating, Meg. You don't talk about someone like that if you *aren't* interested in him," Evie offered.

"Yeah, go for it honey. What do you have to lose?" Carigan said, jumping on the Colton bandwagon.

If only she knew. If only they all knew. She had been in McKenzie Ridge for months now and felt safe. Nothing had happened, and she wasn't willing to add the "yet" to the end of that thought. Maybe there was room to explore Colton Sparks.

Sam decided to be the voice of reason on this one and offered her two cents, "Honey, he has waited his whole life for what he wants. He'll wait for you if you need more time."

She smiled at her friends and said, "Maybe. Now, let's get back to planning this shindig!"

Excitement over the added formal event to the Holiday Fair line up was overshadowed by the flooding thoughts of Colton. Feeling more relaxed in her circumstances, compliments of her friends, the idea of pursuing him seemed more realistic. She would be just as careful as she already had been and not take unnecessary risks. It was as much for his sake as her own.

* * *

A SUBTLE KNOCKING SOUND CAUGHT HER ATTENTION ON THE drive home. It escalated to a loud thump as her car began to shake, getting harder to control. She pulled to the shoulder of the old back country road and searched for her phone. Stepping out of the vehicle, she noticed the source of her delay—a flat tire.

She wandered around the car, circling it several times, holding her phone in the air, searching for a signal. She had no idea how to change a tire and couldn't even look up a "how to" video without a phone signal for internet. Deciding which was closer, town or home, she went to pull Jax from the vehicle and head one direction or the other when Blake and Morgan pulled up, parking behind her.

"Need some help?" Blake asked, stepping out of the police car.

"Yes! Perfect timing! My phone doesn't work out here for some reason."

Blake held up his phone, had a clear signal, noting Morgan doing the same. Her surprised and slightly bewildered look suggested that she found the same.

"How can I help? Need me to change it?" He asked.

"Would you? Free coffee and Danish for a month if you do!" She offered in exchange for help. "I was going to call Colton, but…" She held up her phone, showing her excuse.

"I would do it for free, but since you offered, I'll be in for that coffee and Danish. Fritters from Baker's are our usual, but my arm can be twisted for your strawberry cream cheese Danish," he said with a smile.

"Which means we will still get fritters from Baker's, and he'll eat a Danish, too," Morgan joked, leading Blake to nod in agreement.

Megan laughed, enjoying their banter. "I'll be sure to set one aside for you each morning."

Meg caught Morgan up on the discussions and decisions made at the Holiday Fair meeting while playing with Jax. Like the others, Morgan was looking forward to the formal event that was scheduled to follow the week-long festivities. The annual event was about to step it up a notch with a little Megan flare.

Blake had helped himself to Meg's keys and then the trunk in search of the tools needed to change her tire. There was a small suitcase stashed in the far back of the trunk that struck him as odd. He was ready to ask her if she was taking a last-minute trip and where she was going when he noticed another bag…a bag of money.

It wasn't a small stash, easily explained as a bank deposit from Blooming Grounds, unless she had been collecting it for months. No, this was a large sum, enough to live off of for several months. An amount one would need to disappear in a hurry.

The uneasy feeling that had drifted in and out the past several weeks returned and settled deep in his gut. Her subtle paranoia and anxiousness, the behavior the night of the accident in front of her shop—it was all adding up. What was she running from…or who? A young woman with a toddler in tow and a trunk full of supplies and cash had red flags flying everywhere. He really didn't know enough about Megan to draw a conclusion one way or the other. The only thing he knew for certain was that if he said anything, she would be gone before he could finish his sentence.

He didn't want to spook her, but he couldn't help her if he didn't know what was going on. He stopped to look around the area, taking in anything out of the ordinary, making a note to look into her background. Megan had a secret. Even if she didn't want his help, she had the interest of one of his best friends, and it was his duty to keep them all safe.

He went back to changing her tire, as though nothing was out of the ordinary. It wasn't lost on him that she had a watchful eye on him while talking to Morgan. When he placed the spare next to the car, an obvious wave of relief washed over her. She relaxed as if sliding under the radar with her hand in the cookie jar. If she didn't have his attention before, she certainly did now, and he had a winning poker face.

He finished quickly, loading her bad tire in the trunk while telling her who to go see in town about a new tire. They each said their goodbyes while Blake reminded her of their Danish deal, and they went their separate ways.

As they drove off, Blake asked Morgan, "What do you know about Megan?"

"I don't know. Not a lot I guess. She's from the east coast, lost her sister a year or so ago, ended up with Jax, came to McKenzie for a fresh start. She clearly lived a little higher on the hog than McKenzie has to offer, hence all of Jessie's nicknames for her, but she seems to fit in well. Is there something wrong?" Morgan asked, knowing Blake only inquired when there was reason to inquire.

"No, just curious. She seems like a real nice girl. Sparks has it pretty bad for her," he laughed.

The suitcase and cash in the trunk was for a quick getaway. Was she an abuse survivor or something else? He read people well, *too* well. It haunted him at times, in fact. He didn't feel that she was a threat, but he couldn't always be right.

He felt it deep down. Trouble was brewing, but who was he protecting, and what was he protecting them from? The last time this happened on his watch, someone had died, and their blood was on his hands. It was time to have eyes everywhere, make some phone calls, protect his town and especially his people.

9

———

Not much of a baker, Megan grabbed a variety of goodies from her shop, remembering how fond Colton had been of the delicious delectables at the tasting. It was a small thank you for all that he had done in the passing weeks, like staying with her when she didn't want to be alone. Reality was, it was an excuse to go see her guy. She had missed him. He was finally off shift. It was the longest 48 hours she could remember.

If she were really honest, she even missed the animals. She stopped at Paisley's Pupcakery before leaving town for the day to grab some special treats for Colton's animals. A clever spin off of the trendy cupcakeries popping up every-where, Paisley's was a fun shop that posed as a pet bakery. It was known for its organic treats that were even suitable for humans, or so Meg was told. It was a little different than your typical pet shop but perfect for the tourist town, appealing to just about every demographic.

Excitement shot through her at the sight of Colton's truck – he was home. She knocked but received no answer. He told her before to let herself in, so that's what she intended to do.

Greeting her furry friends first, she passed out mini pupcakes to each, followed by "Bruno Bars," which were the equivalent of animal friendly biscotti.

His house was quiet, drapes still drawn, not a single sound, not even the shower. She crept to the kitchen where she could leave the treats as a surprise, assuming he must be napping. Duke had followed her in, distracting her with one-sided whispers. When she looked up, she was startled, nearly running into six plus feet of wet, solid muscle wrapped in a white towel at the waist and with one around his neck. Stunned, she dropped the box of goodies at his feet, needing her hands to pick up her jaw, followed by a, "Holy shit!"

He was hot, more than hot. There wasn't a word yet invented that described what he was. His perfectly molded, tan physique was something right out of an art museum. Something to celebrate and appreciate. The water drops were like little drops of desire, tempting her to take a taste. His hair was messy, but even that added to the sinful thoughts dancing around in her head.

So much was said without a word exchanged. He knew he was getting to her and enjoyed every uncomfortable minute. He bent over to pick up the box at his feet, causing her to catch her breath, as if his closeness singed her skin, startling her. When he stood, pink bakery box in hand, her eyes were heavy, lids slow to open, while her mouth remained open. He was giving her a show it appeared, and her body was betraying her every dirty thought.

Fully aware of the effect he was having on her, he played off the moment, milking it for all it was worth. With a wicked grin, locking eyes with her, he slowly lifted a brownie to his mouth, taking a bite. He did his best to torment her with the motions, making her wish she was that brownie. He licked his lips, slow and purposefully, before asking, "Want a…taste?"

Her eyes fluttered quickly, but no words escaped. He moved closer, placing one hand under her chin, tossing the box of baked goods on the table behind her with his other, and pulled her in for a slow, sweet, chocolate flavored kiss. He walked her backward ever so slowly until the back of her legs met the table.

With his free hand, he grabbed her ass, picking her up in quick motion and seating her on the table. He stood between her legs, still keeping a tight hold on her ass while his kiss became hungry and wanton. Her hands glided up his wet body, landing around his neck and then in his hair where she ran her fingers in motion with their kiss.

The rolling muscles and tightness of his body, combined with an assaulting kiss, had her hungry. Relieving the pressure he was creating in her aching core, she lifted her legs, wrapping them around his waist pulling him in closer. She could feel his excitement through her clothes, ready to remove the towel that stood between her and what he had to offer.

His hand slowly made its way down her neck to her collarbone, finally finding her breast. He massaged and tugged through her thin t-shirt, driving her desire to pleasure of epic levels. He was good at this. He was *damn* good.

An abrupt end to their kitchen escapade fell quickly in her lap in the form of Duke. A whine and chirpy bark had their attention when he divided them. Unsure if he thought he was protecting her or just jealous, Colton laughed as he moved back ever so slightly.

"Seems you have an admirer, or maybe a protector?" Colton laughed, scratching the dog's head.

With a winded tone, she replied with a chuckle, "It appears so. I think he wants another pupcake."

"A what?"

"A pupcake from Paisley's. I brought them treats. They're super healthy and good for fleas, shiny coats, and organic… we could even eat them," she said proudly.

"But I don't have fleas," he joked with a serious look.

"Yet. You don't have fleas, yet. And now you won't. You're welcome."

"Go out with me. Dinner. Tomorrow night," he said, quickly changing the subject.

She looked around the room as if the answer, or excuse, was lying around her. She wanted to say yes, but the doubt and hint of fear she had been battling was nudging at her to say no. What they were doing was safe – a date changed everything. It made it harder to protect his heart as well as her own.

"Colton, I…"

"Just dinner, you and me. I even have a babysitter! Come on, tomorrow night?" He didn't yet have a sitter lined up but had a handful of willing and able bodies with a single call. "I'll pick up Jax at the shop so you can get done without distraction. We'll have a guy's day, and then I'll take him to the sitter and pick you up by seven o'clock."

She smiled at the idea of "her guys" spending the afternoon together, just the two of them. He made it all seem so simple, carefree, not a single worry. She wished like anything that she could feel as optimistic as he did. Her conversation with the ladies crossed her mind, and Lou's voice recalled first. She said to live a little, have fun. Maybe it was just that simple.

"Okay…seven it is."

* * *

COLTON HAD PICKED UP JAX AS PLANNED, AND THEY WERE off to do whatever "guys" do in small towns like McKenzie. He had arrived before she was completely ready for the day, caught off guard by her attire – yoga pants and a tank top. His reaction was priceless. He was in fact *speechless*. She would have to remember that. She had asked him what she should wear for the evening so she could leave, dressed accordingly, and all she got was "casual and warm." Interesting.

She was spending the slowest three hours at the shop she had ever counted. Fed up with the day's lagging way, she closed up early so she could get her end of day paperwork completed and the shop ready for the next morning with time to spare. Jason, the high school kid she had working in the coffee shop, was pleased to cut his shift short. High School football was the place to be on a Friday night in the fall, and he was headed there to meet the rest of the town.

Finally making her way through the mundane paperwork that typically didn't phase her one way or the other, she let her mind wander. McKenzie was a delightful town, charming but small. She had been to every eatery in town and tried to decide which would be his choice.

She was rattled from her thoughts when a loud noise from the back caught her attention. She called for Jason, assuming it was him, either making his way out still or just returning for something he had forgotten. The hair on the back of her neck began to rise when Jason didn't reply. More noise sounded, causing her alarm. Colton was due shortly but wouldn't come in the back, and Jason surely would have heard and responded by now.

Nerves getting the best of her, she called out, asking who was back there, voice wavering, revealing her fear. She turned to look outside through the front shop windows. It was near dusk, but plenty of people were out doing the Friday night thing, should she need help.

Slowly making her way to the back room, she scolded herself for making such a brazen move. She paused at the entry, scanning the space, finding everything in order from a distance. Phone in her hand, she moved forward, seeking out the source of the noise.

A sudden movement from behind a large storage rack signaled her that she was not alone. Feet cemented to the floor by fear, she couldn't move. Hopeful that her stillness would leave her unseen, she held her breath until her intruder began to move her direction. All she could see were shadows and perhaps dark clothing. She couldn't make out a face or even see if it was a man or woman – based on general size, it was more than likely a man.

Taking small silent steps backward, she was aiming to turn and run for help when she ran into a solid wall. Large arms encircled her, preventing her from running. The shadowy movement in the distance became frantic. She kicked and screamed as loud as she could before landing an elbow to her captor's gut and stomping his foot in an attempt to get away.

She turned to the winded voice of her captor when he said her name.

"Oh, my God, Colton, I am so sorry!" She looked behind her to where the shadow had danced behind the shelf, but it was gone.

"Remind me never to follow you down a dark alley," he joked, standing upright, still trying to catch his breath.

"I…I…someone was back here, or so I thought," she said, glancing over her shoulder again. "I was going for help, and it was you, but I thought it was someone else…I'm so sorry."

"Someone was in here? Where's the kid?" he asked, with

a look of concern as he moved in the direction she had indicated with flailing arms.

"I shutdown early, so I let him go to the game while I closed up. Please be careful!" She alerted.

She stood there petrified, wondering what he was going to find. Had someone truly been there, or was her imagination antagonizing her again with the fear that had been brewing of late? Eyes wide, a tremor coursing through her, she realized her past wasn't left behind at all. It would likely follow her everywhere, forever.

"There's nobody there. The door was open, a few flower buckets were knocked over along with a box of those paper coffee cups, but that's it. Are you sure you saw someone? We can call Blake…"

"No! No need to bother him. Maybe Jason just didn't close it all the way. I bet a…stray cat got in here or something." She pasted on her best fake smile and grabbed for his hand. "Let's just go. It's fine now."

He pulled her close and landed a sweet kiss on her forehead before leading her to the front of the store so they could leave. Walking through the doorway to the front of the store, she looked back one last time. There may not be anyone in there now, but there was. Someone had been in there.

10

—————

LIGHT CHATTER ENSUED AS THEY MADE THEIR TWENTY-minute drive up the mountain to their final dinner destination. Megan eventually relaxed, not letting the afternoon's events hinder their evening. She finally convinced herself that she was fine in McKenzie, that she and Jax were safe. No one knew where they were, nor could they.

Colton had noticed a distance about her, her mind elsewhere, clearly shaken by what happened at Blooming Grounds. He noticed that before – was it a pattern? Was she afraid of something or just the jumpy paranoid type? She was single with a toddler, in a new town, so it could be both. It was his mission to give her a fun and relaxing evening, despite any earlier hiccups.

Her breath caught at the stunning sight that came into view as they rounded the last curve in the road. They drove through a large wooden threshold, which held a rustic sign that said Pinecrest Ranch. The gravel road grinding beneath them took them to a stunning log ranch house that had beautiful grounds surrounding it and a spectacular snowcapped mountain backdrop.

In the distance, there were multiple buildings that looked to be a mix of barns, silos, and several small log cabins sprinkled about as far as she could see. Horses flanked the north side while cattle flanked the south. A slew of various animals were mixed in between, including a few roaming dogs and wandering cats.

There were fields of grape vines climbing the slight hills, while acres of pumpkins were nestled below. She assumed the cleared meadows scattered about were for other crops that were no longer in season. This place was massive. It was an image right out of Hollywood or a fantasy from a favorite book. Gorgeous.

They drove past the ranch house, following the gravel road to the north, behind the many structures and corrals, and to a field that held dozens of parked vehicles. Colton parked his truck and rounded the front to let her out. A true gentleman.

"What is this place? It's amazing," she asked.

He smiled, pleased that his choice in location met her liking. "It's a Dude Ranch."

"A what?"

"A Dude Ranch. Come on, you've heard of a Dude Ranch. Haven't you?"

"Well, yeah, in movies maybe, but what are we doing here? Are we learning to be cowboys or something?" she quizzed, not sure she was going to enjoy his answer.

"Sort of," was all he said before placing his hand at the small of her back and nudging her along with his charming wink.

"I don't know if I like the sound of this," she chuckled.

Weaving in and out of the rows of cars, their destination finally came into view. They were nestled in the midst of the small log cabins they could see while driving in. There was a large pergola type structure that had something much like a gazebo with an open top right in the middle. There were rows and rows of large family style wooden picnic tables filling the space from one end to the other. They were organized in a sunburst pattern, surrounding the gazebo with stacks of baled hay that appeared to be used as the seating at each table.

On closer look, she noticed the gazebo housed a large, open, fire pit covered with a metal grate used to cook the Texas sized steaks resting on it. They were pulling corn on the cob from the large stock pots cooking over the fire as well. She could see small football shaped objects wrapped in foil, sitting below the grate at the edge of the fire. The same foil footballs were stacked in the buffet line that circled the gazebo…they were baked potatoes!

This place was absolutely fabulous. Colton said hello to the various staff who recognized him in passing as he guided her to a numbered table, holding two place cards that had "Sparks" printed on them.

"Here we are, table 7. After you." He gestured to the makeshift seating, holding her hand to help her navigate her way over the narrow bale of hay that would be her seat for the night.

"This is such a charming place. I had no idea this was up here," she admitted.

"This is Morgan's ranch," he said.

"*This* is Morgan's? She's a cop. How does she do this too? This can't be an easy hobby."

"It's been in her family for generations. It's a real operating ranch that she has employees for. It's also a big tourist attraction as a Dude Ranch. People come from all over and pay to be a cowboy for a week," he laughed.

"This is amazing. I mean, I knew she had horses and volunteered at the equestrian center a lot, but this? Wow!"

"She's an only child, so when her parents retired, it became hers. This is where they feed the ranch hands, tourists staying here, and it's open to the public by reservation for dinner only."

"Like a restaurant…let it pay for itself. Brilliant," she admired.

"This part is only open to the public on weekends from the end of spring until around the first snow, so they will close for the season soon."

"It's amazing. So what do we do, sit here and wait for service, or do we serve ourselves?" she said with enthusiasm, anxious to take in the whole experience.

"A girl after my own heart! Grab your plate, let's go!"

They made their way through the buffet where they gathered very simple options. Steak was on the grill tonight, nothing else. There was a salad with only two dressing options, baked potatoes with all the fixings, and corn on the cob sat at the end of the line. The tables were lined with big baskets of fresh sweet rolls and farm fresh butter. Simple, but plentiful, and absolutely delicious.

The tables were lined with metal pitchers of iced water and clear glass pitchers of sweet tea to accommodate the two glasses set at each place setting. No soda, no alcohol, simple and perfect. This wasn't the bucking bronco hoe down she thought he had brought her to. It was a new kind of elegant – quaint and completely unique.

There were strings of lanterns floating above them. Individual lanterns were hanging from every post and strategically placed at each table for light as the evening sky settled in. Burlap table runners with ribbons of lace woven through them lined the centers of the tables with Mason jar glasses to drink from. Rows of milk glass vases, full of fresh fall flowers, offered a lovely fragrance and punch of color to each table, along with black and white plaid napkins strategically folded and wrapped in twine bows.

It may not be her style, but she found this country chic setting adorable and absolutely charming. There wasn't anything like this, with this ambiance and wow factor, in the city. Maybe small town, simple life living was starting to rub off on her. This gave her an incredible idea for the Holiday Fair's final event.

* * *

Colton was a gentleman, making sure she had everything she needed first. He also made it clear who she was with. He held her hand or had his hand at the small of her back as they made their way down the buffet line. He was sweet, kind, and even laughed at her jokes.

He loved watching her joy flood the place they were in. She laughed all night and made fast friends with everyone around them. Her outgoing spirit was mesmerizing. He couldn't get enough of her, and he was also tired of sharing her.

Dinner was replaced with dessert at the buffet while coffee and tea stations were set up around the perimeter of the pergola, granting easy access to guests wandering the grounds and mingling. Peach cobbler was the featured dessert, but seasonal pumpkin pie and apple pie were served as well. On the side of each plated dessert was a generous scoop of freshly made vanilla bean ice cream. Unable to make their choices, they settled on a dessert each with a plan to share. Colton grabbed the third dessert for good measure.

They found a lovely spot near the log railing that lined the perimeter of the property. This particular railing protected people and animals alike from the steep rocky terrain of the ridge beyond. They took a seat on a vacant bale of hay that boasted the best view on the entire property. The ridge overlooked the moonlit town below, sprinkled with the few city lights there were. A mirror-like maze that was Bear Creek trailed through town, disappearing in the distance while reflecting the gorgeous star speckled sky and silvery light of the moon. It was a magnificent sight as even the newly snowcapped mountaintops at the highest elevations glowed from the same silvery light against its freshly lain snow.

It was a magical night, thoughtfully planned, and neither wanted it to end. From the fun campfire-like singing and mingling with strangers from all over to their sweet romantic spot on the ridge…it was perfect.

Staring off in the distance, Megan said, "I've never seen such beauty. Absolutely breathtaking."

"I couldn't agree more," Colton said, referring to his view, which was all Megan.

"You're sweet. Really, tonight has been…amazing," she confirmed.

"Well, I'm glad you liked it. I had a feeling you hadn't been out here, so it seemed like a good choice."

"It was. Oh, my God, this dessert! I can't believe you stole an extra!" She joked.

"It isn't stealing. It's just…sampling," he said with confidence, taking a hearty bite of dessert.

She laughed at his defense and said, "Well, thank you for inviting me. It's nice to get out and *adult* a little! I love Jax, but tonight was so needed and so…worth it," she finished, locking eyes with him, hoping he heard all that she was trying to say without giving everything away.

"I enjoy spending time with you and Jax. I think you know that by now. Tonight, I just wanted to be with you," he admitted, figuring he had nothing to lose. He wasn't ready to propose anything more than dating but needed her to know that she was quickly becoming a priority and someone he saw some form of future with.

"Colton…" she interrupted, putting her guard up ever so slightly.

"Meg, I know something happened to you or someone hurt you. I see the walls you hold up, the anxiety that it provokes. I'm in no rush to turn this or us into anything you aren't ready for. I want you to know that. Whatever your past holds, you can tell me when you're ready, and maybe you'll never be ready. In the meantime, you can count on me. You can trust me. I won't let anything happen to you or Jax, and you can count on that." His sincerity and vulnerable heart on the line, he said everything she needed to hear.

Tears threatened as his words sunk in, and he found his way to her heart. How did this incredible man find her? He accepted every piece of her without even knowing what he was signing up for. There wasn't a word she could say that conveyed how he made her feel in that moment. She leaned in and kissed him, hoping he read every page of her story and everything she was feeling in that kiss.

Their steamy kiss was interrupted by the ping of her phone. She was reluctant to check it, but it could be about Jax and couldn't be ignored.

"It's a text from Sam," she said while reading it.

"Really, what's it say? Everything okay?" He said with concern.

Megan handed him the phone, smile on her face, so he could read it for himself.

M-

Kids are sleeping in the blanket fort that they

made with D. Can J just stay over? Get
him in the morning after breakfast?
-S

Colton grinned and looked at her. It seemed their evening just got a little longer. He raised his eyebrows, questioning her response. To his delight, she gave him a dramatic nod and wicked raise to her eyebrows. He looked back to the phone and replied,

S-
I love you, girl. We'll see you in the morning!
-C

Colton grabbed her hand and pulled her from her seat, giving her a quick kiss before dragging her through the parked cars, once again, all the way to his truck, causing her to laugh breathlessly the entire way. Once there, he opened her door and lifted her to her seat, giving her one final kiss before he drove them down the mountain.

Megan was certain this was a premeditated event planned by the menacing matchmaker fairies again, but she wasn't complaining. They had already planned to finish their evening with a movie, but both were hoping it would end with a sleepover of their own.

11

———

Colton held Megan's hand all the way down the mountain. He had a smile that wouldn't fade for days as he listened to her contagious excitement over her new ideas for the Holiday Fair, which were inspired by their evening. It was now the "Holiday Hoe Down Bazaar," featuring their first annual "Crystal Showdown Gala," a formal ending to a week-long chain of events. This was one of the best days Colton had for as long as he could remember, and he hoped it wasn't the last.

They ended their evening at his house so they could let the animals in and to bed for the night. Nancy pushed her kittens to the mudroom, followed by the other dogs and Doug the goat. Even Rambo was in for the night, perched at the top of the snuggled up stack of pets in the long, custom dog bed that lined one side of the room.

Megan was impressed by their nighttime routine and found it absolutely adorable. She sat and gave them each good night pets and sweet "good nights," especially Duke… he was becoming quite special to her.

She found Colton in the kitchen, making popcorn and hot

chocolate while gathering a few other movie snacks. They quickly settled on a romantic movie that happened to be a mutual favorite. She was surprised that he enjoyed the movie as well. He was such a man's man but had such a loving, tender heart that it shouldn't have surprised her.

He held her close throughout the movie as they laughed through the humor, held each other tighter through the spectacular love scenes, and of course at the end when she cried like a child over the happy yet sad ending.

"Oh, my gosh. I've watched that movie a million times. I don't know why it makes me cry still! How embarrassing! Ugh, it's just so beautiful though, to die in each other's arms…" She hiccuped on her last word and wiped her tears, laughing at herself.

Colton reached up and caught a runaway tear from her cheek and brushed it away. "It is a really good movie."

"I'm so impressed. Most guys wouldn't watch it to save their lives. Nothing blows up and there isn't any blood or fast cars," she laughed.

"I'm not most guys I guess. I like all the other stuff you mentioned, but there is something about this movie. I suppose I just really want something like that someday. Someone to love forever, through your best and your worst," he said shyly. "Now, I sound like a whiney jackass. Next time, let's watch a movie where they blow shit up," he joked.

"You don't sound whiney. You sound amazing. Like a guy who knows what he wants and won't settle for less. She'll be the luckiest girl around." Her cheeks took on color as she revealed her admiration for him and what sounded a lot like an admission.

He knew her words were anything but a proclamation of love for him, but there was indeed something there, something she felt about him. The eternal optimist that he was, his heart began to do flips as she finally let it be known that she just might be as interested in him as he was in her.

He sat her up from his chest and pulled her close and said, "No, I would be the luckiest man around."

He kissed her. He kissed her full of heart and promise to be whatever she needed him to be for now. His kiss told her he would wait for her, whenever she was ready for more. His kiss was hot and full of the passion he wanted to share with her.

She heard his declaration loud and clear without a single word. She was ready to throw chance to the wind and explore this wonderful man who wanted her as much as she wanted him. He was one of a kind and all hers if she wanted him, and man did she want him.

She turned her body, straddling him on the couch, taking up the heat to epic levels. If he didn't already know what her intentions were, he did now as she pressed her chest to his and slowly slid down his front, making sure to sit right where she could feel his excitement.

His hands rode up her shirt, slowly up and down her sides, finally resting them where his thumbs could tease her hardened nipples. She raised her arms for him, inviting him to strip her sweater from her body, and he was happy to oblige. Her breasts were perfectly displayed in a sexy lavender lace and satin bra with little bows above each breast. Man, he *loved* her underwear. It was the *sexy* expensive boudoir type…it suited her.

She unbuttoned his shirt, pushing it from his shoulders to reveal his Adonis-like chest, hard, rippled abs, and her favorite…his wide, sexy, strong shoulders. He was something to look at, hot as hell, and she couldn't wait to taste every inch of him. She ran her hands down every hill and valley, finding her way to his waist, undoing what stood between them.

Before she could finish, he found the clasp of her bra, freeing her breasts that were as happy to see him as he was them. He closed his eyes and let out a deep sigh.

"You are so damn beautiful. You know it? So beautiful," he said before taking her mouth again.

His hands worked her breasts while he kissed his way down her neck to her collarbone and eventually her breasts. Her head fell back in pleasure as his tongue marked her as his. He stood, holding her around his waist, and walked to his bedroom.

Placing her in the middle of his bed, he slowly undid the rest of her clothing while taking tastes of her along the way. He stood from the bed and finished removing his own clothing, gaining a sigh from his lady, who apparently wanted the joy of doing so herself – next time.

The bright moonlight was cascading in from the large window above his bed, the only light in the room, intensified by the glare off the lake. She stood to her knees, crawling to the edge of the bed, appreciating the show he was giving her. He stood there, looking at her, in all his glory. He was *magnificent*.

She reached for him, unable to wait another moment to get her hands on him. All over him. She found his collarbone and sprinkled sweet kisses and nips along the trail. Her hands traced the length of his body to the impressive 'V' that had her mouthwatering as it led to his hardened length.

He was impressive, more than a handful, leaving her both nervous and excited to explore him more, feel him. He only let her stroke him for a moment before he held her hands, raising them above her head while laying her down. He loved the feel of her hands on him, but he loved to feel her more.

He kept one hand holding her arms above her head, the other skimming her body, leaving a trail of heated skin covered in goose bumps. Her pebbled nipples told him he was touching her in all the right places, her hot and ready folds confirming his thoughts. He gently teased her swollen bud, stroking her in sync with the motions of his tongue.

He let go of her hands, needing to touch more of her. Half on the bed, half standing, straddling one leg with his girth heavily resting on her thigh, he continued his assault, intensifying his strokes and motions in response to the breathy sounds she was making. He slipped one finger inside of her, then two, kissing a trail down her abdomen to where she wanted his mouth most.

She missed his weight on her thigh until she felt his hot breath against her most sensitive parts. His tongue was pure magic as it massaged her in heavy strokes, stopping to tease her hard knot over and over again. One leg over his shoulder, he spread her wider so he could go deeper.

Her body responded to his every touch with such erotic movement, he worried he would be done before he could start. It was hot, it was sexy, and he couldn't get enough. Her body began to twitch when she began to move against his mouth trying to find her pleasure. His fingers slipped back in, one, then two while his free hand made her arch at the touch of her breast.

The sensations were all-consuming, so intense. Her rhythm was fast, her breathing faster, and her cries so sensual, like an aphrodisiac that hardened him to near pain as he tried to hold off his own release. He stroked her harder, faster, responding to her every movement until she cried out his name and shattered around him, riding the waves coursing through her body.

Colton slid her back and crawled up the bed between her

legs, giving her long loving kisses as she came down from her high. He slowly filled her, inch by inch, giving her time to catch her breath. Before he knew what was happening, his tiny vixen had rolled on top of him, taking him all in.

She was hot, wet, and felt like a well-fitted glove covering him. Heaven. She began to ride him slowly, never breaking their kiss. Her kiss became harder, more purposeful as her pace quickened. She sat up, hands on his chest, tossing her head back. She rode him fast and hard. He held her waist, lifting her up and down as he ground into her.

It was so virile, primal even, as they made fast, hot love, both greedy for their finish. With one final thrust, deep inside her, she cried out for a second time. He felt her clench him hard, the waves of her finish squeezing him tighter like a rapid pulse until he followed with his ending, completely spent, completely satisfied, completely smitten.

He rolled her to her side, her exhaustion evident, and held her close. She eventually began to stroke him again, and he complied with her demands. This time, he made slow, sweet love to her long into the night.

12

———

A COLD, WET NOSE LYING ON HER ARM WAS ENOUGH TO WAKE Meg from her sleep. Trying to maneuver under the heavy arm and leg that lay across her body, she turned to find two dark eyes inches from her face, startling her until it licked her chin…Duke.

She turned to see Colton still soundly sleeping and felt content, happy. She could get used to this, wet nose and all. She scratched Duke's ears and whispered what a good boy he was. She carefully found her way out from under Colton, pulled his shirt over her head, and made her way to the kitchen where four little faces greeted her, tails wagging.

"Ah, its breakfast time, isn't it?" she questioned the furry gang before her.

She let them out while she started a pot of coffee and gathered their food bowls to fill. She had watched Colton do this a number of times. Surely it wouldn't be that hard. Their bowls were clearly labeled as was the large eight cup measuring scoop. She stacked them up as Colton did and carried them to the front porch, trying not to spill the contents.

"Shit, this is heavy. It weighs as much as Jax," she proclaimed.

She lined them up, just as Colton would, in size order. She gave them all the okay to eat, including the hand signal for Boss that she learned by watching Colton so many times. Very proud of her accomplishment, she confidently stood, hands on hips, with a satisfied look on her face until she turned to the door to check on the coffee. A chill ran down her spine.

She watched her house in the distance, along with what appeared to be a prowler getting in his dark car and driving off. Who would be out this time of morning? What was he doing outside of his car, in front of her house? She didn't get a good look at him or the car—too far away.

She pushed down the paranoia, reminded herself that she was safe. Nobody was looking for her, and if they were, they couldn't find her. Living alone in a new town was starting to play games with her mind. This wasn't the city—it was a safe little town. "Bad guys" don't lurk in places like this.

* * *

COLTON LEANED AGAINST THE WALL NEAR THE HALLWAY, arms crossed in front of him, watching Megan through the large picture window. He felt her get up – her absence had woke him from his deep satisfied slumber. He wondered how one night with her in his bed could leave such an imprint on his soul that he felt when she was gone.

He chuckled at the sight of her carrying the bulky bowls, balancing them as she made her way through the house. He almost helped her but was enjoying the show. Her final feat, signaling Boss, afforded him a cute little victory dance filled with bouncing breasts and wiggling hips that made the front of his pants twitch and heart swell. He was completely taken by her. He knew he had a lot of love to give someone, but this was overwhelming. He wondered…was it love in such a short time? If it wasn't, he didn't know how he would handle the real deal. This, whatever it was, was powerful and all consuming.

His mood quickly shifted when he noticed her joyful dancing quickly change to stone cold fear. She stood still and became pale, eyes locked on something in the distance. He followed her gaze in the direction of her house. He could see it through the dining room window from where he stood. He saw an unfamiliar car driving in the distance, not sure where it had come from or why it drained the light from her eyes.

He went to her. She snapped out of her somber mood and returned from wherever she had been when his arms circled her waist and a gentle kiss landed on her neck.

"I could get used to that, ya know," she said, finding comfort in his embrace.

"Good, my plan is working," he joked. "Where were you just now? Everything okay?"

"Huh? Oh, yeah, everything is fine. Just lost in
thought is all," she said, reaching one arm around his neck, turning to kiss him.

"You sure? You look like you've seen a ghost," he mentioned while turning her to face him.

"I'm sure." She smiled and kissed him sweetly, trying to convince herself as much as him that all was well.

"Okay, if you're sure," he said, kissing her again. "Thanks for feeding the gang."

Her smile returned with the light in her eyes at the mention of her morning task. "Well, it was my pleasure. I was honored when Duke was nominated by the gang to wake me for food."

"So, it's Duke's fault you left the bed so early," he said, giving a surly look to the dog that lowered his head.

"Aww, it's okay boy. It was time to get up anyway. They are starting to really grow on me. It was fun and quite the work out!" She laughed, flexing her muscles.

He pulled her in for a passionate kiss that she wished could have lasted forever, then said, "Shower, before coffee or after?"

"After, or you'll see a side of me sure to scare you off for good."

"In that case, I'll go first…feel free to join me." He smacked her ass as he went inside, headed for the shower.

* * *

MEG WANDERED THROUGH THE HOUSE, HEADED FOR THE kitchen for that cup of coffee she desperately needed. Grabbing a pastry from the box she had brought over the day before, she sat and thought about the past 24 hours. She really could get used to this, she thought. The companionship, his tenderness, and nights like last night. She knew this was a bad idea, but his hands, his mouth, and his devotion to her left her with a craving for more, much more.

She didn't want to hurt him, and maybe she wouldn't have to. Maybe they could stay this way forever. Forever. That's something she hadn't thought about in so long. The smile it left on her hopeful face was quickly replaced with regret and sorrow when the image of that man in the unfamiliar car flashed through her mind.

"What have I done? Oh Colton, what have I done?"

* * *

Colton had time on his hands, so he was off to find something special. His shift didn't start until the evening, and he'd just dropped Meg and Jax off at Blooming Grounds after picking up the tot at the Taylers'. He was glad he had picked Meg up at the shop the night before as it meant more time with her. She was completely dependent on him, even though for only a few hours. He liked that. He wanted her to depend on him. He wanted to take care of her and Jax.

She was kind and outgoing, and she lit up every room she entered and had everyone around her completely mesmerized by her presence…especially him. Her beauty was beyond the surface, and after last night, she would always be his muse, controlling his every thought. She had him by the balls in a big way, and he was one hundred percent okay with that.

He felt so protective of her. There was something he was missing but didn't know what. Watching her this morning so full of joy, just to see it ripped away at the sight of a car?

Something had a hold of her, and it pained him that she wouldn't let him help. She denied anything was wrong, but this was more than just paranoia. She was *haunted*. Colton wanted to fight her demons and ghosts for her, take her pain and give her pleasure. He would too – he would find a way in.

* * *

Meg loved her shop. It was fun and brought in so many of the townspeople and tourists alike. If they weren't there for flowers, they were there for coffee and a light lunch or treat by day…wine and beer by night. It was new, fresh, and fun. What wasn't there to love about this place?

Today, however, she would rather be somewhere other than Blooming Grounds. Thoughts of the night before had her wanting a certain man. As much as he made an "impression" in bed, it was everything else that had her distracted. He was so gentle and warm, took care of her at every turn. He made her feel special and cherished…something she hadn't experienced until now. She was lost in tangled thoughts of him and how she could make a life with him in it work when an abrupt roar of laughter brought her back to present.

Her cheeks blushed when she noticed every eye, surrounding the corner table she was seated at, pegged on her. The Holiday Fair meeting—all of her friends were enjoying her embarrassment to the nth degree.

"Sorry, what did I miss?" she asked nonchalantly, trying not to trip over her own words.

"I think the real question is what did we miss, honey?" Granny Lou asked with a knowing look and wink.

"I think it's pretty fucking obvious. Princess here got it on with Sparks!" Jessie delivered, straight to the point, crude as can be.

"Wait. What? You knew? I mean what? What are we talking about?" She continued to stammer, giving away everything, which lead to another roar of laughter.

Megan looked to Sam for help but received a shrug and raised eyebrows in return.

"I didn't say a word, promise. I didn't even tell them Jax stayed the night." Sam squinted and made a pained face, realizing what she just gave to the piranhas. The laughter escalated to cat-calls and high-pitched whistles worthy of an obnoxious strip club bachelorette party.

Just when Megan thought her face couldn't get any redder, it had. Evie came to the rescue like a wolf in sheep's clothing, more interested in getting the "dirt" on Princess and Sparks than getting her out of that hole she had been digging.

"Come on guys, leave her alone, poor thing," Evie said,

followed by a subtle pause before delivering the punch line. "She's probably speechless from reading her bible all night."

Boom, there it was. She could almost hear the rimshot on the background drum now. Truth be told, she was enjoying the ribbing her friends were giving. It felt good to be "normal," for a change, and have something she could share with them. Not that she would, but she could give them a teaser and let them wonder while keeping the rest all to herself.

"Okay, okay, I'm caught! Yes, Colton and I went on a very romantic date last night. We were at your Ranch, actually," she said, nodding at Morgan. "It's stunning. What an incredible experience – loved every minute of it! The food…"

"For the love of God, nobody cares about what you ate. We've been there. What the fuck happened next?" Jessie interrupted. "Sparks has been acting like a love-struck ass lately. Please, tell me he got laid and I can expect him to be back to normal on the next call because if I have to hear how friggin' wonderful you are much longer, I'm tossing him in the next fire we're called to."

"Honey, he may need a hit from that fire hose. It sounds like he's got enough heat brewin' already," Granny offered with wiggling eyebrows.

"Holy hell, ladies, leave our girl alone. Don't piss her off, or she'll leave all the Holiday Fair plannin' to us!" Carigan chimed in, hushing the gossip brigade.

"Thanks for the compliment, Meg. I'm glad you had a good time at Pinecrest. You're welcome any time, and you *don't* need a reservation. From what I hear, you guys left pretty close and cozy. No need to talk about what happened after. It's pretty damn obvious by that big ol' smile headed your way," Morgan said, nodding toward the front of the shop.

Everyone looked toward the front entrance to see Colton

walking toward the table, grinning ear to ear with bedroom eyes locked on Megan. He walked up behind her and bent down to give her a kiss while setting a box covered in ribbon in front of her.

"So, what did I just walk in on?" he asked. "Are they treating you okay? Don't take their *crap*. They are like a bunch of bratty sisters."

They all noticed the sadness that crossed her face at the mention of sister, but it was gone as quickly as it arrived. He kicked himself for being insensitive.

Jax ran up to Colton, thrilled to see him, tugging on his pant leg, yelling, "Big fuck, big fuck!"

All eyes turned to Granny Lou and Jessie, each of whom already had their hands up and blaming the other.

"Hey, I say the *F word* a lot but never about Sparks. Geez, guys!" Jessie defended.

Lou was shaking her head with her eyes closed. "I would never...and I'm shocked you assume such a thing from an old lady...please, have some class."

Colton laughed, enjoying the show while he picked up Jax. He decided to let them off the hook this time and said to Jax, "Sorry buddy, no *FIRE TRUCK* today, kiddo!"

Giggles and a couple sighs of relief stretched across the room when Colton cleared up the language as simple toddler talk.

"So what's in the box?" Carigan asked with excitement, getting the group back on topic...the box.

Jessie asked, "Need some privacy? We don't need to know all of your kinky secrets."

"Bite me, Jess," he fired.

"You have Priss Pants for that!" she retorted.

"Touché!" Megan shot back, surprising the group.

"I thought bringing flowers or candy, or even dessert to

the girl who owned the town flower shop with a coffee house inside would be tacky. So I brought you this…open it," he said, nodding to the box in front of her.

Meg slowly opened the box, nervous about what could be inside. What was left after flowers, candy, and dessert? She pulled out a big glass fish bowl, filled with small colorful rocks at the bottom and a fake green plant buried within. There was a clear plastic bag inside, containing water and one blue and purple fish with big fan-like fins. The ladies at the table began to giggle at his gift. Of course, Colton would give an animal in place of flowers.

"What the fuck is she supposed to do with a fish? Seriously Sparks, I'm disappointed in you. Ask one of us next time," Jessie scolded.

"Oh, no, honey. I think it's romantic and just the right kind of gift," Granny rebutted. He was bringing her into his world or inviting her into it, anyway.

"I love it! My first pet!" Megan said, not expecting anyone to understand but Colton. All the shyness she had exhibited, just moments before, dissolved and ended in a long, hard, hot kiss.

"Well, hot damn! If I knew there was going to be a show today, I would have brought my fan and some dollar bills!" Granny hollered with a high-pitched, two-finger whistle to follow, starting a chain of inappropriate cheering and whistling.

It appeared that Megan had just made a decision and followed it with a big statement. She had a man, and nothing was getting in her way, not even her past.

Jessie hollered, "Get a room!" earning her a nudge from Carigan.

"I think it's sweet. Don't be such a cynic, Jess," she said.

Colton broke the kiss with a big Cheshire Cat smile and smacked her ass as he headed toward the door.

"I'll see you tonight before my shift starts," he said over his shoulder.

* * *

"Where were we?" Meg asked, picking up where they had left off as if nothing had happened. Each of the ladies looked at each other, and another roar of laughter filled the space.

She went on to tell them of her plan—the Holiday Bazaar would carry on through the week, as tradition dictated, and now be called the "Holiday Hoe Down Bazaar." The big reveal that put her stamp on the event was the dance at the end of the week, which would be named the "Crystal Showdown Gala."

The old Hickory Hill Barn would serve as their event venue. It was, at least, one hundred years old and had served as a school, a church, and even a barn in its day. It was rustic, worn, and perfect for the glamorous event, even if she was the only one who could see the glam in that old building at the moment. Much of her plan was inspired by Morgan's ranch setting. Tables would be adorned with burlap and lace, along with shabby-chic center pieces, adorned with holiday red and white flowers, with strings of crystals anywhere they could stash them for their hint of chic.

She found antique chandeliers online for a steal to replace the stock barn lighting, her contribution along with the flowers. The event budget could handle the rest if area businesses donated wine, champagne, and beer, all local of course. Bakers donated desserts while local restaurants all chipped in for dinner service. Doc Charles, from the hospital ER, and his band agreed to donate their services as the entertainment for the event. She even managed to collect silent auction items from local businesses, as well as some not so local, but needed everyone's help to gather more and handed a list to each of them to call on.

They all sat speechless, in complete awe of what this mad woman in front of them had accomplished in such a short amount of time. When she asked if they had any questions, she found a table surrounded by gaping jaws and wide eyes. Shock washed over them, and only crickets could be heard. It seemed they had a real party planner on their hands – this was the *real* Meg Johnson.

13

COLTON WAS PLEASED WITH HIMSELF AND THE PERFECT GIFT he put together for Megan. Her reaction was more than he imagined. Given that kiss, it seemed he was getting through those thick walls of hers, and he just might get to keep her.

Sure, he had his fair share of women in his life, but none compared to her. Not even a close second. From the moment he first laid eyes on her at Dawson and Sam's wedding, he knew she was special, and he needed her in his world.

He noticed her reaction to the "sister" reference. He felt like an ass, given she had lost her only sister a year or so ago. The more he thought about it, however, the more her response nagged at him.

Sure it was natural to react to the loss of a loved one with sadness, but something felt unsettled. Was there more to the altered state of her emotions as quick as it may have been?

He noticed it more than once…and more of a fear than a loss. Her smile dimmed, remembering he had to work and that she wouldn't see him for 24 hours. He read that loud and clear. He felt bad at her disappointment but pleased by the fact that she would miss him. Progress…or, was it? Maybe it was more about being alone than his being gone.

What was this anxiety that seemed to be appearing more often than not these days? The closer they became, the more he noticed it. Where security should be settling in, he saw angst.

He was breaking through mountain high barricades, but there was still something there, something deeper, something bigger than the both of them. He could feel it. He would find out, he would help her, and she wouldn't have to worry again if he had anything to do with it. He would protect her from whatever was being thrown her way.

* * *

MEGAN FOUND HERSELF WATCHING OUT THE BACK WINDOW, staring at the lake and the vast forest beyond. Completely lost in thought while feeding Jax on autopilot. She pondered what life could be like with Colton around and why she already missed him terribly after only hours. His shifts were typically 48 hours on and 48 hours off, but tonight was just a short shift. He and Jessie were covering for a couple of the guys from the House who also worked with the high school football team. Trained EMTs, they acted as team trainers and went with the team to their second round of state playoffs. Small town, big deal.

She thought it best to keep things platonic – it was safer that way – but their night together was a total game changer, and she was no longer in charge of her heart. It seemed he was. He was a mile long list of things a girl could want. She was safe in McKenzie, Jax was safe, and they were building an amazing life with friends and people who cared for them as she cared for each of them.

So what was the hang up? Why was she still at battle with herself, despite the choice to move on with Colton and explore what they had? She was stuck in McKenzie Ridge regardless of her outside circumstances—she was there to hide, and she could stay even when she didn't need to hide anymore. Either way, she was safe. Her new life was falling into place, and she finally felt like she was on the right track.

So, why did she have that overwhelming sensation resting in her gut, telling her to run, fast, and not to look back? She had felt, more than once, someone watching her, but there was never anyone there that she could see. That forest would be a great place to sit, watch, and hide.

* * *

COLTON WAS PREPARING FOR WORK WHILE A CERTAIN WOMAN lingered in his thoughts. He settled his animals for the night, but one in particular was resistant. He found Duke perched on the front porch, watching Megan's house. Duke was well behaved and well trained, familiar with their routine, but tonight he was defiant. He refused obedience, refusing Colton's every command, responding with deep throaty grumbles and whimpers. It was more than obvious that Duke was fond of the lady in their life, but this was ridiculous.

"Come on boy, you can watch her from inside," Colton begged.

"You're going to make me late, Duke. Inside!" he demanded with a clapping of his hands to motivate the dog.

Still nothing but a moan.

"Look, I get it. I want to see her too, but we have stuff to do…" He hesitated to finish, realizing he was in full negotiations with a dog over a woman.

"What the hell am I doing? He's a fucking dog. Get it together, Sparks!"

He reached down to grab Duke's collar and lead him in, but his hand was met with a sharp, tooth bearing growl. It appeared that Duke was giving Colton a big "fuck you" and was perfectly fine where he was.

Colton was stumped. Duke had never reacted to anyone that way, much less him—none of his animals did. As he stood there, hands on hips, watching his dog protect Megan from afar, an uneasy chill made its way down his spine. He understood the instincts of animals, trusted them. He had witnessed, many times, the mysterious intuition of animals providing positive outcomes to less than good circumstances.

Was this what Duke was doing? Did he know something? What had he seen that his humans may have overlooked in the daily shuffle? His mind probed the odd behavior of his dog while memories of Megan and her anxious, even paranoid, behavior wandered through his mind. How many times had she brushed off such behavior, claiming nothing was wrong, leaving him unsettled and suspicious? He was certain something was haunting her. Did Duke know what it was? It was time to find out.

* * *

A LOUD, QUICK KNOCK AT THE DOOR STARTLED MEGAN BACK to the present from her daydreaming. She sat frozen, staring at a jabbering spaghetti faced toddler, smiling ear to ear with his toothy grin, wrinkled nose and all. Oh, to be carefree like Jax, not a worry in the world. She wished her biggest worry was clean pants and a full belly. But no, right now, her worry rested on what was on the other side of that door.

Another knock came, this time more urgent. She crept to

the door, back against the wall to the right, trying not to be seen through the narrow window that lined the left of the door. An image suddenly appeared, causing her to scream. A bark followed – it was Duke. Her reaction caused a few pictures to fall from the wall she was sliding down. The noise and the scream instigated more pounding on the door with Colton yelling her name, asking if she was okay.

"Hi. I wasn't expecting anyone," she said, answering the door.

"Are you okay? I thought I heard something break and a scream?" he asked, extremely concerned.

She stepped aside, opening the door wide, letting them in and said, "Oh, that was me. I was feeding Jax when I heard your knock. When I saw Duke's shadow jump in front of the window there, it startled me," she admitted with a laugh, pointing to her fallen pictures.

"Why are you so spooked? Did something happen?" he asked, looking around.

"I guess I just wasn't expecting anyone, and I never get company at this hour. It was unexpected is all."

"Well, this guy wouldn't go inside tonight. He seems spooked, himself," Colton shared. "He wanted to come here. I think we have a bit of a crush going, and I'm losing my dog to a woman."

She knelt to one knee, letting Duke lick her cheek while she rubbed his ears, and said to the pup, "Is that true, Duke? Or is he just using you to come get a kiss goodnight?"

"Well, I was thinking maybe he should stay with you tonight. You can keep each other company, get him over whatever is bothering him, but I'll take the kiss while I'm at it." He pulled her into a tight embrace, rubbing his hands down her back until they landed on her ass. His kiss was urgent and promising all the passionate things that were to come.

"I'll see you two in the morning!" he promised, swatting her on the ass as he went.

"Well, aren't you a nice surprise! Jax, we have company!" She hollered, leading Duke to the kitchen to find Jax.

* * *

Colton wasn't convinced by her story. Between Duke's behavior and her reaction, he was certain something was wrong. If they weren't already short staffed, hence him working the extra shift, he would have stayed and figured it out. She didn't need to live in fear—he would protect them, care for them…she just needed to let him.

Tomorrow, he thought, tomorrow he would get to the bottom of it and figure out what had her so worried. He gave one last look before driving off. He was glad that Duke was there. Something wasn't right. He knew it like he knew how to breathe.

* * *

Sitting around a table at the House, Colton shared his suspicions with the gang. They each took turns, hearing what he had to say and offering their advice as they saw fit.

"So, she hasn't actually said anything was wrong, and you haven't witnessed anything. Just all voodoo, psychic 'feelings'?" Jessie asked.

"No, I haven't seen anything *happen* – just seems anxious a lot, easily startled. She plays it off like it's nothing. I feel like it's something though," Colton replied. "Am I just over reacting? You make me sound like a pansy ass."

"Well, you are a pansy ass, but…" Blake chimed in, "…to be honest, I've noticed it a little bit, too."

"I think we all have but come on. She loses her sister like a year ago, inherits a baby, and moves across country. That would make anyone a little paranoid," Morgan threw in as her two cents. "The moving cross-country thing has me a little baffled, but everyone deals with grief differently."

"Maybe she left because of someone, like a dude. Maybe she wanted to be as far away as she could. That's pretty much McKenzie!" Jessie said

"Like an abuser?" Morgan asked, her voice a mix of sympathy and anger. "Oh, God. I hope not – not Meg."

Blake rubbed his chin, considering what was being tossed around, trying to pick his words carefully before saying, "She fits the profile. At the very least, she fits the profile of a runner. We just need to figure out what she is running from. I can do some digging, Sparks. You should know what you're getting yourself into, man."

"Whoa, I don't know about that, you guys. Checking up on her like that? What if she finds out?" Carigan warned.

"What if she finds out, and she's not hiding

anything…that's worse. Your ass is on the street," Morgan agreed.

Dawson stood, puffed out his chest and went all alpha. "But what if there is something to find? What if she is in danger? Or worse, what if she did something? How does he protect her from something if he doesn't know what it is?"

"Dawson has a point, man. A few clicks on the computer, maybe a phone call or two? You say the word," Blake offered.

"I don't know. I trust her. I'm more worried than anything. I appreciate the offer, man, but let's wait. It could just be my own insecurities kicking my ass," Colton admitted.

"Offer stands," Blake said, slapping Colton on the shoulder before leaving the table.

Blake understood his friend's hesitation, but he had that same gut instinct that something wasn't right, and it certainly wasn't out of sympathy for Colton's insecurities. It was because there was something off, and any one of them could be in danger, especially Colton. He planned to do a little digging, see what he could turn up. He would decide then if he should tell Sparks about the suitcase and money in the trunk.

No need to give him more to worry about or to spook a runner…for now. In the meantime, he would watch out for his friends and his town. Something didn't feel right.

14

———

After several games of fetch with a very willing three-legged dog, Meg put Jax to bed for the night. He would sleep well after a night of chasing the dog and endless belly giggles. The two played so well together, and it was a fun way to fill the rest of their evening.

Megan had to admit to herself that she did indeed feel safer with Duke there. Not sure what it was about him that offered such security, she decided not to mull it over or dissect the issue. He was there, and she was happy for it.

Duke spent the evening going from window to window, room to room, sniffing at each door, as if making his rounds. Several times. She managed a little quiet time after Jax went to bed and put in a movie.

Negotiations with Duke began regarding his pouting and not being allowed on the furniture. He wasn't allowed at home, so it wouldn't be right there, either. He sat at her feet with his head in her lap, giving her puppy dog eyes. Of course, he had that down. He was a dog.

As the night wore on, she gave in and quickly had a 75-pound lap dog laying across her legs through the rest of her movie. He even whimpered and licked her tears during the sad scenes. Who knew one of her favorite new friends in this town would be a dog?

When she felt her eyelids drooping, Meg gave in to the exhaustion that had been hovering and made her way to bed – Duke on her heels. She was feeling a bit unsettled, despite the happily ever after she had just watched on TV. Her body was craving rest, so to bed she went, hoping rest would ease her brewing anxiety. Her plan to stay up late and exhaust herself in an effort to sleep long and hard through the night was only partially successful. She had the exhaustion down, but the rest was an epic fail.

Getting on her own nerves, she told herself to get it together, reminding herself of the same thing she had repeated for months—she had been in McKenzie nearly a year. She was careful. Nobody knew who she was. She was safe here. Maybe this was just her clingy subconscious wishing she had a big strong man beside her. Since when was she the needy type?

She settled into bed and gave in to more thoughts of Colton and their night together. He was an amazing man—kind, thoughtful, nurturing, and protective. He was an equally amazing lover, putting her needs and wants first, seeing that she was thoroughly sated and completely taken.

He was what most girls wished for. She had him, and he wanted her…not for her money, not for her name. Granted, he didn't know about that part of her life, but if he did, she knew he wouldn't care. He just wanted her for her because he was one of a kind, special. She was falling…hard.

The butterflies that thoughts of him created quickly disappeared at the low growl coming from Duke. She lay still as a course of fear whittled its way in. Duke shot up and charged the doorway, barking ferociously. She sat up and gathered her blankets around her, trying to find her way through the panic that was threatening, low in her gut.

"What is it boy?" She whispered, her voice shaking, barely audible. She waited for him to answer while Duke just looked at her, head tilted, likely thinking the same thing she was. "Seriously, Meg, get it together. This isn't fucking Lassie!"

The growls continued with intermittent barking, causing her instincts to kick in and take over. She dialed Colton. Glad she wore yoga pants and a tank top to bed, she slid her arms into a sweatshirt and moved to the bedroom doorway, just behind Duke. While she was waiting for Colton to answer the line, her gut was screaming at her to run...run like hell and don't look back. Her heart, however, said wait for him.

* * *

Sitting around the table, shooting the shit, the gang waited for their uneventful shift to finally end. Colton broke away from the conversation when his phone rang, startling him at such a late hour. When Meg's name ran across the screen, an icy chill settled in. He knew something was wrong. He answered the call but was overwhelmed with the sound of Duke barking hysterically in the background. He turned to his friends, concern crossing his face, gathering everyone's attention.

"Meg, what's wrong?" He questioned. Only the sound of her breathing greeted him. "Meg, talk to me. What's wrong, baby?"

The sound of his voice brought her comfort, and his endearing reference gave her a voice. She began to whisper, her fear evident by her shaky words.

"Colton? Colton, something is wrong. Duke. He is

running from door to door. He is trying to get out." She paused as reality set in. Her whisper became breathy and faint as she delivered her fearful assumption. "I think someone is out there."

Colton knew something had been off earlier that day – for days really. He should have trusted his gut and not left her. Hell, he should have listened to his fucking dog! He turned to the group, who was already giving him their full attention from his few concerned words and body language.

Blake, the least surprised by this call, stood and moved closer to his friend. If his suspicions were correct, he was about to go and arrest a bad guy. He radioed Dawson and Carigan, who had been out on an invalid assist call, to see where they were en route. They would likely be the closest.

Although not protocol, this was personal, and that's what they did in this small town. They took care of each other, crossing the lines of career when needed. They were all highly trained as search and rescue – they all trusted each other in any capacity.

"Have you seen or heard anything outside?" Colton asked.

"No, I was starting to fall asleep. He insisted on lying at my feet, was fine, and then sprung up out of nowhere. I've never seen him like this, Colton…I'm so scared," she admitted with a small sob.

"Okay, honey, stay put. I'm comin'," he replied as he moved toward the door, Blake following. "Where's Jax?"

Her voice back to a barely there whisper, she replied, "Sleeping. I'm grabbing him now."

As Colton gathered his things while keeping Megan calm on the line, Blake had reached Dawson and Carigan on their way back to the house and only a short mile or so from the sparsely developed area both Megan and Colton's houses populated. With a quick update from Blake, they turned around and headed east to see if they could intercept the problem for their friend.

"We are pulling up now, Blake," Carigan reported. "We can see the property now. All looks dark at Sparks' and Megan's houses. We'll do a drive by and circle back so we don't spook anyone," she finished.

"Sounds good, O'Reilly. I'm headed that way with Sparks, five minute ETA," Blake updated, certain that there was more going on, and Tayler and O'Reilly were about to stumble upon it.

"Be careful. Watch your backs. I don't feel good about this," he finished before turning his attention back to Colton.

They made it to the door when Dawson radioed in, changing a suspicious hunch to an emergency. "Guys, we have flames lighting up the garage—see it through the side window! Appears contained to the garage. Get out here! We're getting them out…" Dawson shouted, the waiver in his voice indicating he was running.

The gang suited up and took their places, headed to help one of their own. Organized chaos ensued as they made their way the short trek across their small town. Carigan could be heard over the radio, yelling at Megan to open the door, her ferocious pounding heard while Duke's frantic barking made its way through too. Emotions ran high as they listened to the events unfolding just miles from them.

"Meg, open the door. Dawson and Cari are there to get you out. There's a fire, Megan. You need to get out! I'm on my way!" Colton pleaded, trying to remain calm. He could let the terrified emotions run later when both Megan and Jax were safe in his arms.

Right now, he just needed to get to them. If anything happened to them, he wouldn't forgive himself for leaving them alone. They had become his world, his everything, and now their lives balanced in peril.

He could hear her jagged breathing, but she wasn't responding. "Baby, please, answer me. You need to get out! Where are you? They'll come in and get you. Megan…"

He was cut off by the last thing he would hear her say before his world shifted upside down.

"Fire…" was all she got out before she heard the deafening sound coming from the front of the house. It was a loud, ear-piercing bang that left her ears ringing in sharp pain.

Colton heard the explosion through the phone, but more so, outside the vehicle he was traveling in. He was close enough to hear it but not close enough to help her. What was worse was that he no longer heard Megan or Duke over the phone.

He picked up the radio and called to Dawson and Carigan. The line was dead, no response. A feeling of angry panic filled him. His girl and his friends were off the radar. He was paralyzed by the fear and the idea that each of them could be badly hurt…or worse. Tears stung his eyes as he accelerated, willing his truck to get there faster. He knew loss, knew abandonment by those he loved, knew loneliness and not having anyone to love or love him back…he wasn't ready for a repeat of those lessons.

His attention was brought back to the radio when static, followed by Carigan's voice, brought him some relief.

"Colton, we're almost inside. Dawson broke through a window. We'll find her!"

That was the last he heard from the scene until he came upon it himself. Just moments later, the cavalry quickly jumped into action, battling the wicked flames.

Going against protocol and ignoring his responsibilities as part of the team battling the inferno, he raced to the window, yelling Megan's name. He was met by Dawson, who obviously took a hit by whatever just happened. He had superficial cuts on his face, a nice gash on his forehead, and bloodied arms that appeared to be minor at first glance.

"We found her. Cari is with her…sort of…hurry!" Dawson led Colton to the back of the house, both running and coughing as the smoke offended their lungs. They finally stood in Megan's bedroom, only to find Carigan knelt down, one hand out in front of her, sweet talking a growling, teeth baring, pissed off Duke.

"She's in there," Carigan said in a soft calm voice, slowly pointing to the closet door Duke was bravely guarding. "He's guarding her, protecting them. I called for her, but she won't come out."

"Are you sure she's…" Colton began to question.

"We cleared the house. All that's left is that closet and our brave boy here," she responded, cutting him off.

Colton moved closer, not sure how to approach his own dog. He had never seen him behave in such a way. He said his name a couple of times, called him a good boy, and even told him to come. Duke did not budge. He called for Meg and didn't get a response.

Relief struck when he heard Jax's faint cry and Megan consoling him, rather loud for someone hiding, when it struck him…the explosion. She couldn't hear them, which meant Duke probably couldn't either. Instinct set in, and he decided in that moment there really was purpose in everything. Having a deaf dog at home, who only responded to hand signals, he thought surely this could help with Duke.

All of the animals had witnessed the communication between Colton and Boss. He hoped like hell this was the answer. They needed it to be. The smoke was thickening throughout the house, and breathing was becoming somewhat labored.

He knelt down before Duke, gaining his direct attention. He put up a hand, signaling him to heel. Duke remained where he was but stopped growling, tilting his head in confusion. Colton raised his hand again, giving the same signal. Duke paused before finally moving to where Colton was kneeling. Slowly Colton reached for Duke and quickly scratched his ears before signaling him to sit and stay. Duke obeyed.

He made his way to the walk-in closet where he found Megan curled up with Jax in the back corner, tears staining her cheeks, pale from fear. He moved toward them, quickly sweeping them up in his arms when she finally let out a defeated sob that broke his heart. Carigan moved in behind, reaching out for Jax, waiting for permission to remove him from her petrified grip. She reluctantly let him go, and Colton lifted her, carrying her to the large window Dawson had cleared so they could safely leave the home and avoid the smoke.

Dawson carefully helped Carigan out, holding Jax until she was on the other side and could carry him to the ambulance. Colton wasn't letting Megan out of his arms. Dawson, completely understanding, having been there before himself with his now wife, Sam, simply supported him. He offered balance as Colton escaped the near tragedy, grateful to have his life in his arms.

Making their way around the smoky house, opposite the side the fire was blazing, Megan and Jax were taken to the waiting ambulance to be checked over. As they rounded the corner of the home, Duke turned around and took off at a dead run, barking, making his way toward the nearby wooded area. Obedient to a 'T', this was out of character, and Blake had a hunch that he was chasing more than a squirrel or nighttime creature. Reading his expression and body language, Morgan knew exactly what her partner was thinking.

Tapping his shoulder as she passed him, she ran after the dog, hand on her weapon, her flashlight illuminating the path before her. They finally came to a stop in a clearing where Duke had halted. He was whimpering, first stepping left, then right, he seemed unsure which way to go next. He sat at their feet, looking to them for answers.

"Shit, he's fast for only having three legs!" Morgan said, hunched over with her hands on her knees, trying to catch her breath.

"Christ, no kidding. It's not like either one of us is out of shape, either!" Blake replied, just as winded from their chase through the forest.

"What do you think he was chasing, and how did he lose the scent, right here, there's nowhere to go but on foot," she questioned, although she had a hunch she already knew the answer.

"Fuck if I know, but I think it's a who, not a what," he admitted. "I don't think our friend here lost the scent at all—he's just not sure which one to follow."

The unease Blake was radiating hit Morgan like a brick wall. Blake was highly trained, ex-military, although no one knew exactly what branch or the extent of his service. They didn't know much about his past. He didn't talk about it, probably couldn't. What they did know was that he was never wrong. Blake could feel trouble miles away and weeks in advance. If he was so certain there were too many paths to chase out here, she knew they had someone to look for.

"We aren't going to find what we are looking for out here tonight. They could be anywhere by now. We don't have a team or enough to justify one. Low-key eyes on everyone, Jameson…got it? We have a problem on our hands."

She nodded, and they headed back in the direction they had come. They had their work cut out for them. They were chasing ghosts.

* * *

MEGAN AND JAX WERE BEING TREATED BY DAWSON AND Carigan back at the ambulance when Blake and Morgan returned. Colton was at her side, quickly joined by Duke.

"How are they?" Morgan asked, studying Megan, wondering who would be after her. Random act or someone from her previous life?

"Baby Jax seems well. She must've had him cradled just right – his ears look good," Carigan responded. "But our girl here can't hear over the loud ringing in her ears!"

"We're taking them in, let Doc Charles give them a once over at the ER," Dawson chimed in.

Colton stepped closer, hand on the gurney Meg was sitting on, and said, "I'm riding with you guys. I'm not leaving them." The defensiveness, or perhaps protective nature he had, rang loud in his tone.

"I figured you were, buddy," Dawson replied with a smile. "Can't say I blame you. What about this guy?" He asked, pointing to Duke.

Morgan reached down to give him a long rewarding pet and said, "We'll take him back to the House with us as soon as we are done here. I'm pretty sure he doesn't want to be left alone so soon...poor guy. We'll get him over to Dr. Bain for an ear check, just in case"

"Thanks, guys. Appreciate it," Colton said while bending

down to scratch Duke's ears. "You were a good boy tonight. Good boy, Duke."

"We're about to get crowded. Sparks. You're a trained medic. You're riding in the back with our two guests," Carigan ordered, giving Jax a quick tickle to the tummy. "Tayler, shotgun. Grab a kit and clean up those wounds. Looks like you're getting some stitches on that big forehead of yours tonight. I'm driving."

"I have a big forehead?" Dawson asked, rubbing his head.

"Just get in, ya jackass," Carigan scolded, getting a laugh. She wasn't one to swear, but when she did, it was smothered in her Irish dialect.

Dawson fired back, "Such an angry leprechaun, O'Reilly!" then ran to his side of the truck to avoid her wrath.

She closed the doors to the ambulance, jumped in, and drove off. Blake and Morgan watched the ambulance leave with their friends inside. They were glad their injuries appeared minor and were hopeful they would check out as such.

"Did you notice how she wouldn't even look at us?" Morgan asked. "Of course, you did. What am I saying?"

"Yeah, I noticed. Something is going on there. She had a chance to say something and didn't. She's afraid. Really afraid," he said, scratching his chin.

"Victim or perp?" she asked, hoping it wasn't the latter. She had really come to like Meg and didn't want to find that she was a criminal.

"I want to say vic. Remember that day, on the side of the road, with the flat tire?" He questioned, jogging Morgan's memory. She nodded in response, acknowledging the incident.

"When I went to pull the jack and spare from the trunk, there was a suitcase and a bag of money."

"On the run," she stated, rather than questioned. She was trained to recognize that as a classic symptom or behavior of an abuse victim.

"It gets better. It wasn't a random flat tire. It was intentional or appeared to be," he offered. "I noticed a dark sedan off to the side of the road, just beyond where we were. It was there when we arrived but turned around and left after we got there," he finished.

"If they were already there, why didn't they offer to help?" Morgan questioned, catching on.

"Exactly. I wasn't sure it mattered until now. I think we need to look into Megan Johnson a little closer. We may have trouble in our town, and our friends are in the line of fire," Blake said, obviously worried.

They would do their job, follow the clues, and not say a word until there was something to share or someone to arrest. Blake's intuition ran deep, almost too deep for his liking, and he didn't like the weight this left in his gut.

15

SEVERAL DAYS QUIETLY WENT BY, AND MEGAN HAD FOUND herself going stir crazy. Her house was uninhabitable, and although everyone from Granny Lou to even Jessie offered to put her and Jax up until the repairs were done on her house, Colton wouldn't hear of it. He had every reason in the book, pleading his case as the most logical host.

He used everything from it being easier to oversee repairs, given the proximity of her house, to Duke and the other animals missing them. She concluded that it was less about the animals and more about him needing her close. He had been hovering, waiting on her hand and foot, even had friends over to "visit" when he had to leave. She didn't need a babysitter, but given the circumstances, she understood why he felt she did.

It had been a horrifying night, sheer terror as she felt her past closing in on her with nowhere to run but a closet. The investigation had finally closed as a gas leak from the furnace in the garage. The majority of the damage was isolated to that area and the two interior rooms that butted up against the garage.

The rest of the house was fine other than the smoke damage, which was easily repaired, considering. Her car, although in the driveway at the time, sustained damage from the heat of the blaze. Funny, her instinct was to run, but her means to do so wasn't available to her – irony at its best.

So here she was, roaming from window to window, looking for cars that didn't belong or strangers who were up to no good. Time certainly wasn't on her side. If this was indeed a warning, or worse, an attempt on her life, it was only a matter of time before her number was up. He – or perhaps it was "they" – would be back.

She didn't want to run. She loved her town, her shop, all of their friends. This community felt more like home than anywhere else. So did he. He was her heart, and she couldn't bring herself to break it. Maybe she could stay. Maybe, she thought, she should tell him. He said he wanted to protect her, take care of her. Maybe he *could* help her. But, would it be worth putting his life at risk too?

Construction was due to start on her house in the coming days, and she would be able to move back in by Christmas. She wasn't sure how she felt about that. She had managed to settle in at Colton's quite nicely, and her nerves had calmed, allowing her new perspective. It had been a random accident, the investigation confirmed it, and she was determined to keep her demons at bay, taking away the power they had over her. She had become her own worst enemy, turning nothing into a bunch of somethings.

Eventually, sometime soon, she would talk to Colton about her past. It was the final nail to be put in that coffin before she could truly leave it behind and move on. The nagging guilt of carrying such a dramatic secret was the source of her short comings. It made her anxious, fearful, and suspicious when there was nothing to worry about to begin with. Telling him everything would free her of that bondage that held her trapped in her own circumstance. For now, she was safe. More importantly, she was happy.

Happy had been a distant friend until now. She finally felt content, felt like she belonged, felt like she was wanted for more than her money and status. Colton made her genuinely happy and made her realize there was more to her than those things too. He was healing and exactly what she had needed at such a vulnerable time, allowing her the clarity to see her purpose and that she was fulfilling her destined role, here in McKenzie Ridge.

Sharing his bed each night made her happy too. She was done running. She was ready to start really living and own her new life. No regrets.

* * *

While Meg was working, Colton found himself sitting with his pets on his front porch, twiddling his thumbs for the first time in his adult life. He never sat alone on his porch, talking to his animals…bored. In a matter of just a few months, Megan turned his world upside down. He couldn't even remember what it was like before her. She filled the gaping hole he had been carrying most of his life. She was his missing piece…she completed him.

Getting Meg back to work today was a good idea, he thought, but he couldn't help but worry. It was hard to leave her, but he knew he couldn't hover any more than he had. She was getting restless. He could *see* it, *feel* it even.

Something had not been right about the fire, despite the "accidental" nature. Her reaction was another issue. Sure, fear made sense, but she was absolutely spooked, petrified, like she had seen a ghost. Rather than run from the danger, she hid in the middle of it.

He pained for her, ached for answers. He would do anything to take that fear away. He waited his entire life for her, and he wouldn't let anything happen to her. He would take her demons, fears, anxieties, hurt, and pain and absorb every last bit of it for her. He knew the night they met, months ago, that she was special—she was his.

Colton had fallen harder each day since that first meeting. Love at first sight is such a cliché he didn't think he believed in it, but he did believe in fast love. He was in so deep he ached for her. Everything she felt, he felt deeper.

He knew she had fallen for him but wouldn't let him in entirely. She was afraid to. It wasn't only obvious to him but to everyone. He saw it on their faces, in their words, in their hugs goodbye. She had a family here, and it started with Colton.

He would find a way to get through to her, get her to open up. He couldn't have another night like the night of the fire. Colton had lived through enough loss in his life, and he was done with it.

He would do anything for that woman. He would chase her to the ends of the earth and back, over and over again. It made him sound weak, needy, and insecure, but Colton was anything but. His vulnerabilities were what made him strong and made him the right man for Megan. He loved her.

He couldn't imagine a life absent of Meg. He wanted to love her forever. All Colton needed to do now was get through that stubborn wall of hers and convince her that she needed to love him forever, too.

* * *

MEGAN CLOSED BLOOMING GROUNDS EARLY TO PREPARE FOR the ladies to arrive for a meeting. Colton stopped in to pick up Jax so the ladies could have their committee meeting in a kid-free zone. He noticed the bottles of wine and glasses set on the table. There was beer as well…Jessie.

He was glad she was cutting loose and having a relaxing night. He held her close, giving her a detailed promise of what was waiting for her at home. He lifted her off the ground while he gave her a preview by way of a steamy kiss that would blush the cheeks of just about anyone who may have walked in on them.

When he set her on the table, facing the front of the store, she noticed a man staring at her from across the street, causing her to gasp. She pushed Colton away and stood, frozen in place, shocked. Colton grabbed her shoulders and asked what was wrong. He turned the direction she was staring and saw a lone car pass by and wandering tourists.

"Meg, seriously, what is it?"

"Oh, sorry. I thought I saw someone standing there, but I don't know where he went?"

Colton turned again. There still wasn't anyone standing there, just the passersby and light traffic. Nobody was standing there, watching them. Perhaps she was having a flash back, he thought.

"I'm sorry, Colton. It must have been a shadow or something, I don't know. I just thought I saw someone out of the corner of my eye. I didn't mean to worry you!" She wrapped her arms around him and let out a deep breath. This really needed to stop happening, she thought.

"It's okay." He kissed her for reassurance. "You just need a break. Have fun tonight. I'll see you later."

With one last kiss, he propped Jax on his shoulders and

went for the door just as the ladies started filing in. She wouldn't be alone, providing them both relief.

16

———

BLOOMING GROUNDS RESEMBLED THE LIKES OF A HOT HEN house. The final committee meeting for the week long Holiday Hoe Down Bazaar and Crystal Showdown Gala was underway. Their meeting was accompanied by an impromptu "wine tasting" that may or may not have made their little meeting more of a girls' night drink fest. The more they drank, the louder they got and looser the conversation.

Megan was especially loose and on glass number who knew what of wine. She needed to get lost in the alcohol and forget her troubles for the night, which was a recipe for disaster in the making. She knew the man across the street was real. Like the last time she caught someone watching her, she found him familiar but couldn't place him.

He wasn't a customer – that would have been an obvious connection. Who was he? Why was he looking in her shop, and where did he go? Maybe she *was* losing her mind. Time for another drink.

"It sounds like everything is on track!" Sam said to the group while clapping her hands. "This is going to be our best year yet!"

"I'll drink to that. It's going to be fan-fucking-tastic!" Meg deadpanned, lifting her glass to all the ladies around the table. All eyes were wide and jaws dropped. "We are going to celebrate this shiizt," she finished before tossing back her glass and chugging the last of her wine.

"What the hell? Fancy Pants just dropped an *F bomb*? Oh, this is good!" Jessie joked, laughing hysterically at her swaying and slurring friend.

"Oh, honey, I think it's time to switch cups. Let's get you some coffee!" Evie said, moving to the barista bar to make the much needed sobering sauce.

Her giggle wasn't as subtle as she had hoped. She had to agree with Jessie. *This* was funny, right up there with toddlers swearing. You know you shouldn't laugh but can't help yourself because it's so shocking when it happens.

Jessie grabbed an open bottle and reached over to fill the glass Meg was twisting upside down and shaking violently, as if it just needed help to refill itself. Meg let out a slushy sounding hiccup that ended in a little burp that was so out of character, it even caught her by surprise as she quickly covered her mouth, trying unsuccessfully to stifle her giggle. Burping had never been funny until now.

"Here ya go, Princess! I got you, girl!" Jessie said with a mischievous laugh while filling that glass back up. It earned her an excited, wide-eyed giggle from her schnockered friend.

Carigan weighed in on Jessie's doings. "Jessie, come on. I don't know if that's such a good idea. She's already pretty hammered." Her disapproval was anything but believable. Her smile wide, laughing while a two handed, wine drinking Megan tried to line her glass up with her mouth.

"Oh, she'll be fine, won't you honey?" Gran asked, tossing her own glass back. Her "arthritis" must have been acting up again because her glass wasn't filled with wine or beer, but she was clearly just steps behind Megan in the sloshed department. Gran drank for medicinal purposes only, after all.

She just carried her inebriation a little better, more experience. Lou Shaw was no dummy. Once the coffee came out, she knew the liquor was done for. If she fed the girl wine, no one would be watching her. So, enabler was her mantra for the evening, mostly because she didn't bring the bottle of booze that compliments coffee.

"Megan, lets sober you up sister. Have you even been drunk before? Oh, my God, honey let's leave our shoes on," Morgan pleaded until the shoes proved to be a walking hazard. High heels and drinking didn't mix, especially with a virgin drunk. "Better yet, you sit. I'll get the shoes."

While Morgan helped with the shoes, the rest of the group chuckled. Meg tossed her head back, eyes closed, and swayed to the music only she could hear while stroking the top of Morgan Jameson's head. Morgan froze, gazed up through her lashes with a shocked look and said, "Are you..." She paused, scanning the table before pinning a *what the fuck* look back on Meg. She finished her thought with, "...are you *petting* me? Is she *petting* me?"

The table of women roared with laughter, Jessie in particular. She handed Megan her wine glass, looking for more cheap entertainment at her friend's expense.

"No, I'm *HUGGING* you!" she replied, wrapping her arms around Morgan and pulling her in for a hug. "You guys are the best. Really, the very best. I love you guys!" She declared, letting Morgan out of her vice-like grip.

"Holy shit! This is epic! Tell us more, Priss Pants. Tell us everything!" Jessie instigated, pouring herself another cold one. She enjoyed being fairly sober. She was glad it wasn't her about to deliver on the truth serum.

"Jessie, that's enough. Poor thing is completely shit faced. We can't let her go home like that!" Carigan reasoned.

"Like hell we can't! Sparks will fucking thank us. If she *loooves* us, this *can't* go bad for him. Look at her! Who the eff is she dancing with? Oh, my God, where's my phone? I need to record this!" Jessie blurted while shuffling things around, looking for her cell phone on the table. "FOUND IT! Yes!"

"Jessie, put it away! That's low, even for you!" Morgan scolded.

"Ahhh, come ooon! Don't be such a piss…piss…priss pants, Morgie!" Megan slurred, pointing her thumb back at herself. She stood in a not so steady manner, ready to address her friends with a heartfelt speech.

"Loook, I'm just so happy, and I love you guys like sisters, even though you're not my sisters, but if I could have more sisters, you guys…would be my sisters!" She shouted the last few words with an emotional conviction that was as much sweet as hilarious. Jessie was holding herself at the waist, lost in her fit of laughter. Granny Lou kept fist pumping above her head, shouting yes, amen, and hallelujah. The rest of the ladies just sat there, hands over mouths, trying to stifle their laughs, each afraid to look at each other and risk completely losing it!

"You guys are my bitches! Not like my *side* bitches – you're like my *main* bitches, but in a totally platonic hetero way!" Meg proclaimed.

Just when they all thought she was done pledging her love for them, she delivered her grand finale, and was it ever grand. "Even Jessie. That's how much love there is 'cause she can be a total bitch, but that's what makes her Jessie and why everyone loves her, so it's alllll gooood."

All eyes shifted to Jessie, who wasn't laughing anymore, like a deer in headlights. She had a sharp glare on the wino in the room. If looks could kill, Megan Johnson would be dying a slow, painful, heinous death. Jessie glanced around the room, taking in all the looks of concern. Morgan was halfway standing, ready to prevent a punching versus hair pulling brawl, when Jessie blurted out a deep roaring belly laugh that shocked them all, sending them into fits of tearful laughter.

Megan was on a roll, enjoying her freedom to say whatever crossed her drunken mind.

"Yeah, well I love you too, Princess, even if you annoy the shit out of me with all of your proper bullshit. Christ, now you're making me all sappy, so fuck off…and stuff!"

"I knew it! You *do* like me! This is the best fucking night. I really like using that word. I get why you use it all the time," Meg admitted.

Snorts and more laughs encouraged her to continued, fist in the air. "We are like a really small gang of really awesome bitches!"

"Kind of like Colton's animals, they're a small gang." She laughed to herself at the inside joke about the animals, oblivious to the fact that Colton and Blake had just walked in and stood behind her completely shocked by her final declaration. "I love the animal gang. I love him, too."

Gasps filled the room, Colton the center of their attention. Stunned didn't begin to describe the look that washed over his face. His eyes were wide, eyebrows raised, head tilted, mouth wide open. The guy was floored and completely speechless.

"What's wrong Sparks? You okay there buddy?" Jessie

questioned with an unflattering snort that caught Blake's attention.

"Was that a…snort? Did you seriously just snort?" Blake said with a laugh.

"Fuck off, Coop!" she replied.

Colton stood before the group pointing to Meg, and then the table littered with wine bottles, looking back and forth trying to put together the obvious.

"Did she…" he began to ask, pointing at Meg then the table again. "Is she…" His shock and confusion landed back on Meg. "Did you guys get her…drunk?"

Everyone spoke at the same time, some offended by the accusation, some, finding it hilarious.

"We didn't get anyone drunk, Sparks," Evie defended. "We've all been drinking, and well, I guess we didn't realize she was such a light weight, and maybe we lost count of how much she had."

He counted the wine bottles, noting the beer and bottle of whatever Lou was sneaking back into her rather large bag.

"Holy shit, that's like nine bottles!" Blake said, laughing.

"Oh, yeah, and Fancy Pants here polished off close to two herself, I'm guessing!" Jessie offered, not helping matters. "I got it all on video. We can review the footage to better determine her level of indulgence…when she's sober of course!" she said with an asshole smile.

"You taped it? Jesus, Jess…dick move, even for you!" Colton shot back.

"What? Why does everyone keep saying that? It was *funny*. She loves everyone, or didn't you catch *that* part? You're welcome, asshole." Jessie wasn't mad. She was rather enjoying the show and Colton's state of bewilderment. She was pretty sure he had no clue what to do with her now.

"Heeeeey! I wasn't expecting you here!" Meg said,

approaching Colton, pulling him into a big awkward hug. She grabbed his face and planted a big sloppy kiss right on his lips, complete with dramatic sound effects and all. Colton's surprise was made obvious by his stiff posture and rapidly blinking eyes.

"High five, Blake! Isn't this fan-fucking-tastic? This Holiday bow down, blow down, whatever it's called is going to be amaze-balls! Right? Where's my *Amen*, Lou?" Megan said with a half turn, pointing an extended arm to Granny Lou.

"Amen, Pussy Pants! It's going to rock, girl!" Gran tossed up the classic rock and roll gesture of two fingers and bobbing her head as if at a metal concert.

"Uhh, isn't it…Priss Pants?" Blake asked, shrugging his shoulders when Colton gave him the stink eye.

"Pfffft. I think Lou is a little tiiipsy!" Megan joked, in a sing-song voice, completely unaware of just how tipsy *she* was.

She began to fall back, losing her footing a bit, landing right in Colton's arms.

"She's completely shit-faced, man!" Blake laughed.

"Yeah, I can see that. Thanks, Captain Obvious," Colton rebutted, balancing a three sheets to the wind and giggling Megan.

"We came down to see if anyone needed a ride home. Saw the bottles out earlier. Didn't expect this though," Colton laughed, finally, the humor of it all settling in.

"I'm good, Sparks. Didn't have much. I'll get Gran and Evie home. Why don't you leave Jax at my place? I'm sure he's asleep anyway. I think you are going to have your hands full with our drunken friend here," Sam offered. It was pretty obvious that Meg was about to have a really bad night, complete with rooms spinning and toilet hugging.

"Are you sure? I'm pretty sure this one is going to pass out cold the minute we hit the road."

"Nope, I insist. The kids love having him anyway! You guys go."

"Dude, Sam's right. Jess, Cari, Jameson, and I will deal with this and lock up. We got it man," Blake finished.

"What? Why the hell am I cleaning?" Jessie fitted.

"Because you're a pain in the ass and owe her a solid. Delete that video, too," Blake scolded as he received the middle finger wave from Jessie.

"Jessie," Megan whispered for all of Oregon to hear. "It's a good plan – you get to be alone with Blake. I see how you guys look at each other. You go, sister!" Megan gave an awkward, wide-mouthed wink, accompanied by a thumbs up.

She finished with more loud whispering, "Later, Blake. Thanks for…all of the everything! Keep your gun to yourself, if ya know what I mean…she's secretly a good girl!"

"Okay, on that note, we're out of here. She's done enough digging for the night!" Colton threw Meg over his shoulder with an awkward grin. Her last sharing episode was bold. He was afraid of what she would say next.

Megan was hootin' and hollering all the way to the truck, smacking Colton's ass with one hand, and awkwardly fist pumping the other.

"He has his hands full, doesn't he?" Morgan asked as everyone burst into laughter when she started blowing kisses from the sidewalk.

17

———

COLTON DROVE ALL THE WAY HOME WITH A SMILE ON HIS face. Sure Megan was out of her mind drunk at the moment, but he heard her loud and clear – she loved him. She may have a hard time owning her deepest most raw feelings when sober, but alcohol tends to be the liquid courage one needs to let their heart sing. He had felt it as much as he had felt her resistance, a true battle of mind versus heart.

Maybe now he would have an easier time getting through those mountain high walls of hers so he could help her with whatever had such a haunting hold on her. Her odd behavior earlier in the evening, before the meeting, or party rather, had left him uneasy. She thought she saw someone or something. He didn't doubt her sanity in the least, but he was concerned about whatever or whomever had her spooked lately.

He wanted to relieve her of her fretful burdens. He would show her that she didn't have to live in such dread and worry and that he would carry the burden for her, if needed. Protecting her and Jax would show her that she didn't need to live in such a bubble of fear anymore. Her past couldn't hurt her – he wouldn't let it. Whatever it was, near her again. It was past time to have a come to Jesus conversation about it, and soon they would, when she was sober.

Colton looked over at her and laughed, her window was down, hair was blowing, and she was singing and dancing along to her own music, assuming the wine told her she could dance. Man, he loved her…even drunk as a skunk.

Driving home with the window down on a cool fall night went a long way with Megan's "condition." It appeared that she was still rocking a great buzz, but she was a bit more "together." Getting herself up the steps and inside the house was a much easier feat than climbing into his truck and negotiating her seatbelt had been. As it turned out, the seatbelt was indeed just a seatbelt and not a kinky game he was playing as he locked it around her. She needed much less help with this round.

As over the top and out of character as her behavior was, he rather enjoyed the fun, light hearted way she had about her. Of course, it was good for the laughs, but he enjoyed seeing her carefree for a change. She landed in the living room with a plop on the floor, smack dab in the middle.

"Hi guys!" She shouted gleefully as the animals surrounded her. Each one hesitated ever so slightly, taking turns sniffing her, unsure what to make of her disposition.

"What's wrong? It's just me but a funner me. Who wants to play? Oh, wait, who wants a *treat*?" That had their attention. Ears perked, they followed her to the treat jar.

She even attempted to give Boss a hand signal which was more of an obscene gesture than signal of any kind. Boss cocked his head to the side, unsure what he was being told to do until he looked to Colton for help. Colton signaled accordingly, and Boss lined up for treats.

Colton couldn't help but watch in wonder. Where on earth had she come from, and how did she find her way to him.

Amused by her dancing around with the animals and silly chatter with them, he found himself completely taken by her. That wasn't the alcohol – that was genuine. The wine just gave her the freedom to express who she really was.

She was stunning inside and out…her heart as big as her fussy, yet fun, personality. Even intoxicated, he was mesmerized by all that she was. In that moment, he realized just how deep he was in. He knew, from a young age, what heartache was, to be unwanted, to be abandoned. She literally held his heart in her hands, and it scared the hell out of him. He didn't remember life before her and couldn't imagine one without her. He prayed, "Please, God, let it be her. Let me keep her."

* * *

MEGAN WAS HAVING A GOOD TIME, PLAYING WITH COLTON'S pets, laughing at anything and everything they did or didn't do. She couldn't remember a time where she felt so light and unburdened. She also couldn't remember a time where the floor seemed to move beneath her feet or the room tilt with every turn.

Moving floor and walls aside, she couldn't help but notice Colton watching her every move with that adorable half-grin of his that showed off a single dimple on his left cheek. The more she played and moved about, the more intently she noticed him watching. He was fucking hot. His beautiful golden eyes and thick lashes could go from adorable to sexy and mischievous at the flip of a damn coin.

She felt like flipping that coin and betting on mischievous. She moved closer to him, ever so slowly, admiring the view he provided. She elicited a twitch of his pecs, and then biceps, with the sway of her hips that accompanied every step.

When his eyebrows rose, she knew she had his attention. The shifting in his seat and uncrossing of his legs let her know she had *all* of his attention. Standing in front of him, she took a wide stance, with one hip cocked. Her hands ran up her hips, to her ribs, and she slowed her drift over her breasts while licking her lips.

Her seductive glare never lost eye contact until she closed her eyes and tossed her head back as her hand coursed over her collarbone. A breathy sound escaped her while her hands released her hair from the top of her head letting it fall slowly around her shoulders. A provocative shake was added, inviting a touch of allure.

Her movement increased from a simple sweet sway to a heated captivating charm that held his fascination with every swivel and grind of her hips. Hands making their way back down, pausing again at her breasts, she held them together while gifting him with a little shimmy. She pulled the hem of her shirt, betrayed by her liquid courage as she fumbled it over her head in an awkward and uncoordinated move. He gave her a chuckle, finding her attempt at sensuality absolutely adorable. Even if the shirt debacle was a sharp reminder that his sexy little vixen was a *drunken* little vixen.

She earned points for her recovery when she slowly turned, watching him over her shoulder as she released the front clasp of her white lace corset style bra, and let it fall to the ground. Her erogenous movements continued as she fumbled with the fly of her pants, finally succeeding.

She slowly moved her perfectly fitted black pants over her ass, and down her hips, revealing the perfectly matching white lace, cheeky panties she had on underneath. Fancy Pants just took on an entirely new meaning. He appreciated her finer tastes, especially in underwear. She was so fucking sexy, smoldering.

Her arousing show continued with a perfect view of her ass when she bent over to free herself of her pants. God have mercy. Knowing exactly what she was doing, she slowly stood, dragging her hands up each side of her legs to her ass where she made a point to drag her nails as she moved her hips in a sexy response. She traced her way past her hips and beyond, covering each breast before finally turning to him.

Her seduction merged from bold and enticing to sweet and shy. Her full lips slightly pouty, doe eyes twinkling, she tilted her head down, watching him through the thick lashes of her heavily hooded eyes.

"You're beautiful. Come here," he said, reaching for her. He landed a hand on each hip and pulled her in. His mouth found her abdomen, hands drifted to grip her ass as his kisses trailed down past her navel.

Freeing her breasts, her hands ran through his hair and held his head, encouraging his descent. Every ounce of pleasure he offered was happily accepted, and she greedily wanted more.

A slight stumble in lieu of her sway was a harsh reminder of her state of mind. She was drunk, and he was a gentleman. He kissed each hip before resting his forehead against her stomach.

"What…what's wrong?" she asked with a confused look and concerned tone. "Did I do something?" she finished, feeling a sense of insecurity.

She placed one knee on either side of him, straddling him where he sat, trying to keep the mood heated.

"No, baby, it's just that it wouldn't be right of me to take advantage after you have…well, after the wine, honey." He tried to deliver his conscience gently and honestly, in a way she would understand despite her inebriation.

The fact was, he respected her far too much to make a

cheap move and have his way with her in this condition, and it wasn't his style. Sure, they had made love plenty of times before, but she was fully aware, more than a willing participant. She seemed to know what she wanted, which was, apparently, him since she was undressing him. She began to nibble on his ear, then jaw, and so on. She was so damn tempting, had him hot and ready, but he would never give her a single opportunity to doubt him or their relationship. She meant more to him than the hot and dirty sex she was offering.

"I'm not drinking wine anymore. I've moved on to hot, kinky, sexy time with my guy," she said in a seductive whisper while peppering his neck and shoulder with kisses.

"I'd love nothing more than to spend the rest of the night making love to you on every surface of…" He paused as she quickly stiffened, looking him dead in the eye with big eyes.

The color began to drain from her face, and she started to sway as tears welled, and eventually slid down her cheeks.

"Megan? Are you okay, honey? I promise I want you. I want you *real* bad. I just…"

And then, it happened…all down the front of both of them. Megan Johnson couldn't hold her liquor, literally. Barely sober enough to be horrified by what had just happened, she began to sob. She tried to get up unsuccessfully, which just worsened the mess since she was still pretty inebriated and apparently not done getting sick.

Shocked, Colton sat still, waiting for her to be done before he stood, holding her while she still straddled him, and carried her to the bathroom. He gently set her at the tub's edge while he started the separate shower. While it warmed, he disappeared to the living room to quickly throw towels over the little bit of mess that didn't land on either of them.

Thank God for wood floors and leather furniture. He'd finish the rest in a few.

He returned to a now steamy bathroom and a mortified Megan, slouching in front of the toilet, head resting on the cool toilet seat. His heart broke for her, trying to escape her worries for the night only creating new ones. He removed his clothing, then the one garment she still had on – her strip tease paid off in one regard tonight.

Sweeping her up, he cradled her in his arms and walked into the shower with her. He stood them both under the warm water, waiting for it to wash away all that plagued her. Her silent cries were given away by the shaking of her shoulders. He kissed her forehead and sat them both on the built-in bench.

"Honey, I've been thrown up on before. Comes with the job. It's okay."

She sniffled and looked to his eyes and said, "But it's not. It's not okay. I don't deserve you. You don't deserve this," she said while scanning her hand from head to toe, indicating that she was *this*. "I have baggage…I'm a mess. I don't belong here. I'm just drunk trouble, and I have throw up in my haaaair."

"Megan, honey, you're a dream come true. You belong here. You and Jax both, and…"

"The BABY! Oh, my God. I lost Jax!" She shot up, only to fall right back to where she had been sitting.

"He's fine! He's fine!" He comforted, wrapping his arms around her. "He's with Sam and Dawson for the night." He kissed her shoulder as she relaxed back into him.

He spent the next several minutes tending to her, washing her hair, massaging as he did. Then, he carefully washed her head to toe, making sure she felt his devotion. She may not have it all together at the moment, but the wine wouldn't last forever, and he wanted to be sure she would remember the good parts of the night, like *this*. He wanted her to remember how much he took care of her, carried her burdens, mostly. Most of all, he wanted her to remember he loved her.

After towel drying her body and slipping one of his shirts over her, he tucked her in for the night. He promised to return quickly when she reached for him. He made his way to the living room to finish cleaning up and to grab her some Tylenol and water. She would need both after this.

When he returned to his room, he crawled into bed behind her, only to find her fast asleep. He smiled at her. So peaceful, so beautiful. He put the pills and bottled water on the nightstand within her view and reach, should she wake before him.

Before he lay down behind her, he dropped his head, landing a sweet kiss on her shoulder, then whispering in her ear, "You do belong here, with me, always. You're the dream come true that I've waited my entire life for. I'll take care of you every day and love you forever and beyond."

She scooted back nuzzling, her backside to his front before whispering back, "I love you too, Colton."

He lay beside her, held her close, and fell asleep with his girl in his arms and a smile on his face.

18

———

MEGAN WOKE TO AN OBNOXIOUS NOISE, ASSAULTING SMELLS, and unrelenting light. When she found her way from under the blankets, she was able to identify her annoyances as birds, breakfast, and what would typically be beautiful fall sunshine. She was pretty sure the devil himself was tightening the vice on her head while turning up the volume on the rest of the world. "Friggin' birds!"

Memories of the night before swarmed through her head like a bad movie. Hopeful her memories were exaggerated versions of truth, the way she felt told another story. How humiliating. Flashes of Jessie laughing at her and petting Morgan sunk in first. The fist pumping with Lou and declaring her love for each of them paled in comparison to her ultimate humiliation. The most painful of all...those three little words she delivered after a high five to Blake. She told Colton she loved him.

Truth be told, she did indeed love him. However, that was not how she wanted to tell him – with an audience who had video evidence. She closed her eyes in shame, scolding herself for being so irresponsible, and then she remembered her dance. Planting her face in her hands, she recalled every detail of her little dance of seduction, which was bordering cheap porn star quality. Then, it hit her, her grand finale… epic embarrassment. She threw up all over the man she had just declared her love for. She was winning. Why couldn't she be one of those drunks who forgets everything instead of remembering in high def?

"You don't like birds?" Colton asked with a puzzled look on his face. "I brought you breakfast if you're up to it."

Startled, she quickly tried to hide her face in shame at the sound of his voice. She smacked her mouth open and closed trying to identify the wretched taste that was foreign until now, and to clear the dry cotton sensation that made her tongue feel glued to the roof of her mouth.

"I usually like birds just fine. They are just louder today than usual. Shouldn't they have flown south by now? Ugh!"

She couldn't help but notice how sexy he looked half-dressed in gray sweatpants resting low on his hips. She felt like shit, but she wasn't dead. Nor was her libido which was causing all kinds of tingling in all the right places. Who knew sweatpants were the new sexy? He needed those in every color, she thought.

"Take the Tylenol…you'll feel better. Think you can handle a bit to eat?" He gave her his 100-watt smile, dimple included, and placed a large lap table between them on the bed.

It appeared that he thought of everything, and it was set up as a mini family style buffet. He prepared bacon, a bowl of fresh fruit, scrambled eggs – that would be a hard pass – as well as a couple pastries, and some oatmeal with fixings on the side. She smiled at the last plate, her favorite…toast. He knew her so well, made it just the way she liked it, slathered in a heart attack worthy amount of butter and almost burnt. He gave her a wink and a smile when she went for the toast.

"I wasn't sure what you would feel like, so I went with a variety—should have known toast would be your pick," he said.

"You can never go wrong with toast. This is…" she said as she took a hearty bite, froze, stopped chewing, and made a sour face. "…disgusting!"

Colton's face went from happy and light to serious and concerned. Alcohol, hang over – of course, it tasted awful. Everything would for a while. He laughed as she quickly chewed and reached for her coffee. Another bad move. She sat back, watery eyes, with her hands over her mouth.

"Honey, you've never been drunk before, have you?" he chuckled.

"Is that what this is? The wine? What did I do to myself? Oh, my God, I *need* coffee, but it's…not coffee. It's poison!" she proclaimed.

"Stick to water for a bit, and try getting some of that toast in. It'll go away soon," he assured her, even though she wasn't buying it. "Are you still up for heading over to Portland? I can just have Sam and Dawson pick up the equipment for the House, and I'm sure they'd have no problem picking up that donation you needed for the Bazaar, too."

"No!" Her reply was more of an urgent yell than she intended, but she had been looking forward to this trip to the city for over a month now. "They have a real mall there, and boutiques…are you kidding me? I'm *not* missing it! I need something to wear to the Gala that isn't flannel or covered in faux fur!" She joked as she tossed a grape into her mouth, making that sour face again.

Her unease over the previous night's blunders dissipated as an overwhelming rush of excitement took its place. A real mall, with real stores, full of impractical shoes, and a lot of non-flannel.

The two finished their breakfast and picked up where they had left off the previous night before the alcohol interfered. She may have been slightly hung over, but that couldn't dampen the ache he caused her in all the right places. Both had been hot and bothered with no relief, making their good morning romp in the sack just that much more satisfying.

* * *

AFTER A STEAMY TRYST IN THE SHOWER, THEY BEGAN THEIR day and prepared for their long-awaited trip to Portland. Colton cleaned up breakfast, surprised at Meg's packing progress when he returned to the bedroom. He leaned against the wall and watched her work with a smile on his face. She had piles of clothes for her and Jax, organized by day, it appeared. If he didn't know any better, it looked like she was working on his pile as well.

He could really get used to this life. Hell, who was he kidding? He already was. Maybe they wouldn't be able to fix her house, and she could stay with him forever.

"What are you looking at?" she shyly asked, knowing it was her.

"My beautiful girl… I could watch her for hours," he replied, in all honesty.

"Folding clothes turns you on?" she joked. "I'll remember that."

"No, just the girl folding. I'd pair up every last stray sock for the rest of my life, if that's what she wanted," he declared.

She knew full well that he wasn't volunteering for laundry duty and that he would do whatever it took to make her happy. That was Colton Sparks, genuine to a fault, and a heart with more love to give than any one person deserved. Truth be told, she would do whatever it took to make him happy and keep him forever. Even face her past.

* * *

Colton left Meg to finish packing and prepare snacks for Jax. She had brought what they needed from her house, for the day to day, over the last several weeks. She hadn't brought a suitcase that was large enough for three, however, in the many trips and heaping loads of "stuff." Being alone his whole adult life, he only had a small carry on size, enough room for clean underwear…typical guy.

On his way to pick up the little guy from Sam and Dawson's, he offered to grab her large suitcase from the office closet at her house. When he climbed the steps, he noticed something wedged between the screen door and front door. He stopped and looked around briefly before continuing to the door. He grabbed it before it fell to the ground when he opened the screen door. It was a newspaper, the Community and Lifestyle section, folded in fourths.

He looked around once more – still nothing – nobody was around. Not a thing out of place otherwise, even though someone had clearly been there. An eerie sensation crept up his neck, leaving him with hair-raising goose bumps down his arms. There were eyes on him. He could feel it, but where?

They were surrounded by forest. The next house was a good distance beyond Meg's. He moved inside, out of sight, and gave this random section of paper a closer look. It was the New York Times. Where would that have come from clear out here? Furthermore, the date was from nearly eighteen months prior, almost to the day.

Someone had left Megan an old paper from New York.

Everyone in town knew she was staying with him and where her shop was, so why leave it here, like this, anonymously? He scanned the few pages, more than once. Nothing stood out, but there was clearly a message here, or why leave it? He could ask Megan, but she was finally starting to settle and wasn't as jumpy as she had been until last night.

She thought she saw a man watching her, but nobody else saw him. They thought she was just flashing back to the night a man was hit in front of her shop. A man who had died and had yet to be claimed, identified or match a missing person report, country wide. That chill reared its ugly head again. There were clues all around him as he stood in her house. He just needed to find them and hope she still trusted him later.

She wasn't telling him what he needed to know, and he had a sickening feeling whatever haunted her from her past was now hunting her from afar, lurking right outside. He needed to find it, and fast. After searching everywhere he could imagine, he had nothing. Back in her office, paper still in hand, he sat back at her desk without a single fucking clue.

He stared at the paper again, scanning the pictures a little closer. On the front page, he took a pause and looked closer at a picture of two women. One was looking awkwardly to her right, talking to someone. The other was looking directly at the photographer with a well-practiced smile.

They appeared to be at some sort of event, something elaborate, given the attire. The headline read, *"Local Socialites, Killed in Fatal Car Accident."* The opening statement read, *"Prescott sister, and a minor child, killed in a tragic accident last Tuesday evening when an unidentified driver lost control and ran the vehicle off the road."*

He hesitated, looking at the picture again. The woman looking back at him was somewhat familiar—who was Lydia Prescott and her sister, Trinity. What did this have to do with

Megan? He looked up, staring at the large cork board that rested on the wall above her desk, lost in thought. He was trying to piece it all together, but at a loss, he was clearly missing a piece. Was it this article that she was supposed to see? The rest of the articles were related to local park dedications, a golf tournament fundraiser, and the like. Or, had he missed the mark completely?

He stood to leave, determined to figure this out when they returned from their trip, when a piece of paper on the cork board caught his attention. There was a post-it note with Jax's pediatrician's number covering the note below. Peeking from the side of the post-it, he read *"O'Reilly."* He removed the post it to reveal *Declan O'Reilly* followed by a phone number.

Declan O'Reilly? As in, Carigan's brother, Declan O'Reilly? How would Meg know Declan, and why would she have his number? She didn't know Carigan until moving here, and Dec hadn't been home in years.

Nobody knew what he did, really, including Carigan. Blake knew him well – he knew all five of the O'Reilly brothers – Dec particularly well, which suggested that Dec was from a similar background. Top secret, probably military…the kind you don't talk about and doesn't show up on any government paperwork, and completely badass scary.

Colton grabbed the paper from the board. He had another stop to make.

19

<hr>

After picking up Jax from Dawson and Sam's, Colton found himself headed to Blake's cabin, reeling with concern and questions. The cabin was secluded, away from the masses, kind of like him. Blake liked his privacy. What was once a hunting cabin – was now his quaint and isolated home that rested just outside of town in a wooded area along Bear Creek.

It was simple but charming, sparse furnishings, very tidy, not a TV that could be seen but plenty of book filled shelves. Colton was always surprised by how simple Blake lived. It actually suited him.

As Colton pulled up out front, Blake was already standing in his yard to greet them. Knowing Blake, he probably had the property rigged with booby traps and alarms, letting him know a mile back that someone was headed up his long drive from the road.

"Hey man, what brings you guys out here?" he asked Colton, giving him the standard "Bro" secret handshake. "Give me knucks, little man," he said to Jax, putting his fist out to bump with the toddler, who was happy to comply.

Blake may be on the quiet side and a bit introverted, due to his own demons that he kept locked away, but the kids always brought out a side that the group of friends rarely saw from their ultra-macho, gun toting, badass friend. As oversized and intimidating as Blake looked, the kids only saw a big teddy bear they adored.

"Not much, hell…" Colton stopped to correct himself. "Man, I need a favor, a big one," he finished, hesitation surrounding his words.

"Need a beer for this?" Blake offered. "More importantly, will I need a beer?"

"Go for it, but I'll pass. We're headed to Portland with Dawson and Sam to pick up the new equipment, long drive," he replied. "Look, it's about Megan…"

"Man, please, don't bring me your girl problems. That's Dawson's department," Blake said, cutting him off while grabbing that beer after all.

"Coop, it isn't like that. This is unofficial, official business. I need you to look into something," Colton said, defeat sliding off each word.

"You're finally here to talk about it, huh? About time," he replied, leaving Colton a bit confused.

Blake knew it was only a matter of time before this conversation would take place. Something was going on with Megan. He felt it in his gut and was already a step ahead of Colton.

"Okay, tell me what's going on. I'll do what I can. You know that," he said, tossing back his beer.

"I think there is someone after her. I don't think the fire was an accident either," Colton admitted.

Blake sat on the leather chair, nodding for Colton to take a seat on the adjacent matching couch. "Okay, that's a pretty serious statement. What do you got?" Blake asked, leading

Colton to believe he was completely in the dark and unsuspecting.

"You know there have been odd little things, right? She gets pretty anxious and worked up over nothing, or so it seems. Well, she's trying to hide something," Colton said, his words full of guilt.

He felt as if he was accusing her of doing something wrong, even though he didn't know if she was or wasn't. Truth was, he knew very little about the woman he adored, the woman he loved.

"Okay, so, people can be a little…paranoid in nature. That doesn't mean anything is going on beyond that," Blake countered, challenging Colton to give him something he could work with. He had his own ideas about what was going on but wasn't one to put words in other's mouths or plant negative ideas.

"True. Look, my gut says something is wrong, really wrong," he offered. "A while back, I caught her in the back room at her shop, scared shitless. She thought someone had been there, but I couldn't find anything but a few buckets knocked over that could have been from her. Then there was the John Doe hit in front of her shop."

Blake interrupted at the mention of the unidentified man, deceased, still unclaimed at the county morgue. "You noticed that? He was looking right at her with that smirk as he was dying—it was odd, out of place. Her reaction…"

"Was off," Colton finished. He felt like he was betraying her, talking about this, but he knew it was for her own good. "I know seeing something like that is shocking, but she seemed to check out. The rest of the night she was afraid, haunted almost, like she had seen a damn ghost, man." Colton went on to tell Blake about the rest of the small, but noticeable things he had encountered over the past several months – which she swept under a rug – ending with today's discovery.

He handed over the newspaper that was left at Megan's door and the slip of paper he found with Declan O'Reilly's number on it. The odd discovery when snooping through Meg's things was that she had very few files or pictures, none of which dated before her time in McKenzie Ridge. It didn't have to mean anything. For all he knew, there were boxes containing old tax returns, credit card statements, and her birth certificate laying in piles of ash from the fire. His hunch was that he was really reaching and those things just didn't exist.

"You know this is Declan, Carigan's brother, right?" Blake questioned with a raised eyebrow and hint of irritation. "You know who he is…why someone would have this number?"

"No, Blake, I don't. I don't know much about the guy anymore. All I know is he is always *on assignment*, whatever that means! Given you seem to know, I'm going to guess it's some top secret bullshit that screams danger and blowing shit up!" Colton conceded, showing how worried this really had him. "So, are you going to tell me, or do I get to guess?" he finished with a slice of sarcasm, completely irritated by Blake's evasiveness.

Blake ran his hands through his hair with a sigh and then rested his elbows on his knees while rubbing his hands together. He wasn't sure what to say next. He wanted to tell his friend what he knew and what he suspected, but would it do any good or add worry to an already troubling situation.

He tried to keep his own past hidden, afraid to let anyone in so they wouldn't get hurt, but he cared deeply for the people in his little circle. He would do anything for any one of them, especially if it kept them safe. He had to tell him…tell him everything, even if it revealed a little bit of himself.

"Ball." Jax's favorite word and favorite toy had been offered as if to help ease whatever stress was streaming through him. Blake smiled, something he didn't do often, took the ball and picked the tiny tot up to put him on his knee.

"Okay, I'll look into it more. Truth is, I already have been. I can't find a damn thing on Megan Johnson. Everything starts here in McKenzie." Blake paused to study his friend, gauging how much more he should or shouldn't say. "I already knew a lot of what you told me, I've noticed it for some time, been watching for it even. Do you remember when Jameson and I saw her on the side of the road? Flat tire?"

"Yeah, nail in the tire, no cell service…what about it?" he asked anxiously. "I'm not going to like your answer, am I? You have the smug, this will piss you off look on your face," Colton finished, unable to decide if he was dreading or intrigued by the pending answer to his question.

"Smug? Screw you, Sparks. Look, when I got the jack out of the trunk, there was a suitcase." Blake noticed Colton's blank look and shrug. It may seem insignificant to him, but it was a noteworthy clue in context. "There was also a bag – with a *lot* of cash in it – stashed in the side compartment with the jack."

"Can you, I don't know, cut to the fucking chase here? You've lost me on all this vague, I found a suitcase, crap. We aren't all GI Joe bad-asses, Coop, what's up?" Colton fired, fed up with dancing around the issues at hand. He needed answers, and he needed them now.

"She's a runner. It's a classic sign. Keep essentials at the ready at all times, and cash is untraceable. You can just up and leave at any minute and be in the wind, completely off anyone's radar in a matter of minutes, really." Blake delivered the blow as directly as he could. Straight to the point, no fluff, it was out there.

He waited, gave his friend a chance to process what that meant. Colton was already so invested in Megan and Jax – surely this realization would come with some form of denial and maybe even anger. So he waited, let him reconcile the facts and the emotions that were sure to follow.

"What? Running from what? What am I up against, Coop?" To Blake's surprise, Colton wasn't angry but devastated, likely by the idea that the woman he loved could and probably would be just gone one day, untraceable.

Abandonment and loss was no stranger to Colton – they were a thieving whore who stole all that you had to offer emotionally, able to devastate and even ruin you. He hadn't been ruined…damaged but not ruined. This could ruin him. He had been an orphan his entire life – this could leave him an orphan in love.

"I don't know. I thought a bad relationship, maybe an ex, but when I couldn't find a damn thing on her, I figured this was bigger. You don't just come up with an identity and cover your tracks like that without help. Someone hid her," he said, holding up the paper with Declan's name on it. "The day I changed her flat, I noticed a dark car parked just up ahead. It left when we stayed to help. It turned and went the other way. There's nothing on that road for a few miles, Sparks. Who just sits there and watches a stranded woman and child and does nothing?"

Blake's story stung. Colton knew something was off, that she had a past that confined her to fear, but this secret? This was huge. This was the type of burden that movies were made of, and she was the star of the show. How did she hide it all so well? More important, why did she hide it from him?

"You said a dark car? A few weeks ago, I caught her completely stunned, another one of those petrified moments of hers. She said it was nothing, but I remember seeing a dark car driving down past her place. Do you think it was the same car? Wait, the fire! You don't think…" Colton's disappointment transitioned to some form of fear at that realization. It was the type of fear that instigates a deep-seated demand for action. The kind that felt barbaric almost, an animal marking and defending all that was his from an imminent threat.

His straightened posture, puffed out chest and furrowed brow gave it all away. If it hadn't been obvious before that he was madly in love with this woman, it was absolutely undeniable now.

"Whoa, before you start beating your chest and go half-cocked with guns blazing, we need to take it down a notch. Got it?" Blake cautioned.

He waited for his friend's response, lifting his brow as a prompt to answer. He finished his thought at Colton's returned nod. "I'm certain it's all related, especially given the accounts you are sharing today, but who and why?" Blake asked.

Colton stood, postured like the halfcocked rooster Blake warned him not to be. "Let's go find out! Come here Jax." He reached for the boy, ready to confront the only one who had answers.

"Wait a minute!" Blake said, putting his arm around Jax, indicating they weren't going anywhere. "If she hasn't told you anything yet, I guarantee you, confronting her like a pissed off ape will make her run," Blake reasoned.

"How the fuck do I protect her if I don't know what I'm protecting her from, man?" Colton yelled.

His plea was desperate, concern and impatience evident in his tone. Blake felt for his friend. It actually pained him to see the devastation and reverence eating away at him with such momentum. As much as Colton wanted to protect his world, Blake wanted to protect his, which was their group of friends and his town. The danger might already be in McKenzie and would be whether Meg ran or not.

"You can't protect her from anything if she's gone, man. Don't spook her. For now, take your trip, don't say anything to her, and keep an eye out. I'll call Dec and see how much danger she's in and if it's already here. For now, we'll assume she's still hidden," Blake said matter-of-factly.

"If it's not already here, it's coming. I feel it Coop," Colton confessed.

"Yeah, I agree. Do you have cell service out on Mountain-view Road?" Blake asked at random.

"Yeah, there's a tower right there…" Colton didn't need to finish his answer to see where Blake was going with his inquiry. If cell service was plentiful in the area where Megan had a flat tire, why didn't her cell phone work? Jammer. Whoever was in that car had a jammer, blocking her signal. She was a sitting duck until fate stepped in and sent Blake and Morgan.

Blake read Colton like a book, saw clarity cross his face as he put the puzzle pieces together. He knew they were dealing with something much bigger than a pissed off ex-asshole. This was sophisticated shit. It was good that they were getting out of town for a few days.

Blake planned to call ahead and give his buddy, Dean with the Portland Police, a heads up, should trouble follow them.

"Hey, Colton?" Blake hollered before he climbed into the truck and drove off. Colton turned to acknowledge him with a half-smile and nod.

"Her tire...those nails were intentional," he said as a last warning.

"Shit."

* * *

Colton drove home by way of Mountainview Road, clearly a glutton for punishment. He realized there would be nothing to see from the tire incident, but it gave him a few extra minutes to digest all that he had learned and reconcile the emotions it generated. He had no doubt Megan was his one true love. Only problem was that she obviously wasn't Megan Johnson. So, who was she?

He decided to make a phone call, get someone on his team so he wasn't fighting these ghosts alone. He needed someone he could count on to have his back. He needed an extra set of eyes.

"Hey, Daws...look man, we've got trouble, and I need your help."

20

THE TRIP FROM MCKENZIE RIDGE TO PORTLAND WAS beautiful. The highway was lined with gorgeous forests reflecting every shade of green, rocky mountainsides carved out by flowing waterfalls nestled in niches, and the most gorgeous valleys as far as the eye could see. Their descent from the mountain was breathtaking at every curve. Its only downfall was that it was roughly four hours long. Four hours of forest, waterfalls, deer in the distance, a few random lakes, and a very bored toddler.

Fortunately, Megan and Sam planned their departure around nap time and brought tablets loaded with favorite movies and shows. They would have to execute the same plan on the return home…break up that drive. Deer are only interesting the first ten times when you are five and under, come to find out.

"You've been quiet, Colton. Is everything okay?" Megan asked with concern.

"Huh? Oh, yeah. Everything's fine, babe." He reached for her hand and held it tight before leading it to his soft lips for a kiss. Colton took in the smile she repaid him with, and his heart stung a little. He reminded himself that he was protecting her. He wasn't intentionally keeping a secret for any reason other than her safety.

"I'm just watching the road. People get impatient, and that doesn't mix with a winding mountain highway," he offered with a smile of his own, hoping he was selling his somber mood as being a cautious driver.

"Okay, if you're sure there isn't anything else?" She asked.

"Well, there is one thing," he said in all seriousness as he gave her a quick concerned glance. "I'm trying to decide where I'm taking you on our date," he admitted.

Meg's eyes grew wide, and her smile brightened, excitement radiating from her like a ray of sunshine.

"Date? You didn't tell me about a date!" She clapped her hands and squealed, quickly covering her mouth and looking to Jax, hoping she hadn't disturbed him.

"Dawson and I worked it out earlier. We will be in town for three nights. Tonight, we'll get everyone settled and just eat at the hotel, maybe take the kids to the pool. Then the next two nights, we'll take turns with the kids, so each of us gets a date night in the city," he said, tossing her a quick dimple bearing grin and a wink.

"This is so exciting! I can't wait to see where Sam and I end up. I mean the possibilities are endless for a couple girls in the city!" She exclaimed.

"Sam? What? You want to go out with Sam? I thought we…" He was cut off by a boastful laugh, the best sound in the world.

It was carefree and light today. He loved seeing this side of her. He hoped by the time they returned to McKenzie Ridge, he could take every worry away and give her endless amounts of days like today.

"Oh, you think you're funny, huh? You just wait until tonight!" He warned while reaching over and tickling her ribs, prompting her to laugh again.

He couldn't wait until tonight when he would hear all the other joyful sounds he could get her to make.

* * *

PORTLAND WAS NOTHING LIKE ANYTHING MEGAN HAD experienced—big city amenities at every turn, but without losing its small-town atmosphere emanating everywhere. There were charming small boutiques, restaurants, and businesses nestled between the various high-rise buildings.

There was a fair mix of modern and eclectic, boasting both swanky vibes and those of comfort. The diversity of its buildings, people, and ambiance were exhilarating. West coast living was something she could really get used to.

They landed at a hotel that faced a stunning waterfront which divided the city's east and west sides, lining as far north and south as the eye could see. Boardwalk-like paths traced the water with various fountains and park-like areas all along the way.

It appeared to be the epicenter of the city as the many joggers, walkers, and families told a story of its relevance. Even in the cooler fall weather, the stunning array of vibrant reds, yellows, and oranges topped the trees that likely contributed to the draw of the crowds it hosted.

Valet took their keys while bell hops took their bags as the couples made their way into the posh establishment that would be home for the next few days. As the others ooh'd and ahh'd, Megan simply felt at home in response to an element of her former life. She had been accustomed to a lifestyle that delivered such privileges. It was like riding a bike.

She fell right back into the comfort of such as soon as she walked through the revolving door.

With a deep relaxing breath in, she felt the weight of her world fall from her shoulders. It offered a chance at familiarity, like a teaser from her past. Even if only for a few days.

The now joyful group made their way to the top floor where their bags already awaited them in their adjoining, yet separate, rooms. This was the life.

"Wow, you guys really went all out!" Sam said.

"If I didn't know better, I'd think this was more of a romantic getaway than a business trip."

"Why can't it be both? A little mix of business and pleasure!" Dawson asked while wrapping his arms around his wife, giving her a toe curling kiss.

"Ewww!" Ellie shouted, reminding everyone of the tots in tow and that the romance was limited to the scheduled trading of children.

"Yeah, what she said! Get a room!" Colton said sarcastically, high fiving little Ellie.

"I have a room, you're standing in it, asshole!" Dawson shot back with an ornery grin and wink for his friend.

"Ummmmm…twenty-five cents to the swear jar!" Ellie scolded for language.

"Dude! Ellie…really?" Dawson questioned, shocked by his daughter's scolding.

Hands on her hips and a sassy cocked head, she replied in all seriousness, "I'm not a dude…I'm a princess!"

"Yeah, twenty-five cents to the swear jar you big jerk. Princess Ellie Lou said so!" Colton agreed with his own ornery flare. "Wait, is jerk a bad word, squirt?" he asked and swooped her off the ground, tickling her belly.

"Stop, stop, Uncle Colton! You're gonna make me wet my drawers!" Ellie pleaded between giggles. "It's a not nice word but not a bad word, so you get it for free and a warning. If you say it too many times though, you'll get in trouble and hafta put a money in a jar. Do you have a jar Miss Megan?" She asked.

"I'm afraid we don't. We better get one!" Megan said while elbowing Colton.

"No bad word jar?" Ellie asked, eyes alight with shock. "Can I come to your house?"

The group laughed and laid out their plan for the evening as well as the rest of their trip. Meg was looking forward to the next several days. Tonight, would be all about family at the hotel. They would eat in and let the littles swim to get their pent-up energy out after such a long car ride.

The next two nights, the couples planned to swap children, each taking a nice romantic evening sans the littles. Megan couldn't wait for her night out with Colton. They were beginning to feel more and more like a family, and it scared her less and less.

Despite the many highs and lows over the past few months, it felt right. She wanted to be there with him, no longer prepared to run. She was ready to tell him everything. She knew he would understand, help her even. Maybe, just maybe, they could find a way to forever.

21

Portland was an amazing host. While the men tended to business for the House, training on their new equipment they were to bring back, the ladies explored the town with the kids. The city gave them plenty to do by day, and at night they had each other.

Loving this woman of his was easy. He knew he loved her but discovered just how head over heels he was for her during their getaway. He was completely enchanted by her, consumed with her. The overwhelming energy and excitement she shed was contagious and hard not to fall for. His thoughts were often nothing but her, and he could spend the rest of his life that way without a single hesitation or complaint.

He hoped that her carefree spirit would follow them home. Meg was truly and thoroughly happy, unafraid and relaxed. She would always feel that way, from this day forward. He would see to it. As soon as they returned to McKenzie Ridge, he would know what he was up against, what threatening entanglements he would have to rid her world of to keep her. Until then, they had today.

"So then, there were naked women everywhere and they were shooting cheeseburgers from their big…" Dawson said with excitement as they leaned over the railing of the firehouse dock that sat right on the river.

"Uh huh. Wait, what? Cheeseburgers?" Colton asked visibly confused.

"I was talking about these new devices we're taking home, and when *uh huh* came out every three seconds, even when I wasn't talking, I thought I'd screw with you a little. Let me guess, Meg? You didn't even blink at the naked women comment." Dawson laughed, impressed and amused by his own corny jokes.

"Sorry, man. Yeah, I'm just thinking about everything. *She's* everything I've been waiting for, man. My whole life. I keep thinking about how quickly it can all be gone, ya know?"

"I hear ya, man. I went through that with Sam. I never thought I would get married, much less have a family. Then, she had the accident, and my world fell apart." He offered his experience as understanding. Dawson could absolutely relate to what Colton was feeling, even if their circumstances were different in nature. Loss is loss no matter how it happens.

"I remember. That was rough, man. Look at you now— married with two kids. I've always wanted that. Growing up without a family was rough. I couldn't wait to have my own. Then, I got all of you guys, but ehhhh," he joked, earning a punch to the shoulder. "Now I feel like I just might have it, and the shit hits the fan. Of course, I pick the girl that's running," Colton said in defeat.

"Don't think like that bro. It's obvious how much she loves you. If she didn't have whatever this is hanging over her, you'd be locked up in a ball and chain. Coop will figure out what's going on, and we'll all help her through it, man.

You deserve to be happy, you both do. I want you to have what Sam and I have. I've got your back, man…we all do…Meg's too," Dawson said with an encouraging pat on the back.

Colton was the emotional one of the bunch, with a big heart that was always resting on his sleeve. He wasn't used to being on this side of sensitive, especially when it was coming from Dawson, alpha heart breaker turned pansy puss softie.

He appreciated his friend's words, however, and appreciated the truth within them. He could count on the gang as much as they could him. Before he could say another word, Dawson stood and began unbuttoning his shirt.

"Whoa man, I'm all for the bro bonding bullshit, but…" Colton said, hands up with a shock stricken look crossing his face.

"Shut up, asshole! I'm showing you something!" Dawson countered.

"And I'm not interested, Tayler. Leave your clothes on," Colton said, backing away.

"Seriously, Sparks…look, you idiot!" Dawson replied in irritation.

Colton reluctantly looked at what Dawson was showing him under his shirt. Much to his surprise, his once larger than life, man's man of a friend, revealed the most ridiculous thing he had ever seen on a grown man. Especially one of his stature and swagger.

Uncontrollable laughter consumed him to tears while Dawson stood, hands on hips, staring at the blue sky above, jaw clenched. As Colton started to catch his breath, Dawson finally broke through with a big F.U. look and spoke.

"Are you done, jackass?"

"Is that? Is that a…pixie?" Colton asked, referring to the tattoo resting on Dawson's upper chest.

"Yes, dickweed. It's a *fairy*. Ellie Lou was obsessed with them and thought that I was one, remember? It reminds me of who I am and what I'll fight for every day of my life. That's why it is next to that scar where I took the bullet for her. Truth is, they are my life, and I'm nothing without them, so I'll gladly be a fairy, wear a fairy, whatever it takes to keep what I have," Dawson said, his words full of compassion and love. "So fight for what you want. If she runs, chase her. Be her fairy, man." Dawson added a shit eating grin to the last part, trying to lighten the mood without losing the message.

Colton stood silent for a moment. He looked to Dawson and then the ridiculous fairy on his chest before looking off into the distance as if all of the answers rested on the water before him.

He looked at Dawson in all seriousness and said, "I'll fight for her. I'll be a damn fairy and fight!"

Dawson rolled his eyes, and punched Colton's arm, nodding his head indicating it was time to go. "Let's go find our families, see what kind of damage they were able to do."

Colton fell into step with Dawson, letting his words roll over him…his family. His heart swelled beyond measure at that thought. Megan and Jax really were his family.

Clarity sank in, defining why the secrets and fear affected him so deeply. It was less about her not trusting him or keeping secrets and more so about something much bigger. The new emotions coursing through him were about a threat against what was his, and he didn't recognize it sooner because it had been foreign to him before now.

His frustration and even hurt was because something was wedging its way between him and his family, threatening it before he even realized he had it. He meant what he said – he would fight for it. He would protect what was his.

There wasn't a single ghost, demon, or angry ex that

could get in his way. No, they were his responsibility now, one he gladly accepted. He would guard his world, his family, at any cost.

"So, ball and chain? What kind of kink stuff are you and Sam into, anyway?" Colton poked, keeping a straight face.

"Fuck you, Colton."

"You owe the swear jar like fifty bucks now, pretty sure a fairy dies every time you drop an *F bomb,* too." Colton joked, lightening the mood, taking on the day in an entirely new light.

"I hope Meg hangs your ball and chain from your dick, asshole."

* * *

MEGAN AND SAM HAD SPENT THE BETTER PART OF THE morning exploring the various shops downtown Portland had to offer. They found everything, from darling clothes and interesting toys for the kids to candles and fancy lingerie, on their adventure.

Megan was especially fond of the lingerie shop. Not only was it something severely lacking in McKenzie Ridge, unless you were a Big Box store, cotton staple kind of girl, but her date with Colton was only hours away, and she wanted to wear something extra special.

"Well, this is the last shop before we head to 'Kid Korner'," Sam said as they approached the last boutique on their list. "Let's see if the perfect dress for the Gala lives in here, shall we?"

They explored the racks of designer items like hungry wolves in a chicken coop. Arms were weighted down with loads of stunning dresses and outfits that couldn't be found in a shop back at home. There wasn't a need for such extravagance in McKenzie. Megan was in her element – this was her kind of shop and her kind of clothes…chic, designer, couture, and expensive.

She wouldn't have many opportunities to wear things like this in lumberjack nation, but she did have a few tastings coming up at Blooming Grounds, and maybe it was time to bring a little flair and elegance to the Ridge. If she was going to stay there, which she desperately wanted to, why not add her own bit of culture and sophistication?

Her shop was proof that there was room for fun and flair —the tastings were a hit and a great tourist attraction. Hell, it was a flower shop that hosted a coffee house that served bistro-style food options. If *that* didn't say something about room for change, nothing did. A little lingerie and designer store front could succeed there too.

Her thoughts went a step forward, thinking about their next stop, *Kid Korner*. An indoor play place for kids and mommy groups alike was genius. Especially in an area that experienced four real seasons of weather that had limited outdoor access to burn off energy on any given day.

Every thought included Colton. Perhaps he was the reason she had suddenly become a small-town business mogul in her mind. Pursuing these potential opportunities was really an excuse to plant deep roots and stay exactly where she was. Sure she missed the amenities of her former life and would love the convenience of some of them in her new one, but truth be told, small town living, the simplicity of it, had really grown on her.

He had grown on her. She couldn't imagine a future without him, but there was still that nagging awareness – no matter how badly she wanted a life with him, she could be putting him in danger – the whole town, her friends…they could all be at risk. She needed to find a way to protect Jax, protect her new-found family, and keep the man she never thought she would find.

"Where did you go, girl?" Sam asked.

Caught off guard, Megan danced around the question with hmm's and haa's.

"I don't know, just thinking of a lot of things really. Like why doesn't McKenzie Ridge have an indoor play place for kids and mommy groups?" Megan started, listing her pros and cons for Sam. "Between locals and tourists, I think it would do really well."

Sam raised an eyebrow at her friend, partly due to interest in her idea and in part calling bullshit on her bullshit excuse for her distraction. Something about being in Portland had brought out an enthusiasm she had not seen in Meg before. It also brought brief waves of sadness that would wash over her.

"That's a fantastic idea. Actually, I would take the kids there in a heartbeat! I'd even be interested in partnering up on a project like that! Let's cut the crap though. What's really going on with you?"

Stunned by Sam's observation and blunt nature, Meg felt like a deer in headlights. This, she supposed, was the consequence of staying in McKenzie and letting people in. They get to know you, and your secrets become harder to hide.

"Wha – what do you mean?" she asked, trying to buy herself some time or even avoid the question all together.

"Honey, you go from happy and in the moment, to lost and distraught. Talk to me…how can I help?" Sam reasoned, her plea genuine and sincere.

"Ugh. It's that obvious?" she answered, desperate to spill all of her secrets to Sam. She was like the sister she had lost several months before, but she couldn't tell her a thing. If she were to tell anyone, it had to be Colton, first.

"Yes, it is. I know there is something or someone that

seems to burden you, but I want you to know, if you ever want to talk, I'm a great listener! I just want to see you happy all of the time, not just most of the time," Sam said, grabbing Meg's hand, giving it a loving squeeze.

"Thanks, really, that means a lot, and I'm sure I'll overwhelm you with my crazy eventually, now that the offer is out there," she laughed, trying to shift the seriousness looming over them. "Look, it's just a lot of things, some I can't really talk about. Some…well, Colton." She hesitated at his name, not sure where to take the conversation next.

"Colton. That part is obvious. You smile, laugh, and seem happy when you are around him or talk about him, then something just changes. What's that all about? It isn't the animals, is it?" Sam joked, earning a laugh over Colton's furry gang.

"No, not at all. I love the animals, surprisingly enough! Who knew? Ha!" She chuckled. "He's…amazing. Beyond amazing. There is something so special about him…I just can't get enough. I didn't think men came like that. He's so caring, nurturing, and loyal even, but still carries that macho charisma that makes my heart skip a beat. It doesn't hurt that he's spectacular to look at!" she said, as a sense of flowing warmth coursed through her, followed by tingling goose bumps that threatened to take her thoughts elsewhere.

"I'll give you that. All the men in our town are pretty to look at!" Sam agreed. "You're right though. He is all of those other things, so what's the problem, honey? After the other night, we *all* know you love him!"

"Oh, yeah, there is that. I was hoping I remembered it wrong!" Meg admitted, burying her face in her hands from embarrassment.

"Oh no, you were the highlight of the night. You love all

of us, even Jessie. You also love *F bombs*, Colton, and his small gang of animals.

"There isn't a problem…*that's* the problem! I moved to McKenzie for a fresh start, and here is this perfect man – it's like he was made for me. And, he loves Jax so much. I'm just waiting for it all to fall out from under me, you know? Like I don't deserve him…this is only temporary." Sadness rushed through her last words. Saying them out loud for the first time was like a punch to the gut.

"Of course, you deserve him. You deserve each other. I've seen it!" Sam declared. "Honey, he loves you and Jax. You guys just fell into this beautiful rhythm like it was meant to be! That man would die for you!"

"That's what I'm afraid of," Meg admitted before she realized what she said.

Her reality and her fantasy to stay put in McKenzie were colliding. She didn't mean to show all of her cards, but she nearly did, and she needed to fix it fast. *Nobody* could know her truth.

"What? Why would you be afraid of him dying? Are you in some kind of *trouble*?" Concern laced Sam's words, and she stood taller as if ready to help her friend in battle.

Here was Megan's moment of truth. Her opportunity to come clean and no longer carry this ugliness alone. She could trust Sam, she had become more of a sister. *All* of the ladies in the group had – even Jessie – she was just the bitchy, sarcastic one.

She looked at Sam, then Ellie and baby Gavin, and decided better of it. Her burdens were her own, and there was too much to risk if Sam knew, starting with those precious children.

"*No*. No…nothing like that. I meant that I'm afraid of being so invested and it not working out. It would be devastating for both of us." There it was, a half-assed lie and only a partial truth. Megan was getting *too* good at deception. It made her stomach turn, but it was worth every lie if it meant everyone she cared about was safe.

"Meg, don't give up before it even begins. Give it a chance. Colton is one of the best people I know. He adores you. Just let the relationship find its way. Colton is worth it, and so are you. Don't let your past dictate your future. I did, and it nearly cost me Dawson," Sam offered.

Megan finished zipping the side of the dress she had been trying on and stepped out from behind the dressing room curtain. Sam's eyes grew large and mouth opened wide. Her breath was swept away by a heavy gasp at the sight of her friend.

"That's the one, hon!" she said with a big smile. She began to clap her hands and jumped up and down.

"Oh, honey…*that* is *thee* one!"

Meg turned to look at herself in the three-way mirror. Her smile reached from ear to ear at the reflection before her. This was indeed the one. It was stunning and perfect for the Gala!

"Ohhhh, Miss Megan, you're a princess!" Ellie Lou's words came at a near whisper, in total awe, impressed by the gown as well. Ellie speechless was a first. Ellie and Sam stood side by side like two peas in a pod, sharing the same expression that revealed their satisfaction in the final dress.

Megan turned to the girls, feeling confident in not just the dress but her choice to follow her heart and stay in McKenzie Ridge with the man she loved. They would find a way!

"You're right…" she said, turning back to her reflection with a new certainty and brashness. "About everything!"

22

Nerves. A shit-ton of ragged nerves plagued Colton heavily. He didn't understand why his collar felt tight, even with the top button free, and why the hell his palms were sweaty, but they were. He and Megan had been out many times, made love many, many times. Hell, they even lived together at the moment! This night was no different than any other, or was it?

Maybe it was different now. Maybe the uncertainty shifted, and rather than chasing what he thought he wanted, it was now about keeping what he had and making it his. He had loved her all along, perhaps since the beginning, but now he was committed to fighting for her. Whatever it took to get through to her, to get her to trust him with her past, whatever it may be, he would do it. Tonight, he didn't just tell her he loved her, he showed her.

His attention shifted to the adjoining door to Sam and Dawson's room where Meg had taken Jax an hour earlier and got herself ready with Sam's help. He didn't think she needed help—she was stunning in yoga pants and an old t-shirt with messy hair and no makeup on. She was perfect.

When she walked through the door, though, he couldn't breathe. He stood there, dumbfounded and speechless, overwhelmed by the image in front of him. He'd take yoga pants and an old t-shirt any day, but this exceeded perfection. She was hair raising and spine tingling, drop dead gorgeous. He was out of his league…far, far out of his league.

She stood before him in a black satin cocktail dress with a deep V neckline that revealed her ample cleavage and bare shoulders. The full skirt landed mid-thigh, showcasing her sexy toned legs as she posed with one hand in her pocket. She turned in sky high heels that he hoped she would leave on all night, even in bed, exposing the same deep neckline on the back of her dress. Her perfectly kept hair lay swept to one side, exposing her elegant neck, which he couldn't wait to taste.

"Wow! You look… You look…" Meg's smile faded at his expression and loss for words.

"What? I can change. You don't like it?" she replied, losing her confidence.

"NO! I mean, no, its… it's… You look amazing! I don't think they've invented a word for you yet," he confessed. "I think I need to change though. Everyone will wonder why the homeless dude is following the stunning woman everywhere," he said, motioning at his dark pinstripe slacks and white dress shirt.

"No, you look handsome. Dashing really," she added.

Exchanging pleasantries and compliments, as they were, felt much like a cheesy prom or first date. His palms began to sweat again and his pants became tighter. How the hell was he going to make it through dinner? Ice water, lots of ice water, he decided. As if she knew what he was thinking, she cocked her hip, hands at her waist, and gave him a sultry look that was enough to make him chant grandma over and over in his head to avoid an embarrassing reaction. He was so screwed, figuratively and hopefully literally before long.

Dinner was spent amidst light conversation and heavy flirting. She told him about her indoor play center for children that would appeal to parents and tourists alike. He was fascinated by how her mind worked, how quickly her ideas came to life, how vivid they were. The space next to Blooming Grounds was coming vacant, something that rarely happened in McKenzie.

She thought it would be the perfect place for the new venture. She even thought about connecting the two at the bistro so food and coffee could be available on both sides. She was impressive…he could listen to her forever.

They finished their meals and decided to take their desserts to go. It was getting incredibly hot inside, and neither could sit comfortably. They had walked to the nearby water-front eatery since it was a clear, albeit cool, fall night. The benefit was obvious – the cool air allowed them each to breathe and chill their libidinous highs, but the walk, short as it may be, felt like miles.

They made their way back, taking in the romantic ambiance the city provided at night. There were many lit bridges crossing the river, joining its two sides, and crystal clear lights adorning the trees that lined each side of every street. Musicians, with their fedoras turned up for a quick tip, played the light jazzy music that set the mood. The enchanting, clear sky was speckled with a sprinkling of glowing stars across its belly with the moon full, casting a stunning, glassy reflection off the river, providing a romantically lit path home.

He stopped her just before the hotel to watch the steam roller paddle boat cross the water, loaded with party goers, as it passed under a bridge. This night couldn't get any better…

with clothes on, anyway. He held her close, his piercing gaze pulling her in for a kiss to beat all kisses. He landed hard, purposeful, and rich with promises he'd yet to make but fully intended to deliver.

Her arms craned his neck, hands running through his hair. She pressed her chest to his, accepting what he was offering, teasing him with an offer of her own. His hands moved from her ass to her sides where they continued their ascent, clear to her breasts. His thumbs softly caressed her taught nipples through the material barrier. He took credit for their hardened state and the soft throaty moan, despite the cool air.

He had her pinned against the railing at the water's edge beneath a tree, blocking any onlooker's view with his large physique. He pulled away slowly, her arms dropping to his waist in disappointment. He cupped her face in his large hands, thumbs stroking her lips to her cheeks, and he stared into her eyes, searching for words that would say everything she meant to him.

"I love you, too..." she said, hearing every word that he didn't have to say. She felt his heart in everything he did, and the look he had told a love story that there weren't enough pages for.

It was one you could only feel and maybe get a shy glimpse of if you looked hard enough. It was bold, all consuming, and passionate. She did...she loved him...loved him so hard.

"You love me? Because of wine again, or..." He asked with his grin that promised her trouble.

She tilted her head and attempted an offended look and slapped him on his ass. He chuckled at her response, then pulled her in for another kiss. This time, it was soft, slow, and filled with forevers. It took her breath away. This time she broke their kiss and tried to regain her balance.

"Not because of the wine but because I really love you. I loved you the other night…" she said with a laugh referring to her drunken confession. "I think I've loved you all along."

He kissed her forehead and leaned his head to hers. Staring into her eyes, he took in everything she said, reconciling each word. She was his angel…everything want, need, and desire…and she loved him.

"Megan, you have no idea what hearing those words means to me," he said. Taking a moment, he looked to the night's sky and gathered his thoughts, trying to prepare the appropriate words to help her feel what he felt. "I knew you were mine the first night at the wedding. You are my dream come true, my beginning and end. You and Jax both. I don't remember my life before you and can't imagine the rest of my life without you."

He continued to pour his heart out to her, knowing his words were sinking in when the tears, collecting in her beautiful golden eyes, finally welled over, streaking her cheeks. His plea to stay, not to run, to let him battle her past with her and protect her was out on the table. He prayed that his words were heard for what they really were, a beautiful overture to trust and rely on him…to stay forever.

"I know something frightens you and that you'll tell me when you're ready, but know I will keep you safe, protect you from anything and everything until my last breath. I'll fight for you forever," Colton finished his final appeal as sincere as could be, hoping it was enough.

She shook her head, looked down then around her. How did she end up here with this perfect man who was everything every girl dreamed of, yet he wanted a broken, damaged, imperfect her? That small voice in the back of her mind chose that moment to make some noise, reminding her of what was out there and waiting for her, hunting her. It was telling her to run and take the danger with her.

She looked up, got caught in his irresistible gaze, and her heart took over. He said he would protect her…he said he would listen when she was ready. He said forever.

"Colton, I…I have so much to tell you, to share with you. I am so afraid…" She stopped to take back the control she was giving her enemy, unwilling to spoil their amazing night with her dramatic story. How did she tell him everything without compromising anything, their safety specifically?

"Meg, there isn't anything to be afraid of, together. The only thing that frightens me is a life without you," he finished with a whisper, words desperate yet full of reason.

She smiled, her grip on him tightening and she nodded her head again, "Okay," she said with a breathy laugh. She was ready to fight back and no longer live in the shadows, hiding from everything that wasn't even there.

"Together…we'll do it together and chase our forever!" she declared.

Colton picked her up and swung her around shouting, "Woohoo!"

His joyful behavior drew smiles and laughs from passersby as she tossed her head back and laughed at his reaction. She felt like a princess whose fairy tale was finding its happily ever after.

Colton grabbed her hand as he set her down and ran across the street toward the hotel, dodging cars as they went.

* * *

STANDING IN FRONT OF THE ELEVATOR, WAITING FOR ITS arrival, they both hoped it was late enough to manage a solo ride to the top floor. As a couple approached, they each held their breaths until the twosome passed the elevator and moved on to the lounge. Childlike grins crossed their faces as if they had just gotten away with making out under the high school bleachers.

The numbers above the elevator doors slowly decreased with its descent. Hand in hand, they quickly charged their car, pausing only to let the lone Bell Hop by. Cheeks flushed, breathing heavily with anticipation, they anxiously waited for the doors to close.

Colton reached to the button panel, hitting their floor number first, then the button labeled *'close door'*, rapidly as if it were a video game. As soon as they were closed and the first bit of motion ensued, he spun Meg around with her back to the wall next to the panel of buttons. She let out a lusty gasp when he held both of her wrists above her head, and his other hand snaked down her body slowly, purposefully, feeling all of her with seductive intention.

He took her mouth fast and hard while his free hand made to play with her breast. She arched her back, pushing her chest to his as if compelling him to increase his touch. His lips trailed her jaw, biting and nipping as he found his way down her neck. His hand traveled south, finding her sweet spot through her dress, her desire obvious from the heat of her body and the sounds she was making.

She felt his length harden against her thigh, pleasing her and assuring her of his intentions. Her breathing became heavier as the pace of his hand increased, and his mouth found her breast.

"Screw it!" Colton shouted, releasing her hands so he could hit the stop button on the elevator and finish what he started. This late at night with such a large bank of elevators, surely they had time on their side before it would be needed. She grinned at him, pleased with his idea, hoping it meant a first-class finish. Before she could catch her breath, he had her mouth on his again. He pulled at the top of her dress, exposing her bare breasts, no bra.

"Holy hell!" he said through heavy breaths at the sight of her.

She grabbed the railing, dropping her head back when his mouth found her breasts, picking up where he left off. He reached for the hem of her skirt, pulling it up high enough to reveal another desirable treat. Her barely there lingerie was equal parts kinky and deliciously seductive. Black lace everything.

It appeared his temptress did indeed have a bra, of sorts, on after all. It was a cupless corset that matched the delicate pair of frilly, lace, cheeky panties she was made for. The final touch was a garter that attached to her thigh high stockings with black, satin bows holding the two together.

He loved all of her fancy underwear on her as much as off of her. There was nothing more sexy. He would work around it – for now. Her sexy lace told a story of a woman who already had this night planned, and it included this very moment of seduction.

"Baby, you are beautiful. You *do* love me!" he said, appreciating her finer tastes and the twitch in his pants that they caused.

Her smile gave her away. She did indeed plan this for him, which earned her a reward. He slid his hand beneath her dainty panties and stroked her heated mound that was more than ready for him, making him smile. He watched her heavy lids drop in ecstasy as her mouth puckered, releasing her breathy sounds.

He increased his pace, making her bite her bottom lip and move against his hand, hungry for more. He took her hardened nipple between his teeth bringing her to throaty moans.

Unzipping his pants with his free hand, he readied for her release. Her body quaked as she let go and rode the waves of her pleasure while he picked her up and wrapped her around his waist. It was hot, it was primal, and it was fast.

He had never experienced such raw and pure pleasure as he made bawdy, hungry love to his girl. Maybe it was being in the elevator and the thrill of potentially getting caught. Or, maybe it was the start of something new…their declared love and commitment to a forever, transcending limits that were no longer. They leaned against the wall, Megan still in his arms, trying to catch their breaths. His face buried in the crook of her neck, he began to chuckle.

"I didn't see that coming! That was…" He was cut off by a bell ringing, over and over. They quickly adjusted themselves, and Colton hit the button to go.

Panic washed over her, fear they were caught and the humiliation that was to come. She watched Colton just stand there with a wicked grin, watching the numbers change as they climbed to each floor.

"Colton, why are you smiling? We just got caught… Got caught… Well, you know!" Megan said while frantically waving her arms at the wall indicating the scene of the "crime."

He let out a laugh and pulled her in by her waist, planting a kiss on her lips.

"What? What are you doing? Oh, my God, stop! We're caught. Don't make it worse!" she scolded as she slid her arms between them, landing her hands on his chest, pushing him away. He laughed harder and pulled her in tighter.

"Colton!" she shrieked in panic.

"It's fine, darlin'. We aren't in trouble. It's just the alarm that sounds when an elevator car has been sitting idle too long. It's so they know when or if there is a problem.

We're moving now, see?" he assured, motioning to the lights above still moving steadily.

She relaxed in his arms, flooded with relief, and finally accepted his kiss.

"Are you sure?" she asked, hanging on to a final thread of doubt and worry.

"Honey, I'm a fireman. We respond to elevator calls all the time. I know what the bell means and also when an elevator has cameras," he said with a wink.

"Cameras?!?" She questioned, pushing him away again, searching her surroundings for any form of surveillance.

"Relax," he chuckled. "We were the only two people watching."

Her cheeks blushed at his comment, and a warm tingle rushed through her at the thought of what that steamy scene must've looked like. Holy hell…sex in an elevator. Just as her wits returned and her brief humiliation subsided, the doors opened to their floor.

They stepped out, arm in arm, when Dawson walked straight into their path, bucket of ice in hand. He grinned as he walked by. Megan looked everywhere but at him while Colton gave the standard "bro" head nod. Just as their paths cleared, it happened, instant mortification.

"I should have known it was you two," Dawson hollered back, followed by a hearty laugh.

Epic elevator ride behind them, Colton and Megan spent their last night making their love for one another clear, over and over again, their commitment to fight for each other undeniable.

23

IT WAS THEIR FINAL DAY IN THE CITY BEFORE HEADING HOME. Prior to the long drive ahead, they stopped at the mall to gather the last details needed for their upcoming Gala. Megan had not had so many options in one place in so long. She made the best of her time, gathering all of the things she wouldn't have access to in person until another trip came up.

The men tended to the kids at the family play area within the space while the ladies did some serious retail damage. Delivering their bags to the guys, they took off for another round, Meg practically sprinting, dragging Sam along behind her.

"Who is this girl? What did you feed her this morning?" Sam teased, winded behind her friend. "Never mind…don't answer that!" she said with her hands up to deflect any reply.

Colton and Dawson laughed and watched the women hit the next row of stores.

"Meg seems really at home here," Dawson laughed.

"That she does. I guess it's true what they say…you can take the girl out of the city but not the city out of the girl. Or, in her case, the mall," Colton reasoned.

"Well, she seems happy, relaxed even. I take it things are working out?"

"I think so. We talked about everything. She hasn't let me in entirely, but she said she wants to tell me everything. She loves me, wants to fight for us too," Colton said, smiling. "I'd call that progress."

"Good! I'm happy for you. Hopefully, Coop has some info when we get back, and whatever else is looming will be resolved," Dawson said, sincerely wishing that would be the case.

"Look at us…a couple of lovesick bastards talking about our feelings," Colton said, full of sarcasm while rubbing his friend's shoulder.

"Go to hell, Sparks!" Dawson bit back, shrugging Colton's hand off his shoulder.

"Yeah, we'll need to go shoot some shit in the woods when get back and earn some of our man cred back," Colton reasoned.

Then a little voice hollered from under the slide, "Twenty-five cents in the bad word jar. Both of yous!" Caught again by the tutu patrol.

* * *

MEGAN AND SAM WERE AT THEIR FINAL DESTINATION, A bridal shop. The perfect shoes for the Gala were somewhere in this mall, and this was the last store to explore.

"You know what they say…save the best for last," Sam said, trying to add a little optimism to the bleakness of today's shoe shopping.

"They're here. I can feel it! I can almost smell them. Sexy, strappy, mile high, and a touch of glitz!" Megan replied.

Truth was, she was feeling something, and it wasn't necessarily the shoes…but something unsettling, a roll in her gut, and a shiver down her spine. She looked over her shoulder, over and over, finally settling on it just being old nerves.

Acting brave, facing her past, and fighting for her man, was a new concept, less than twenty-four hours old. It would take getting used to.

"What is it, honey? What do you keep looking at? Afraid Colton will see you surrounded by all of these white dresses? I think he'd marry you right here in the store if he saw you!" Sam laughed.

"Huh? Oh! No, nothing like that. Just this weird feeling, probably just tired, not thinking clearly," she said with a superficial smile.

"I hear that! Between mall sprints and, uh, the elevator… I'm sure you're pretty exhausted," Sam teased.

"Oh, my God, he told you? It's not how it seemed! Ahh crap, it is exactly as it seemed, and it was fantastic!" Megan admitted with confidence.

"Whooo, go you! That a girl!" Sam said, high fiving her friend.

"Seriously, we sound like a couple of guys that just scored," Megan laughed with her friend.

It felt good to have this again. As well as someone to talk to, shop with, and confide in. She missed this, missed her sister. She reached for Sam, giving her a side hug and said, "Thank you for being such a good friend. I meant what I said the other night over *wine*. You guys are like sisters. How did I get so lucky to find the perfect guy and the best kind of friends?"

Sam hugged her back and said, "We are pretty awesome. You did get lucky, didn't you!" lightening the somberness the mention of her sister brought on. Megan's loud gasp interrupted the humor. She jumped up and rushed to the wall they had yet to scavenge. There they were, her shoes. They were strappy, high as hell and screaming fabulous glitz.

"They're perfect!" she whispered, just loud enough for Sam to hear.

"Oooh. You really did smell them. How do you do that?" she questioned while admiring the lovely shoes Meg was drooling over.

They were done, had everything on their lists, including the perfect shoes. But, there it was again, that feeling. A chill chased her shoe euphoria right out of her mind. She needed to tell Colton everything, tonight, when they got home. The unease had to be due to guilt, she reasoned. Now that they had an understanding, a chance at a life together, this doubt was just a frigid reminder that she needed to share her past.

* * *

A TEXT FROM SAM PROMPTED THE GUYS TO GATHER THE littles and shopping bags and meet them at the exit. The ladies likely hit a few more small stores on their way because the men made it there first with time to spare. An odd push from fate landed the exit right by a fine jewelry store, triggering curiosity in Colton…rings.

He perused the displays on the outside of the store as reality slapped him like the bitch that it was. Was this what they had talked about? Was this the kind of forever they were fighting for?

He heard her laughter long before she came into view. She rounded the corner, arms linked with Sam, and several more bags in hand. Her pace slowed, her smile faded, and her glow dimmed as she approached. Stopping dead in her tracks, pale as can be. Colton's heart sank.

"Hey are you okay?" Sam asked, clearly confused.

"You look like you've seen a ghost, honey."

Colton stood patiently, awaiting a response, concerned with the sudden change in her demeanor.

That look was all too familiar. It tugged at his insecurities as he wondered if it was the sight of him looking at rings or her past having its way with her again. Either way, it didn't bode well for him. She was looking through him, not at him, another foray against him.

Returning from wherever her discernibly frightened mind had been, she quickly picked up her pace, adopting a fraudulent smile as they made the last several yards to their families. Colton noticed her eyes searching, looking everywhere but at him. He turned to look behind him, and saw nothing, but a man walking the other direction with his hands in his pockets and a bag swinging from his wrist.

Turning back to Megan as she wrapped her arm around him, struggling with that smile, she looked over the group, pulling Jax's stroller close before finally speaking.

"Sorry," she said with a nervous chuckle and quivering voice.

"Babe, are you okay?" Colton questioned, face strained with tension, searching for answers.

She looked past the group again. Dawson turned to match her view this time, noticing her unease. He met Colton's eyes and offered a slight shrug of his brow. He wasn't sure what to make of her behavior, either.

"Yes, I'm fine. I just…just felt light headed for a second there! That's all!" She replied, exercising that counterfeit smile again. "I guess I shopped more than I ate. Oops!"

"Are you sure? We'll grab something to eat when we head out right now. You're sure it isn't anything else?" he implored, hoping she would give him a clue, anything that would relieve him of his worry.

"I'm sure. Let's just go. Food and a nap on the road should take care of it!" she said, pushing the stroller through the exit, side by side with Sam, in an urgent fashion for someone light headed and famished. Her eyes made one last sweep beyond where they were standing before she was on her way.

"Is it me, or is her *ghost* back?" Dawson asked.

"Ghost, or me looking at rings. Maybe *I* spooked her." Defeat sounded obvious in his admission.

"I don't know, man. I don't think she even noticed the jeweler. She had eyes over there," he said, gesturing to the vacant area she had been staring at.

"Maybe," Colton said, lacking confidence.

* * *

MEGAN RUSHED TO THE TRUCK, AND IT STILL WASN'T FAST enough for her liking. Her heart was racing, and her panic all-consuming. It took everything she had to put on her brave face and lie to those she cared about the most. She saw him again. The man who stood outside of her shop, a few nights prior, was in Portland.

He was real, he was following her, and she knew who he was the second he grinned an evil sneer, looking at Jax. She had been found. Her nightmare finally realized.

She couldn't get home fast enough. They needed a head start, and she hoped she had, at least, a brief one. She could figure out the how's and why's of being found later. She was prepared for this, had everything ready to get away without a trace. It was time to get home, grab her bag, and run…again.

* * *

Two long hours passed as fast as a rock melts in winter. This drive was a bitch, and they were only half-way through it. Tensions were high, feelings bruised, and anxiety flowed. Megan spent a good portion of the trip "napping" yet didn't get a lick of sleep the entire journey. Laying her head against the window, eyes closed, was her way to avoid conversation and more lying while she planned her next move.

She hated treating Colton this way – she hated leaving him even more. What had she been thinking the night before? Facing her past? Fighting for forevers? Well, her past was here. It had been right in front of her, at arm's length, all day. The harsh reality was that it had probably been there for months, waiting, reminding her who was in charge, and it wasn't her. Not even close.

Now, everyone was in danger, and it was all her fault. She needed to leave, tonight, before tragedy whittled its way through her friends' lives too. She had already lost enough.

A quick stop at the halfway point for bathroom and diaper breaks finally crept up. She would make a point to be quick because time wasn't on her side, or theirs. It was time to disappear.

* * *

The men stayed with the vehicles while the women tended to the children. Dawson checked his cell phone, remembering a buzz indicating he had a message nearly an hour ago. He pulled his phone to find a message from Blake. Their trip home just got all the more ominous.

Need to talk to you both when you get here,
    alone…
Have info, make it happen
-B

"Oh shit," Dawson said, leaning against the front of his truck.

Colton turned his direction and asked, "What's up? Gotta go? I can watch the trucks."

Dawson gave him an ill-tempered look and said, "No, Sparks…check your phone!"

Colton pulled out his cell phone and scanned his messages. The look on his face was evidence enough. He'd received the same message. He stared at his phone, reading the message over and over as if he might have missed something in that handful of words. He looked up, staring at the wooded area beyond before looking back at Dawson.

"What do you think he found?" Colton said softly with a sullen look that even made Dawson feel bad for the guy.

"No tellin'. Blake makes cake sound dark and painful, so it could go either way, man," Dawson replied, wishing he had something more encouraging to offer.

"Okay, well, I guess it's time to get home." He nodded toward the restrooms, indicating that the ladies were on their way back.

Colton and Meg made eye contact, each giving a look as if they were caught with their hand in the cookie jar. Both quickly plastered on a manufactured smile. Both read trouble in the other's look. She was careful not to ask if all was okay because she already knew it wasn't, and she didn't want to stoke any fires. He was careful not to ask because he knew she was anything but okay, and he didn't want to make her run faster than she was probably already planning.

24

———————

BOTH TRUCKS STOPPED AT THE HOUSE FIRST TO UNLOAD THE trailer Colton pulled, carrying the new equipment. They were greeted by Blake, who had an urgent look on his face rather than his typical glower.

"Hey, man, what's good?" Colton asked, reading his expression as a possible warning.

Blake extended his hand, offering their typical handshake to each, giving Sam and Meg each a welcoming nod.

"Not much – just here to help you unload. Chief wants it done now so training can start first thing,"

Blake said with raised eyebrows, hoping they caught on and would run with the opening he gave them.

"Well, okay then. Sam, can you run Meg and Jax home, and I can drop you off after?" Dawson offered to Colton, working with the opportunity Blake gave them.

"Sounds good…shouldn't take long. We'll be right behind you guys," Colton said.

"Then, let's barbeque! It's chilly but clear today. The kids can play and get all that energy out from the long trip. Blake, we expect you to come too!" Sam said with excitement, not ready for their weekend to end.

"I don't know. I still have a bit of a headache, and Jax is pretty tired," Megan cut in, anxiety flooding her tone.

"That's okay! I'll drop you two off. Go grab a nap while I run to the store and get dinner going!" By the time Jax wakes, the guys will be home!" Sam explained, hopping in the truck while Colton put Jax in the other truck, leaving Meg no choice but to comply.

"See you soon, babe. Have a good nap," Colton said, followed by a kiss.

Megan gave him a weak smile, leaving her hand

on his cheek a second longer than she probably would have if this wasn't the last time she was going to see him.

* * *

BLAKE HAD COLTON AND DAWSON FOLLOW HIM TO HIS OFFICE for a closed door conversation while rookies unloaded the equipment from the trailer. He ran his hands through his hair and let out a deep breathy sigh, searching for a starting point. He picked up a folder and began to thumb through it.

A file that size, after only a handful of days, left a weighted feeling deep in Colton's gut. A sense of despair washed over him. He knew this wasn't ending well for them and had an uneasy notion to get home to her.

"Let's hear it, Coop. That's a pretty hefty file," Dawson said, using the words Colton couldn't seem to find.

Blake took a seat on the corner of his desk, facing his friends. He pulled out several pictures from the expansive file, laid them in a row in front of the two men sitting before him and said, "We have a problem…a big one…"

* * *

MEGAN WATCHED SAM BACK OUT OF THE DRIVEWAY WITH A quick wave and a superficial smile because there really wasn't anything to smile about. Once Sam was out of view, Megan immediately made her way inside to execute her plan. She moved quickly, trying to ignore the pain in her chest that was her heart breaking. The heartache over-took the fear as the idea of leaving Colton and this place behind was more crushing than her past finding her. But, she had to go, had to run…for Jax.

She grabbed an already packed bag from the back of the closet in the room Jax had been using. She tossed it on the bed, opening it to add their basic day to day supplies that they would need in the next 48 hours. The rest she would buy later when she was far enough from McKenzie Ridge to do so, safely.

She changed her clothes to a non-conspicuous pair of jeans, sweatshirt, and sneakers, along with a baseball cap to hold her hair. Getting out of town, unnoticed, was her first challenge. Small towns noticed everything.

She had a second car stashed just outside of McKenzie in an old abandoned forest service garage. It was fueled up and stocked with nonperishable food items, even toilet paper. Staying off the radar meant avoiding people every step of the way. Once she got to the other car, her short life as Megan Johnson would be over, and she would be in the wind, untraceable, again, she hoped.

She paused to look around the room, searching for anything she may have missed. She scanned the various pictures of the three of them that had already begun to accumulate. She picked up a picture of all three of them on the front porch, surrounded by their family of animals.

Tears sprung to her eyes as she heard a whimper behind her...Duke. She tucked the picture in her bag and went to her best K9 friend, bending to one knee. She hugged him, giving him a big loving rub down his back. She scratched his ears and hugged his head one last time and said, "You're a good boy, Duke. Such a good boy. I'm going to miss you so much."

She laughed at herself for getting so choked up and emotional over a dog, remembering her first meeting with their furry, feathery, little gang. She chuckled at how frightened she had been by the gentle beasts whom she now loved as much as the people in her life. She'd come so far, grown and changed so much in the past few months here in McKenzie Ridge. She was going to miss it terribly.

"You take care of Colton for me, okay? I love him so much. I don't want to hurt him, but it's too dangerous for everyone if I stay. Okay? You understand, don't you boy? Forgive me?" Duke gave her another throaty whimper and laid his head on her shoulder. "I know. I love you too, buddy."

She got up on her feet, grabbed little Jax, and hugged him tight. This wasn't just hard for her, but it would be hard for him as well. First his mom, now the new family-like friends they had made who he had come to love and adore. It broke her heart.

"Maybe when this is all over, we can come back here," she said to the tot resting on her hip. She wondered who she was trying to convince, the toddler or herself. Someday. That was a day she looked forward to. Someday meant no more running, no more hiding, no more fear or threats. Someday. Such an ambiguous idea. Her someday could be tomorrow, or it could be 20 years from now. Someday was as likely as chocolate rain, she conceded, not in her lifetime. Such a defeating thought.

Her heart filled with sorrow as she grabbed her bag and headed for the front door. If it were just her, she could stay… she would risk it all. But she wouldn't risk Jax's little life. She would keep her promise and protect him, at her own expense, for as long as it took.

Her eyes welled to the edge of her lids as she made her final pass down the hallway, past the living room and kitchen to the front door. She reached for the door knob, closing her eyes, taking a deep breath, readying herself for what opening that door would unleash.

"Were you even going to say goodbye? Or did you not trust me with that either?" Her eyes shot open and breath caught at the sound of his voice. He was here to stop her. She turned to her left, facing the living room, and there he sat on the couch, waiting for her. "Colton," she whispered.

"I…"

"You were running. Why? I thought we had a deal? We were going to fight," he reminded her, his

voice thick with his pain. "Let me help you."

Large tears finally spilled over, flooding her cheeks like a rapid rainfall at the look of sadness and desperation on his face. The sound of defeat mingled with his words. She hurt him. She knew she would, but she didn't think she would have to endure witnessing it.

"Colton…" She choked on his name, as if it was painful to even mention. "I have to leave. *This* is what I was so afraid of, why I tried so hard to avoid a relationship to begin with… I can't do this. I just can't."

Her own words pained her. Sure, they were honest, but they didn't represent what she really wanted. She couldn't tell him why she really needed to leave. He would try to fight her past for her or follow her. Either way, he was in harm's way, and it could cost him his own life.

She needed to protect him, just as he wanted to protect her. He needed to believe this was what she wanted. She may have said she could fight for forever, but those words took new meaning when that fight followed her to Portland, putting everyone in the line of fire.

Now, she needed to get said harm away from her loved ones. She needed it to follow her away from McKenzie.

"That's crap, Megan, and you know it. Or, should I say, Trinity?" he finished with a near whisper, showing her his whole hand at once. If he couldn't get her to stay because she loved him and trusted him enough to help, then he had no choice but to lay it all out there.

Her face drained of color, eyes glazed over in shock, a wave of nausea rushing through her. He said her name. She wondered how much more he knew and how he found out. He was a moving target now in a mercy situation. He would be used, at any cost, to get to her.

Colton moved closer, reaching for her, aware of the fear he had just instilled in her. She stepped away, back against the door, shaking her head no as the tears streamed fiercely to a near sob. She choked on her words, trying to speak, but couldn't. Everything she tried to protect him from was staring back at her...he *knew*. He was as good as dead.

"No, no, no..." She started in a whisper but graduated to a near yell. "You can't, Colton! You can't know! You aren't safe! You can't fight this for me. It's bigger than us, and it's bigger than this town! You're all in harm's way! Don't say that name again," she cried, uncontrollably. Gasping between her words. "You don't know me, okay?"

"Please, let me in. Let me *help* you. If you won't let me help, then let me go with you. Because knowing you are out there in the world alone, being chased by *this*, will kill me too. I swear on everything I've ever known and loved, I'll keep you and Jax safe. Let me help you carry this weight." Colton's anger and pain had become desperate. He needed her to hear him and let him in.

"Meg, I've waited my whole life for you. I will *not* let it end like this. I will *not* let anything hurt you. Please, baby, please, trust me enough with this. Please, trust that our friends can and will help," he begged, his interest not only to keep her but to keep her alive.

"Colton, they are bigger than us. If anyone got hurt, I couldn't live with myself. I brought this here, and I need to take it away," she said, moving away from him and the door, not sure of her next move but knowing it would be at a run.

She heard the side door to her left open and close, followed by urgent heavy footsteps of what sounded like a herd of people. Panic won, her greatest fear realized, and anxiety took over. "Oh, my God!" She whispered through her shaky words. "They're already here." Her eyes rolled back, eyebrows furrowed, and she gasped for breath before collapsing, completely unconscious.

"Megan!"

25

———

Mumbling in the distance began to distract Megan from her thoughts. He knew. He knew everything, but how. She was so careful, covered her tracks at every turn, just as she was told to. If Colton knew, did the rest of them know? They all must hate her. She'd lied. She was a complete fraud, and now they were all in danger because of her carelessness. She should have left months ago.

The mumbling became louder, so many different voices, but she couldn't quite make out who it was or what they were saying. Her body began to move but not voluntarily. She felt his hands, Colton's hands, on her. Only his touch could warm her to her core and leave her with chilling goose bumps at the same time.

Confusion faded, and reality took over, reminding her of where she was and what happened. Her eyes shot open, and she gasped for air as she sat up, remembering the mob of footsteps charging in. She needed to run, but firm hands held her still while his voice washed over her, calming her.

Colton had her in his arms…the mumbling had been him. Unsure of what just happened, she scanned the room and found that they weren't alone. Dawson, Carigan, Blake and Evie were scattered around the room, all eyes on her, their faces reflecting their concern.

"Easy, honey, are you okay?" Colton asked, a look of trepidation hanging from his troubled stare.

Her heart stung knowing she had caused him such pain. The only man she ever loved. The only man she would love, yet she threw his heart to the ground before stepping on it, breaking it in to scattered pieces.

"I…I think so? What happened? I heard them coming… I thought…" She took in the confused looks, realizing the invasion wasn't the threatening presence she thought it was but just their friends.

Why were they there, she wondered? She looked down, acknowledged she was sitting on the couch, but Jax was no longer in her arms. Panic rose again at his absence. She quickly moved from Colton's sturdy grip, attempting to get away and find her nephew.

"Jax!" She yelled. Colton once again came to her aid, wrapping her in his embrace.

"Shhhh, shhh, it's okay, baby. He's safe! He's safe!" he assured.

As if on cue, Jessie rounded the corner, Jax on her hip with hands full of cookies, along with Granny Lou, her own hands filled with plated cookies. Not sure what struck her as more odd, Jessie holding a child and smiling, or a room full of their friends in the midst of her crisis and great escape, she turned to Colton for answers.

He smiled his warm comforting smile that somehow, despite imminent danger, put her instantly at ease. Morgan walked in, trailing Jessie and Lou, with a serving tray covered with mugs and what appeared to be a carafe of coffee.

"Well, look who is awake!" she said with a smile, offering her the first mug. "Hot chocolate?"

Megan took the mug, thoroughly stumped by the kindness and generosity, given what she had done to all of them. She smelled the warm, chocolaty drink and glanced at it, noticing the marshmallows floating around.

"Don't worry, sweetie. It's safe. We're the good guys, honey!" Morgan joked with a wink before passing out drinks.

"You passed out. I know I call you Princess, Priss Pants, and Fancy Pants, but don't you think the Sleeping Beauty act is a bit dramatic? Even for you?" Jessie teased, offering a small grin. "I refuse to call you that, it's just too ridiculous."

"I'm sorry, I didn't realize I had. Wow, this has been a real shit day!" Megan proclaimed, emphasis on the *shit*.

Granny Lou and Jessie high-fived each other at the use of foul language, even if it was fairly minor. "Appears we're rubbing off on her. She even used it correctly!" Lou joked, causing a group chuckle.

The front door abruptly opened, sending everyone to their feet, Colton and Blake standing in front of Megan while Morgan and Dawson stood in front of Jessie, who was still holding Jax. Sam walked through the door, arms loaded with groceries and kids in tow, confused not only by the unexpected group but the reaction to her entrance.

"I guess I should have bought some more food?" she said.

* * *

Nancy watched the three children play in the spare room that had become Jax's while the adults finally settled around the living room.

"Blake, tell us why you called us all here. The suspense is starting to wear on me," Carigan said, starting the dialogue.

"Yeah, you said it was urgent, so what gives? If you wanted some of Gran's cookies, you would've just stopped by, which tells me this is serious?" Evie offered.

Blake looked to Megan, then Colton, and proceeded with a nod from Colton.

"It turns out we have a little trouble in town…after one of our own," he confessed, gaining everyone's undivided attention.

"Blake, please, I can't let you all get involved. It's too dangerous. I'm not dragging you all in to this, please?" Begging with Blake to spare their group, Meg choked back the tears trying to accumulate.

"Too late now – this is what we do. So, who is going to fill us in? From the looks on your faces, I'm guessing Morgie knows, obviously Sparks, and since Blake called, he's the ring leader. Dish, sweetheart!" Evie said while stuffing another snicker doodle into her mouth.

"Wow, Nancy Drew, great detective work!" Jessie teased with an eye roll, earning her a shot to the head with a pillow, compliments of Everly.

"Now, now, girls, play nice. None of you are too old to put over my knee! Blake, honey, what's all this fuss about? You have about another 10 minutes of my guaranteed attention!" Gran negotiated as she pulled a flask from her purse, pouring a shot into her hot chocolate.

Blake gave her a stern look before turning his attention to Everly. With just the raising of his brows, she put both hands in front of her and said, "I take responsibility for the old woman! I drove her here. I'll drive her home!"

"Oh, fuck-stix, who you callin' old, little lady?" Gran countered with a scolding tone, shaking her finger at her granddaughter, Everly. "This here's just for *medicinal* purposes!" she finished with heavy emphasis on *medicinal.*

"Darn rheumatism is actin' up. Snows comin'." She shrugged and took a healthy swig of her doctored hot chocolate, passing her flask to Jessie.

After a quick use, Jessie tossed the flask back into Lou's oversized purse, witch probably held everything a person would ever need to survive in the wilderness for a week. Jessie took a big gulp of her own doctored hot chocolate before looking to Blake with a smug smile.

"Okay, looks like I have Granny 2.0 over there. You're not driving Jessie," Blake scolded.

"Yeah, yeah, whatever you say, Captain America. So what are we here for? What's up with Fancy Pants?" Jessie replied.

Blake sat, hands folded together out in front of him with elbows resting on his knees. He looked down, let out a deep sigh, contemplating where he should begin.

Megan put a hand on his shoulder and said, "I should tell them. It should come from me, at least, the part I know?" she said with a slight smile to assure him she could do this.

Colton's protective instincts rolled through him. He sat taller, his grip firmer, and he asked, "Are you sure? You aren't alone in this anymore…you don't have to."

"I do, Colton. They need to hear my part from me. Then, they can decide from there what they think of me and *if* they want to be involved." Megan firmly stated, regaining some of her confidence.

"Holy shit! Priss Pants has a secret! I friggin' knew it! Rob a bank or shoot someone?" Jessie half yelled, almost excited that Megan had something less than perfect about her.

"Jessie! Let her talk, for land's sake!" Carigan scolded, her Irish tendencies flaring. "Go ahead love. What's your trouble?'

Megan gave Colton one last look, finding the confidence she needed to bravely say what she hadn't said out loud to another soul. Her secret was nearly free, and its consequences certain. She was fearful of what was to come, but primarily her fears resided in this room. Disappointing those she'd come to love as her own would be her greatest challenge to overcome yet. A squeeze of her hand from Colton raced through her. It was now or never…never no longer an option.

She took a deep, cleansing breath and said, "My name is Trinity Prescott."

26

Huffs and gasps filled the space, defining the element of confusion and disbelief that rested on the shoulders of everyone in the room. Megan closed her eyes, soaking it all in, pondering her next move. She didn't want to hurt these people, defraud them of anything they had built together in the past year or so. She was a perfect contradiction of everything real, everything made up.

The person she was with them, completely real—the person she was in general, a complete fraud. She was entirely made up and whoever the world needed her to be to survive and stay hidden.

"Come again dear? I know I haven't had enough of this here drink of mine to be a little *hoo-hoo* in the head, and I'm pretty sure you didn't fill your mug…have I done lost my mind?" Gran questioned, grabbing Evie's arm, eyes wide with concern. "It finally happened. Oh, honey, it's time for the home, isn't it?"

The group snickered at Lou Shaw's panic, lightening the mood and the blow Meg had just dealt them. Megan was certain it was intentional and Lou's way of helping her through her hardship because that woman was sharp as a tack. That's just who Lou Shaw was, everyone's "Granny Lou."

Everly rolled her eyes at the old woman's dramatics, putting a hand over hers and said, "Calm down. We aren't that lucky, old girl!"

"There you go again! Who ya callin' old?!" Gran shot back, suddenly lucid and of sound mind, apparently.

Megan took a deep breath and dug deep for the courage she desperately needed to finish her confession.

"C'mon Princess, out with it. Who the hell are you, and what is it to us?" Jessie asked with a snarky tone. Megan expected this, disappointment, skepticism, and mistrust. She only hoped that when and if this ever ended, forgiveness would follow.

"I'm Trinity Prescott…well, I was. I am from New York. I had a ridiculously pampered life that I've learned lacked meaning and purpose until now…" She admitted her dislike for who she had once been. She wasn't a bad person, just someone who had been in need of *real* importance and meaning in her life. "About a year ago, my life forever changed when I was left to take care of Jax. That's when I became me, well, Megan."

"Okay, so when your sister died, you changed your name and moved? That's it?" Sam asked, confused by the seriousness if this was nothing but a name change and relocation.

Megan let out a deep breath. She knew they deserved to know everything, and she was tip-toeing around the elephant in the room. It was time to get real and deliver hard truths.

"About that, my sister…" she began with her head tilted down, looking at everyone through her thick lashes, gauging how much she should or could say now, "…is alive and well and on the run, too."

The silence her admission granted was deafening.

"Like I said, I am from New York. We grew up wanting for nothing. Our lives were quite privileged," she began. "I guess you could say we were professional *socialites*. Lydia and I were at every major event or fundraiser, coast to coast, that anyone who was anyone would attend. That was my life, superficial as it gets, it turns out." She took a moment to gather her thoughts and process what she had just admitted to her friends, saying it out loud for the first time.

"Are you okay? Do you want me or Blake to finish?" Colton asked, recognizing the pain it was causing her.

She looked at him as if for the first time, realizing just how amazing this man was. She had lied to him as much or more than the others. He had so much more invested, more to lose than anyone else, especially given his own past. Here he was, worried about her. He loved her so much that he could set it all aside and still care about how difficult this was for her?

He really was her dream come true, and she hoped that when this was all over, they still had a chance at a happily ever after to fight for. She smiled and nodded, holding back the tears his benevolence provoked, and finished her story.

"We had been running into the same crowds, over and over, at the various events, including one man in particular, Esteban Ricardo Valdez. He was from Miami, a major real estate tycoon and land developer type. Lots of money, lots of power, and could charm the pants off a snake."

"He fell for Lydee, hard. They fell for each other, really. I was never a fan of his, couldn't put my finger on why. They eventually married, Lydee moved to Miami and I rarely saw her or heard from her after that." Sadness laced her words as she remembered what it felt like, losing her sister to Esteban. Her best friend and partner in everything was just gone one day.

"She was happy. He gave her a life of luxury beyond imagination, but eventually, the newlywed phase wore off. He was working all the time, and he became distant but very controlling. I rarely heard from her, saw her even less. Things got better again when she became pregnant with Jax. He was overjoyed to have a boy. But again, the baby was born, the newness wore off, and he became obsessed with work again."

"I took a trip to Florida to visit, meet my new nephew. I saw Esteban only a handful of times, in passing, over the course of a two week stay. There were people, mostly men, in and out of their home at all hours of the night. I slept with my door locked it was so uncomfortable. My sister had become a shell of herself, her eyes vacant of joy. She would throw herself at him, begging to be noticed. It broke my heart to leave her like that, but Esteban wouldn't let her come with me for a visit home." She perused the faces that were clinging to her every word.

The looks of shock and surprise stung a bit because she hadn't told them the real shock and awe yet. Digging deep for the confidence she needed, she began her big finale. This would be the true test of friendship, the deciding factor between run or stay.

"After I left, I only knew what little she told me in the few conversations we were allowed. In fact, I'm certain those conversations weren't allowed, and she found a way to call without him knowing."

"Then one night, well after midnight, there was a frantic knock at my door. When I looked through the peep hole, Lydia was standing there. I quickly unlocked the door to let her and the baby in, but when I opened the door, they weren't alone. There was a behemoth of a man who followed her in. He moved past me and began searching my house, checking windows and closing curtains," she said as if annoyed by the giant's actions.

"Lydee was a mess. It took the better part of an hour to calm her down, and even then...she was speechless. The angry giant had to speak for her. His name is Declan O'Reilly," she said, looking directly at Carigan.

The room became still as all eyes shifted to her at the mention of her eldest brother, who was as big of a mystery as Blake was to all of them when it came to his background. It was well known that Declan and Blake were some form of ex-military with shadowy pasts that could never quite be defined. Blake was no longer involved at that level, perfectly content with serving and protecting McKenzie Ridge.

Declan was another story. He was still in deep, so deep that mention of his name brought a new level of seriousness and even fear to the story unfolding. It also brought Carigan's raw emotions to the surface.

"My brother?" Carigan whispered, eyes glistening at the thought of him and what it meant if Megan was involved with him. "He's been gone for years. No one has heard from him other than a few random cards letting us know he was okay. Oh, Megan, you're hiding, aren't you? My brother hid you here! He knew you'd be safe, that we'd watch over you and Jax." A subtle smile stretched across her face, knowing he brought her to them. With all of his resources, he trusted them with Megan and Jax.

"Holy shit, Princess. You're in some deep crap, aren't you? You just might be a little bad ass after all," Jessie said with approval and perhaps a little joy. She was a bit twisted that way.

"Declan told me he had been working undercover as Esteban's hired muscle and driver, mostly for Lydia. That's why he was so familiar. I remembered him from my visit.

"Lydee's confidence was shot, but she was desperate to make her marriage work. So, one night, she made reservations at a Miami hot spot, got dressed up and went to his office building. When she got there, it was obvious there were several people there, based on the cars in the parking lot. Afraid that she was interrupting a meeting, she had decided to leave until her insecurities got the better of her, and she went inside to see if he was with a woman.

"He wasn't in his office, though. Nobody was." Megan stopped and found her way back to the present.

The ugliness of what occurred that night was festering in her stomach and trying to wretch its way up. The thought of her sister so desperate, fused with what she would stumble upon, brought on an unimaginable pain and even guilt she had yet to explore.

Talking about this for the first time was good, a burden she wouldn't have to carry so deep anymore, but it forced her to stop and look at what had happened in the hours leading up to her life forever changing. Something she had neglected to do until now, it had been too overwhelming to do alone.

"Something had caught Lydee's attention, a commotion of sorts, so she followed the sound. She began to hear voices the further she got away from the offices and closer to an area that was under some sort of construction. A remodel or something. She heard tools, power tools, followed by yelling and even screaming.

"She continued to follow it and found her husband. He was cold, had dark empty eyes, evil. She had never seen him like this. Angry, sure, but never this. He was someone she hadn't met before.

"There was a man lying on the floor and blood everywhere, she said. Another man was standing before Esteban, crying and had wet himself. His men were crowding the room. She didn't understand what was happening. Who was this man? How could he stand there and not do anything?

"Then it happened...Esteban raised his hand, holding a gun, and shot the man on the floor." Gasps of shock interrupted her story. Jaws were dropped, eyes wide, and tears streaking faces. It wasn't until she stopped that she realized her own tears.

"This sounds like something out of a movie, things that you don't believe happen in real life. Her husband? I just can't imagine," Sam said, wiping her tears.

"It startled her. I mean who wouldn't have been scared? She made a noise just loud enough to make eye contact with one of Esteban's men. He heard her, saw her even. She turned and ran...she left, didn't look back. She went straight to the police station. She hadn't been there long when in walked the man who saw her. She was afraid Esteban sent him to get her, but he hadn't. It was Declan." More sighs and sounds of shock interrupted as they took in what had just been said. Declan had been working for Esteban, but undercover. She needed to clarify his role, if for no other reason than for Carigan's sake.

"Declan had been undercover over a year, trying to bring Esteban down. When he saw Lydee, he went after her. The local PD was corrupt. Esteban had people paid off everywhere. She was now a key witness to countless crimes, and if she told a soul, her days were numbered. Dec got her out of there and put her and Jax in protective custody. They showed up at my place hours later. The only way Lydee would go into hiding was if Jax was safe, far from her, and I was safe, not to be used as a means to get to her and Jax if he found out we were alive."

Evie chimed in, losing the path Megan was leading them down a bit and asked, "What do you mean 'if he found out you were alive'?" her fingers doing air quotes around Megs repeated words.

"He thinks we're all dead. Lydee left a note saying she was coming to visit me, that she brought Jason to drive them and keep them safe," Meg answered.

"So, Jason is really Declan, my brother?" Carigan asked.

"Yes, Jason is Declan. They think he's dead, too," she whispered, trying to lighten the blow to Carigan that her brother is assumed dead to a big part of his world.

Blake stepped in and took over. It was evident Megan was exhausted, rehashing a horrible past and speaking her truth. The details he could handle. Reading his friend's body language as he did, Colton knew she was done, for now, and pulled her into his arms and just let her cry. It's what she needed to do to clear her mind and cleanse her soul. After a year of carrying this weight all on her own, she was free. She was no longer hiding out in the open amongst her friends. She was free to be herself, let them in…let him in. She just wanted to keep them safe.

"Here's the deal…Esteban is a really bad, fucking dude. He's tied to the Cartels, even double crossing each, pitting them against each other while he swoops in and does his own thing. The fact that he does that openly, without fear, speaks volumes to how deep his ties go and the pockets he's in. He has been untouchable until now. His wife's testimony was the final nail in the coffin, but then he went underground." Blake delivered the facts, no fluff, no emotion, just hard truths.

"He played it like a grieving widower, but we suspect he didn't buy the whole death thing. As far as the world knew, Lydia Prescott-Valdez was killed in a car crash while visiting her sister. Also deceased, sister, Trinity…" He gestured to Megan, indicating her role.

"Also deceased, the couple's infant son and the family

driver. That's how they pulled O'Reilly out from cover. They think he's dead, but he's really Prescott's handler while she's in witness protection."

Morgan stood and pulled out a newspaper, held in a clear, plastic, evidence bag, and passed it around the room. "This paper showed up on Meg's porch a few days ago. This is what the world heard, but who put it on her porch all these months later?" she questioned, although the answer was obvious.

"That was on my porch? When? How?" Megan's panic returned. They had been at her house, on her front porch, so close to Jax and her.

"I found it when I went to grab the suitcase for Portland. I took it and Dec's number to Blake before we left. I'm sorry… I knew something was wrong, but finding those two things? He needed to be involved," Colton said apologetically but matter-of-factly.

Megan stared at him, searching for reasons to be upset with him for keeping something so important from her, but she couldn't. He did exactly as he said he would, protected her and Jax. He knew she'd run if she knew, and he couldn't protect her if she did. Her shock and subtle sense of betrayal quickly dissipated when pride and love overshadowed both. She gave him a sweet smile, revealing a true understanding and appreciation.

"So, wrap all this up and put a pretty bow on it, boy. What does all of this mean? What do we need to do to keep her and the baby hidden?" Granny Lou asked. "I got me a .38 special. Pack it in that there bag all the time. You all should be packin' heat, too. This is some bad news headed our way. We gotta shoot them where they stand…get their asses first!" she said, throwing her fist in the air for dramatic effect.

Evie rolled her eyes at her half-buzzed Gran and said,

"Hand it over," holding her hand out. "The purse, old lady… hand it over. It better not be loaded this time."

"Sweet Jesus in the morning, what good is a gun if it ain't loaded, Everly Louise? I declare you young people think some hoodlum will wait patiently while you find your bullets to load it before he attacks. They're called bad guys for a reason, and it ain't 'cause they got manners!" she finished with a shake of her head, pulling her purse a little closer with her foot.

"Wait, your middle name is…Louise?" Jessie asked with a snicker.

"And what's wrong with the name Louise, Jessica Mable Clarke?"

"Not a friggin' thing, Granny, especially when you're locked and loaded over there. Well played, old woman!" Jessie conceded, hand up in front of her.

"Mable? Really?" Blake asked with a look of disgust. Given Jessie's tempered, foul mouthed nature, anyone would find a name like "Razorback" or "Drill Bit" perfectly acceptable, but Mable?

"I'm afraid it's already here," Megan said, getting back to business. "I saw a man in front of the shop a few nights ago before our meeting.

"The night you got shit faced?" Jessie asked.

"Yes, Jessie, the night I got shit faced," she answered with a snarky tone. "I couldn't place him, even thought he was familiar. He was in Portland today, twenty feet from us as we were leaving. I knew exactly who he was then – one of Esteban's men. He found us at the mall on our way out of town, which means he likely followed us the entire trip."

"That's why you were leaving," Colton said as a statement rather than a question.

27

THE CULMINATION OF WHAT THAT MEANT PATCHED HIS HEART a bit. She wasn't leaving because she wanted to, but because she thought she had to, in order to protect him. There was no greater love than loving someone so much you can leave them for their sake, despite the ache it left you with. Selfless and completely Meg.

"They are here. Have been for weeks. The John Doe who was hit in front of Blooming Grounds was part of Esteban's team. The sightings Megan has had and the intruder in her shop? Then, the flat tire that Morgie and I rolled up on? They were sitting right up the street, jamming your cell signal even. They didn't expect us to show up," he said, going down his list of unknown run-ins.

What he had to say next was probably the toughest to deliver. "The fire wasn't entirely a gas leak. It was set up to look like one in hopes that you would have slept through it long enough that it was too late to get out. Or, to flush you out into the dark with nobody around so they could grab you. You have Duke to thank for that one. They've been playing with you," Blake said.

"Why? Why not just take Jax and go? Nobody would've known a thing until they were long gone," Carigan asked.

"To test her. See who she told. Determine what they would get away with and who else they would need to deal with to cover their tracks. They probably hoped it would flush her sister out of hiding, too. These guys are known for their sick sense of mental torture. When they had trouble getting to you because all of us were showing up, they were probably trying to get you to run so they could catch you in between cities." Blake knew he was laying it on thick, didn't need to go into such detail, but he wanted her to be fearful, to let her guard down and let them help. If not for her own sake, then for Colton's.

Blake may stand in the background and keep to himself more than the others, but he cared for his friends and would do anything for them. Seeing Colton hurt wasn't in the cards. That went for any of them, physically or emotionally…not on his watch.

"So what's next, Coop?" Dawson asked.

Looking at his watch, Blake swiftly moved to the kitchen where he shut off all the lights while he made his way to the back door. He turned off the back porch light and unlocked the door. He returned to the living room, closing all the blinds and curtains along the way and turning on all of the front lights to offset the light and shadows emanating from inside.

"What is this? Are we having a sleep over, or what?" Carigan asked.

"Hold that thought, O'Reilly," he replied, watching the time on his wrist.

Footsteps across the deck could be heard at the rear of the house, causing Dawson and Colton to stand in defense. Gran grabbed her bag and pulled it close, digging for her gun.

"It's not in there, Gran. Everyone sit – it's okay," Blake

warned, lifting his shirt to reveal his steamy washboard abs and Granny's gun in his waistband, sending her into a cantankerous fit and leading everyone else to a chuckle.

The footsteps became louder as the rear door opened and closed. Light mumbles could be heard, and the steps lightened to fewer as the movement got closer. In the archway between the dining room and living room stood a larger than life, six foot plus, brawny man with rich, copper hair, a lightly bearded face, and familiar emerald green eyes. His muscles had muscles, and his presence was that of three men.

Megan's eyes grew huge at the sight of him. She grabbed Colton's hand and squeezed. Before she could get a word out, Carigan stood, moving swiftly toward the man, sobs escaping her typically collected self.

"Declan Farrell O'Reilly!" she announced before wrapping her arms around him. He held her tight and folded into her. The emotion he felt could be seen by all when his large, edgy demeanor shrunk to a soft, teary eyed man who had clearly missed his baby sister.

Movement caught everyone's attention as a nervous woman shifted from behind him, stepping into the light. She was petite and curvy, with chocolate brown hair, familiar, golden eyes and turned up nose.

"Oh, my God, Lydia!"

* * *

A QUICK REUNION COMMENCED, FULL OF HUGS AND handshaking. Declan said his hellos and Lydia said her nice to meet yous. There wasn't a dry eye in the place when Lydia sank to the floor in tears after being reunited with her son.

The children were eventually put to bed for the night so

the grownups could continue the briefing of sorts and devise their plan. Without a mention, it was clear to all just how significant this circumstance was if it pulled Declan and Lydia out of hiding. There was only one reason to do so, and that was to use them as bait. Dangling that carrot before the metaphoric rabbit meant the rabbit was indeed there to tease and trap.

In other words, it was time to pull Esteban out of hiding once and for all. It appeared he was right under their noses and had been for some time. They were playing with Megan, toying with her emotions all these weeks, to accomplish one of two things: one – get her to run and lead them to Lydia, or two – dispose of Megan and use Jax to pull Lydia out of hiding.

Declan and his team would do one better. Now that Esteban and his posse were in McKenzie Ridge, they would beat them at their own game and dangle her in front of them to pull Esteban out of hiding. It was so simple and obvious that it was bound to work. They would be looking for hidden traps and complex plans, so they wouldn't realize the game was being played right back.

"So that's the plan? Do nothing?" Carigan asked.

"We aren't doing nothing – we're provoking their next move," Declan answered.

"Dec, that sounds like poking a bear for fun. If we aren't ready for them to swing or don't see it coming…" Colton's concern was obvious and received plenty of nods from around the room.

"I get it, but we know he's here or, at least, nearby, or his men wouldn't be here, playing as they are, making themselves known to her. These aren't just his minions. These are his closest, most trusted associates. They don't go anywhere without him and vice versa," he offered as peace of mind to the group. "The advantage we have is I'm here, my team is here, and we have eyes everywhere, and he doesn't know that. We are either going to draw him out or wait for a mistake and let one of his goons lead us to him."

Looking at Colton, Megan grabbed his hands and gave him an encouraging smile. "It'll be okay, Colton. I trust Dec and his team. They got me and Jax out here safely. He's kept Lydee alive all of this time," she offered. "It's almost over. I'm almost free. We're almost free," she said, giving her sister a teary smile.

"Lydia and Declan will remain hidden. We aren't showing Valdez our cards just yet. They will think we are when they follow you guys out of the area, see a few unidentified people in your cars. Change in activity and behavior will be their tip off, or so they think," Blake confided. "Meanwhile, there will always be an agent nearby, watching both of you," Blake said to Megan and Colton.

"When any of you are together, there will be agents. Just know that. Nobody gets hurt – no one – we're taking this asshole down," Declan assured.

"Sounds like a plan. I'll be spending a lot more time with you, Meg," Morgan said. "If they've been watching, they know we're friends, so it won't seem out of place. The key here is never finding yourself alone."

Megan nodded, accepting her new role, which would bring an end to her temporary life. That thought stung a bit as she wondered what it meant entirely. The past year had been a whirlwind of changes, and she was approaching her final act.

"Any questions?" Dec asked. "I need to get Lydia out of here before we start to look suspicious."

"Yeah, how did they find me?" Megan questioned.

Declan smiled and gave a slight snort. "Facebook."

"But, I don't have a Facebook page," she defended.

"Your town does. It seems the town was quite impressed with the new florist in town. Your evening tasting events were plastered on the tourism sites. And this big dance thing you're organizing?" he questioned.

"The Gala… My wine tastings," she whispered.

"McKenzie Ridge has become pretty tech savvy and caught up with social media—we found you everywhere," he finished. "Seems you've really made your mark on this place."

"She sure has," Colton said, grabbing her hand.

"Oh, my God, what about the Gala?" Sam questioned. "Do we cancel? Will it be safe?"

The room filled with emotional responses to Sam's question. They had worked so hard, and this year was promising to be their best yet.

"Business as usual. We send a huge message if we cancel. Esteban needs to think he has the upper hand, the element of surprise, here. We'll have our people everywhere. Undercovers will be there as attendees, some will be placed as workers, and the place will be surrounded. He won't be able to touch the place. We'll stop him miles out in any direction," Declan assured them.

"Sounds like you brought a small army," Dawson joked.

"We did. This guy is done," Dec replied with a smile.

Everyone said their goodbyes, a tearful one as Lydia kissed her sleeping son goodbye, again. They made their way back out the direction they'd come in, surrounded by the extra men who were posted around the perimeter, and down to the lake. They disappeared into the woods where they likely had a vehicle staged, ready to take them to wherever they were staying.

The room was quiet for a moment while they all processed what the night turned into.

"Well then, who wants dessert?" a now sober Gran asked with a wink and a grin.

28

The Holiday Hoedown was in full swing and scheduled to run until Friday. There were booths galore as the towns-people peddled their wares in an effort to raise money for their own pocket books as well as the community holiday outreach charity that was run by the local Police, Fire, and Emergency Medical from the House. All of the handmade jams, coasters, and wreaths would translate into Christmas gifts for the area youth who had less than most.

As a tourist town, they always had plenty of interest and a successful event as tourists planned their getaways around this special, one-of-a-kind affair. The buzz, this year, went beyond the pickled eggs and fried anything you could think of. The newest element, the formal Crystal Showdown Gala, as contradictory as it sounded with its rustic meets glam charm, was a sold out event.

Megan was proud of her contribution to her community, the success of the annual event and the added element of a formal Gala. The Silent Auction of donated goods and outings from the community, as well as a live auction of McKenzie's finest from the House, were a bonus. Meg had her eye on a certain firefighter, and Lord help anyone who tried to outbid her.

They spent each day at the Bazaar, keeping things in order and enjoying their time together. Although not out of danger, Meg felt this sense of calm and peace…like she was finally home. They couldn't tell Declan's team from a townsperson or tourist but knew his men were there, following their every move.

The occasional spine stabbing chill and eerie sense of being followed let them know that danger was still lurking. It was like a shift of the wind, calm and secure to dark and shady. The latter sparked that familiar urge to run, but Colton kept her grounded. He reminded her that they were safe and that he wouldn't let those assholes anywhere near her or Jax.

He really was her everything. He was her manly, take charge alpha when he needed to be, but he was also a gentle, caring man who would stop the world to make her happy. He was her hero in every way. She was glad that he stopped her from leaving. This was the life she wanted. He was the man she wanted forever.

* * *

THE GERIATRIC MAFIA SEEMED TO NEED COLTON AT THEIR booth more and more. The old ladies held their famous baked goods booth, headed up by their eternal leader…Granny Lou. Lou had insisted on walkie-talkies since they were of *delicate age* and *fragile health*…they might need help in a hurry, she argued.

Complying with her request, especially since she had three extra walkie-talkies at the ready, the three men took to their duties. The requests for help usually consisted of lifting, bending over, and taking a pulse or two. Being the people pleaser that he was, Colton made sure he responded to every call, knowing full well what they were up to when they started pinching his ass and getting handsy.

They paid him well, however, in baked goods, reducing him to a new form of male entertainment who worked for lemon bars and brownies rather than dollar bills. Harmless as they were, he finally scolded them for walkie-talkie abuse when the visits to the granny booth reached several an hour.

As it turned out, they weren't calling more often – Blake and Dawson just turned off their radios, leaving all the dirty work to Colton. *Assholes*. He would even the score, but not until he finished all of the rum cake, apple pie, and various cookies and bars he was rewarded with at his last ass pinching. Dirty birds.

Friday night ended with a community cookout to celebrate a successful week, hosted by several different area restaurants and ranches. Booths were closed a bit earlier and dismantled, so everyone could attend. Their final event would be the Gala the following night. It was the last opportunity of the year to hold such an event with cooler days and crisper nights settling in and the first snow just around the corner.

As the final night of the weeklong event, the committee took a moment to acknowledge Meg as their head of committee and mastermind behind all of the new and improved festivities. The local crowd cheered for her, a job well done by their newest member. She was at it again, in her element, soaking up the kudos and best wishes for the final event, tomorrow's Gala.

Colton couldn't get enough of her as she smiled from ear to ear, her joy filling the space. She was amazing, the final piece to his puzzle, what made him whole. Her happiness and new sense of belonging wasn't lost on him. He thanked God every day for bringing her to McKenzie Ridge and making her his…forever.

* * *

COUNTDOWN TO GALA BEGAN THE MOMENT THEY ALL WOKE. The gang, who made up most of the committee, gathered bright and early to prepare the event venue – the women handled the details while the men were the muscle. By early afternoon, they had transformed the eclectic, one-hundred-year-old white building resembling a large old barn or swollen old school house, into a stunning shabby-chic Gala trimmed with vintage and glam flare.

It boasted gorgeous picture-like windows that were enormous in size, stretching nearly to the three-story ceiling and resting across every wall, allowing in the natural light that reflected off the crystals, which seemed to be strung everywhere. It had large rolling barn-type doors that added an element of character you would think clashed with the elegance strung through the building, but it actually complimented it nicely. The day's natural beauty flooded in, reflecting off the various elements scattered throughout the space, offering a romantic ambiance.

The well-worn, white, chipped walls were perfectly complimented by the antique, iron chandeliers that hung from the high, wood beams. The aged, whitewashed, wood tables were strategically placed to maximize seating without crowding the buffet or stage. Vintage metal chairs circled those tables, and they were accented by vintage candelabras, each different and surrounded by fresh floral arrangements.

Crystals hung from each centerpiece and filled the bouquets while simple burlap ribbon and streamers added an organic feel. Each table had a card that looked like a doily with a number in the middle to prompt guests to their purchased seats. A matching paddle was placed in the center of each plate atop the white napkin, with a raffia bow tying them together like a delicate package. The paddle would be used for the live auction…everything had a hint of rustic and a hint of glam.

The second level, something of a large loft, held the bar. It was open for mingling, with limited seats, and perhaps dancing should the lower level dance floor become crowded. Every inch of the venue was well planned and spent. Megan had thought of every last detail and pulled it off with a stunning rustic charm that only she could.

She had transformed an old, often overlooked, eyesore and made it a magazine worthy view that was sure to get more and more attention after this event. It was a breathtaking experience that represented all things Megan—beauty, class, and natural elegance.

"Wow, Fancy Pants… you fucking did it!" Jessie said in awe, which was the highest compliment one could receive from her.

"It's stunning, like gorgeous, glitzy, wedding stunning," Everly offered.

"Yeah, I wish I wasn't already married so I could do it here!" Sam contributed, getting a furrowed brow from Dawson.

"Oh, honey, you done good. You took a bunch of old stuff and spit shined it real good," Granny said, holding Meg's hand in her own, patting with the other, full of pride for her newest handpicked family member.

"It is beautiful, isn't it?" Megan questioned, eyes filling with tears, her heart full.

"Yes, so beautiful," Colton replied, looking directly at her.

* * *

AS THE AFTERNOON EXPIRED, THE GROUP SCATTERED, EACH finding their way home to ready for the event. Colton found Megan sitting on the back porch, staring off in the distance, Duke at her feet, his head in her lap.

"You're spoiled, boy!" He regarded the pooch with a scratch of his ears.

Megan smiled at Colton's presence and playful jealousy of his dog.

"Aww, that isn't possible, is it, Dukey?" she said in a childlike voice.

"Dukey? Sounds like you just called him crap," Colton said, laughing. "At the very least, you've stolen his man card...Dukey..." he finished, as if disgusted, shaking his head.

He smiled and pulled her into him. She closed her eyes and inhaled his freshly showered scent, waking all of her senses – especially those that made her cross her legs a little tighter.

"What has you so distracted? Everything okay?" he asked with a pinch of nerves.

"Everything is perfect," she said with a sincere grin, face beaming. "So perfect it feels like a dream."

He smiled and kissed the top of her head, pulling her even closer. "It is, finally. Now, tell me what you're really thinking about," he said.

"I'm just thinking about everything. The Gala, Esteban, the security everywhere. Are you worried? About any of it?" she confided, feeling a bit insecure.

"No. Esteban is Dec's problem, and he'll get him. His people are everywhere and the best at what they do. The Gala is going to be a success. Some really hot chick did an amazing job planning it," he teased. "My only worry is you, keeping you safe and happy, and making sure tonight is as epic as you are."

"Hmmm, epic, huh? Are we still talking about the Gala?" she ribbed.

"Megan, my heart stops at the sight of you. My world stops if you're not in it. Every promise I've made to you I intend to keep. I have waited so long for you. I will fight to keep you, no matter the circumstance. You never have to worry…that's my job, forever."

She wrapped her arms around his neck, pulling him in for a long, deep kiss full of promises and those forevers. Colton scooped her up and cradled her in his arms, moving toward the door. She tossed her head back, giving him a squealing giggle.

"Stop, I have to go take a shower and get ready!" she bartered.

"Me too!" he shot back with a mischievous glint in his eye, hinting at the ideas for how they could remedy their shower dilemma.

"But you just took one! Put me down!" She playfully struggled.

"It seems I'm feeling a little dirty again, and I promised you epic…" he said, smacking her ass before going inside to fulfill his promise.

29

Nerves - *unrelenting* nerves – plagued Colton while he waited ever so patiently for Megan to finish getting ready for the Gala. He paced the floor, unsure of the source that left him so nervous. He felt like a libidinous teenager waiting for his prom date to grace his presence. He recalled a similar feeling when they were in Portland and he waited for her to be ready for their date. Another milestone evening, another set of nerves, he concluded.

The suspense was killing him. He couldn't wait to see her in "the perfect dress" that she had been raving about since she found it on their trip. Really, he just couldn't wait to see her. Time away from her left a noticeable gap in his heart, a craving that was probably ridiculous in nature, but he didn't care.

Tonight, everything would be different. He planned a dream come true, and he hoped the outside threats didn't interfere with a single moment of this night.

* * *

SHE TOOK ONE LAST LOOK IN THE MIRROR, TAKING A FINAL spin. Satisfied with what she saw, she grabbed her clutch and went to find her guy. She spied her dashing beau standing in the living room, staring out the window. As if he could feel her presence, he slowly turned and drank her in. She could feel his every thought as he soaked in her beauty from head to toe.

Meg's cheeks blushed from the breathy sigh she released when he fully turned to face her. Daily, Colton was a sight to appreciate – in a tuxedo, he was heaven on earth. His broad shoulders and tapered waist were only the beginning. His sleeves pulled ever so slightly at the girth of his arms, and perfectly tailored pants displayed his perfect, round asset.

Her mouth was watering. This breathtaking man was lethal. If she read his reaction correctly, he was impressed by her evening attire and was likely trying to decide what was beneath it – dirty boy.

"Megan, you…you…" When he couldn't finish his statement, Megan's smile faded, insecurities nagging.

"You don't like it," she said, wide-eyed, as a statement rather than a question.

"No! I love it. There just aren't any words worthy of how you look tonight. Stunning is an insult. You exceed beautiful, honey. I can't even keep my thoughts together here!" he said with a nervous chuckle while tugging at his collar.

A satisfied grin crept back to her face. He was speechless, and nervous – mission accomplished.

Her champagne colored dress flowed as she moved. The deep V, Marilyn Monroe style halter revealed a tasteful amount of cleavage while the hi-lo style, full skirt displayed her tanned legs, from the shin down in front, with a trailing train following. She stalled for a moment, popping out one foot, displaying her vintage inspired, rhinestone clad feet before spinning, revealing his favorite part of her ensemble.

The halter met at her neck and a tie at the waist to hold her dress closed, revealing an entirely bare back that he would enjoy resting his large hands on all night. He loved her hair pinned high and looked forward to nipping at her long, sweet neck while dancing with her, slow and close.

She gave him a perfect pout and watched him through thickly lashed, hooded eyes, finishing her seductive sway, making her way to him. She wrapped her arms around his neck and pulled him down for a heated, intimate kiss that lacked nothing. His hands caressed her back, moving up her sides to stroke the sides of her breasts that her dress left exposed, leaving a trail of goose bumps in his wake.

"We're never going to make it to your Gala if you keep doing this to me," he said, leaning into her so she could feel how turned on he was by her.

"It wouldn't be the worst idea we've ever had, handsome," she flirted.

"Oh, no, honey. This is your night. You save this…" Colton said, biting her lip with a kiss, "…for later." He grabbed a handful of her ass, pulling her in for one more teaser of a kiss.

* * *

Ooh's and ahh's filled the building as tourists and locals alike entered the first annual Crystal Showdown Gala. The group of friends gathered near the entrance to greet those who arrived and direct them to the various areas of the venue. Jessie, being Jessie, pointed out the bar only.

Megan was overjoyed by the flattering first impressions of the party goers.

"Wow, toots, you nailed it! We're going to have to keep you around!" Morgan teased, pulling her into a sweet side hug. "Careful, no wrinkles," she joked, referring to her stunning evening gown.

"Am I the only one shocked to see Jessie in a dress?" Carigan asked.

"Nope! Don't worry – it's still her. I'm sure she's wearing combat boots under there!" Sam chimed in, half surprised but mostly amused.

"It's not even short and skanky…or black! It's like a princess threw up on her!" Evie added, arms crossed, drink in hand, assessing her friend.

"And it's…pink?" Blake interrupted in a soft, admiring tone, unintentionally drawing all eyes and knowing grins to himself. "What? I thought the color pink died when she put it on," he recovered.

"Yeah, yeah…I'm in a fucking dress, I have heels on, and I'm wearing…gasp…make up!" Jessie tossed back, sarcastically, putting her hands over her mouth as if she was shocked by her own admission. "Get over it, assholes!"

And there she was, like the foul-mouthed, hard-ass, bar brawling Cinderella she pretended to be.

"Geez, if we throw water on her, will she melt?" Morgan teased.

"Wrong effing fairy tale, Officer Tits," Jessie fired, pointing to the ample cleavage Morgan displayed in her red satin strapless gown with the hand that wasn't holding her bourbon and water.

Morgan scanned the group and followed their eyes down to her display, shrugged her shoulders and brow and said, "Touché!" before saluting Jessie, taking a long swig of her matching bourbon.

"So, how were all the kids, Ev? More importantly, how

was Lou when you left?" Dawson asked of Evie, who lived with her grandmother.

"Evie took a long pull from her glass of Champaign with a dramatic eye roll. "You mean Gran and her team of old bitties…the wrinkled nanny brigade?" She questioned. "Let's see, there were, at least, two ass grabbing warnings for I don't even know who before I left. As I pulled away, Gran was hanging out the windows, tossing plastic bags of cookies into the bushes."

"Cookies in the bushes?" Colton questioned with a bewildered look on his face. "They promised to stay sober!"

"Oh, they were sober. That's what makes it so embarrassing. She's throwing cookies at the men Declan has posted outside…in the bushes! I heard her ask the two inside if they knew CPR and how to give mouth to mouth!" Everly finished, taking another long drink, emptying her glass.

"Sounds like we may need bail money before the night is over," Sam joked.

"I don't know. Her cookies are really good…it may be enough!" Blake said in all seriousness. "What? I'm just saying these guys are used to dealing with hoodlums like Valdez—I'm sure they can handle some little old ladies."

"Go Gran and the mafia!" Jessie said with a laugh, clearly the only one who found the humor in dirty old ladies and their antics. She was likely taking notes of her own.

* * *

DOC CHARLES AND HIS BAND, THE SCALPELS, PLAYED throughout the evening while event goers enjoyed fabulous food, dancing, and mingling. The last event of the night was the live auction, emceed by the town's Mayor, Jed Baker, of

Baker's Bakery. Up for bid, McKenzie Ridge's hottest. First hottie of the night, none other than Blake Cooper.

"Does everyone have their paddles ready? This one should go quickly!" Jed said, voice full of venom. Blake shot him a go to hell look, fully aware of where Jed's haste was coming from.

"Alright, do I have five dollars? Surely we can find *someone* Officer Angry *hasn't* pulled over…five dollars folks. You get a pizza dinner, generously donated by Ponderosa Pizza, and a ride along with Officer Stickler here!" The banter between the two, genuine as it was, surprisingly engaged the crowd, drawing quite the bidding war over a very chafed Blake Cooper.

The wannabe Barney Fifes fell out of the bidding early while a few hot and bothered women battled over the now, Officer Hottie, doing great things for his alpha ego.

Finally reaching the five-hundred-dollar threshold, with no end in sight at five-dollar increments, a familiar voice shouted, "One thousand dollars!" while holding up her paddle. Jessie Clarke.

Blake's eyes took on a smoldering gaze while a devious grin crossed his face. Not even Jed Baker could rain on this parade.

"Seriously? For *him?*" Jed questioned in confusion.

"Yes!" Jessie replied. "Someone ought to put an end to this! For the kids and all…" Jessie retorted, giving the two bickering bidders the stink eye daring them to top her bid. As expected, they didn't cross the town badass who made grown men cry.

"What the hell, Jess? You know that's *Blake*, right? Something you want to share with us about you and Blake?" Carigan asked in shock.

"What, did you see those vultures bidding on him? I saved his ass, and he knows it. He owes me a solid!" she said with a sly grin.

"Uh, honey, you realize you just spent a grand to go on a date with *Blake*, right? A friggin' grand!" Evie said, surprised.

"Yeah, like I said, he owes me...one thousand dollars' worth...owes me," Jessie replied with an ornery chuckle.

"He would have dated you for free," Morgan said under her breath as she sipped on her drink, which earned her a shut the hell up look from Jessie.

"What? Just saying what *everyone* was thinking," Morgan said before polishing off her glass of wine.

The night went on with Sam winning Dawson and vice versa. Even though married, it was all for fun and in the name of charity. Everyone went through their public humiliation as the attendees bid on each of them. Evie won Doc Charles, while Carigan and Morgan were bid on by members of The Scalpels.

The last auction of the evening was for Colton. Best for last, as they say. His popularity as the town's love-struck, dreamboat became apparent when a group of bidders, narrowed to no less than ten women, nearly resorted to hair pulling and slappy hands each bid.

When the bids climbed quickly by one hundred-dollar increments, Megan finally stepped in, doubling the highest bid, offering seven thousand dollars, getting an instant "sold" from an impressed Jed Baker and a sultry, rogue grin from her prize. This would be the best seven grand she ever spent.

* * *

MEGAN MET COLTON ON THE SECOND LEVEL. THE BAR HAD closed as the night was winding down. They had about an hour left before it was officially over. The music played while people slowly made their way out, some hanging around for one last glass of bubbly and dessert with friends.

With the upper level entirely to themselves, they danced to the slow, enchanting music in a seductive embrace. Colton held her head as he kissed her, burning with wicked desire. Her hands roamed under his jacket, dragging her nails down his back through his shirt, teasing him with her sweltering plan.

He rested his forehead to hers and whispered, "You're killing me."

"Good, you want to get out of here? I paid a pretty penny for you, saving you from a group of horny women. I know a way you can start working that off."

Without another word, he grabbed her hand and rushed her to the second story exit. Once outside, he held her against the wall, pulling her leg to his hip while he grabbed her ass. Leaning into her, he kissed her hard – so hard that she let out a throaty moan, dripping in desire. She felt his excitement against her core, upping the ante. A warm tingle that only he could inspire rushed to her center.

Before they gave an Oscar worthy performance on the second story stairs for all to see, he grabbed her hand, running them down the steps to his truck. The chill in the air prompted him to drape his suit jacket over her shoulders before lifting her into the truck. He couldn't get them home fast enough.

"I have something for you when we get home," he said.

"Oh, I know what you have for me, and I can't wait," she giggled.

"You little vixen you," he teased.

"We'll get to that, but I have something else first."

He winked, adding to the anticipation. Tonight was going to be a night to remember beyond the Gala and bedroom.

30

SHE RESTED HER HAND BEHIND HIS NECK, LIGHTLY scratching it the entire ride home. The heat their expectation radiated in anticipation for what was to come was scorching. A single touch, his hand on her thigh, had her squeezing her legs together. Her hand stroking his neck had his imagination wandering and his pants tight.

They furiously pulled into the driveway, skidding to a stop, causing Megan to chuckle while she watched Colton race around the front of his truck to get her door. He helped her down but held her against the truck for a quick reminder of why his actions were so urgent with a long, heavy kiss that lingered, knee weakening and panty melting.

The sounds of a rowdy clan of pets broke the spell, and they moved up the walk-way. Just before the porch steps, arm in arm, Colton stopped and turned to her, holding her hands in his.

"The porch light is out…mood lighting?" he said with a wiggle of his brow before looking up, acknowledging the bright cast of light from the full moon that rested upon the starlit sky.

"It's a beautiful night," she replied.

"You're beautiful," he quickly shot back. "Everything about you. Your kind heart, witty humor, how hard you love. You're the woman I prayed for, the one I've searched for, the one I've dreamt of." He choked on his own words, emotions nearly getting the best of him.

He bent to one knee and asked, "Megan Johnson, will you make that dream come true and be mine forever? Marry me?" He held out a tiny black box, which contained an elegant ring that reflected the

starry sky and made her melt. He took her breath away. Tears streaked her cheeks as pure joy filled her once empty heart. This man, this perfect man, was everything a man should be, and he wanted her.

"Colton, you're my dream come true. You saved me, and I can't imagine living a life without you. Yes, a hundred times...yes!" He stood and picked her up as he went, swinging her around. He let out a yee-haw or a woohoo – she wasn't sure, nor did she care. Her happily ever after just arrived, and she was going to roll in it for a while.

The chaotic riot from the house caught their attention again as they laughed at the sight in the front window that was crowded with their furry family.

"I think they want to congratulate you, future Mrs. Sparks!"

"Well, as the future Mrs. Sparks, I think we need to do something about our fur babies," she said in all seriousness. His smile faded to concern when there was mention of doing something about the animals.

"I think we need to keep one of the kittens, maybe two," she pondered. "And I think Rambo needs a woman, and maybe Doug!" she deadpanned.

Boisterous laughter consumed him. Her admission caught

him off guard but in a good way. "You really are the perfect girl! You can have as many animals as you want!"

He pulled her into his arms and lifted her again before whispering in her ear, "God, I love you...more than I can ever show you or tell you..."

Her body became still and rigid. She began to push away saying his name in fear. That could mean only one thing. He quickly turned, blocking her from whatever, whoever, was behind him. With one hand behind his back, wrapped around her, the other out in front of him, he began to move them back toward the steps.

"Megan, call Blake, tell him they're here. Phone's in my front jacket pocket," he said, sounding completely calm. "Then, get inside, and lock the door. You know what to do next," he assured.

"Colton?" Her voice was nothing but a quivering whisper.

"It's okay, honey. I'm not letting them hurt you. You can do it. That's why I love you so much – you're a *fighter*. Now get inside."

The man stepped into the light, revealing his presence, hands empty. Colton could handle this piece of shit, he thought, or was he without a weapon because there were men with weapons hiding under the veil of darkness. Either way, he was ready and would do whatever he needed in order to keep Megan safe.

A thick, seething accent laced with disgust and anger began to taunt him, "You fucking bitch, did you think I would not find you? Do you know who you are dealing with?" he questioned.

She froze at the familiar voice...Esteban Valdez.

"Apparently *you* don't know who you are dealing with, asshole. You have no business here, so leave. And you'll watch how you speak to the lady," Colton lashed back.

Esteban laughed at Colton's chivalrous attempt, drawing chuckles from all around, hidden in the darkness.

"Do you hear this fucking guy? Congratulations, by the way. I heard your little pathetic, weak, spineless plea for a wife. I am embarrassed for you." If looks could kill, they would both be dead. This man was exuding hate and pure evil.

Megan reached into Colton's coat pocket, ever so slowly, and hit the button for Blake. Then she prayed that he would answer and get here in time. Colton slowly pushed her back, nudging her up the stairs so she could get inside to safety.

"Where is she, Trinity? Where is that bitch sister of yours, and where is my son?" Esteban spit.

"My name is Megan." Not sure why, but that was the only response that came to mind. If she could keep them talking, stall, Blake and the rest could get there in time.

"Oh, for fucking sake…where is she!!" he screamed. The animals were scratching at the door and window, trying to get out. The ruckus got louder and louder, further angering Esteban.

"Shut those fucking animals up!" he yelled.

A cluster of gunshots rang out, hitting the front of the house. Colton threw himself over Megan, protecting her from the attack. A lone yelp could be heard from inside, then silence.

* * *

BLAKE THOUGHT IT ODD THAT COLTON'S NAME WAS scrolling across his screen. He had just spoken to him a handful of minutes before, upstairs. He turned to look above and didn't see anyone up there, nor did he see Colton or Megan amongst the small, remaining crowd. Anxiety filled him. His intuition told him something was wrong. He signaled for quiet, and the group of friends pulled in tighter while Blake answered the call, putting it on speakerphone.

"Cooper," he answered with his typical salutation.

The line was briefly vacant of sound until he heard the gunshots in the background.

"Jameson, get Dec on the line!" he ordered Morgan.

"Colton? Megan? Hello?" His questions went without reply.

They swiftly moved to the exit, finding their way to the vehicles, splitting up between Blake's and Dawson's trucks.

"Dec is on the way. He got confirmation from the men posted at Lou's house. Everyone is safe, and they are on alert. Nothing from Colton's. They aren't responding," Morgan alerted.

"Shit! Let's go! It's going down at Sparks'!" Blake replied. "Dialing you into the call. Morgan, ride with Dawson so you guys hear what we hear. O'Reilly, call it in. We need back up, all hands on deck."

He paused for a minute, realizing what his next statement meant, "We don't know what we are walking in on."

What were they walking in on? Were their friends okay? Was there anyone hurt? Where were Declan's people?

* * *

"Oh, my God, Boss!" Megan shouted, recognizing the deeper, mature sound such a big dog made.

"Go!" Colton said, squeezing Meg's thigh before lunging at Esteban.

Before she could move toward the door, a large man stepped within view just behind Colton. Megan screaming his name in warning was the last thing Colton heard. He turned to see Megan, over his shoulder, getting a perfect view of her horror just before a slicing, sharp pain stretched across his forehead, and everything went dark.

"Colton! Colton!" Megan screamed, crawling toward him, laying his head in her lap. "Baby, wake up! Oh, my God, please, wake up!" She sat back on her knees and looked at her hands. They were covered in blood, and it was staining her dress. He was bleeding. A lot.

A shrieking laughter pulled her from thought. She watched Satan, himself, double over in laughter as if the events of late were nothing more than a sick joke. Evil and hate spewed from his face, causing her stomach to roll in disgust. She gently laid Colton's head on the grass and ran for the front door.

She needed the gun. Then she would shoot the son of a bitch herself. She made it to the top step before her feet were pulled out from under her. She hit the deck, face first, and the wind was knocked out of her. Gasping for air, she tried to scream, remembering the cell phone she dropped near the steps.

God she hoped Blake had answered. She kicked and fought, pleased with the heel she landed on Esteban's face. One of his men grabbed her by her hair and stood her to her feet, causing her to scream in pain. Lip bleeding, face aching, she spit right in Valdez's face.

"You smug son of a bitch. Do you ever do your own dirty work?" She spat, referring to the hired muscle holding her back.

Esteban laid the back of his hand across her cheek and slowly dragged it down her face, not stopping as he reached her chin. He continued his disgusting descent until his hand reached her breast, and he began to stroke her through her dress.

"Ahh, I see why he is so fond of you. Beautiful and feisty," he said while massaging her breast. Tears streamed down her face. She turned, unable to look at the vile man.

"I think I'll have my way with you before I kill you, see which sister is better."

She turned and spit in his face again at his remark. Anger like she hadn't seen consumed him while he wiped the saliva and blood from his face with an expensive silk handkerchief from his suit pocket. He carefully folded it and returned it to its place in the front pocket of his suit jacket. He paused for a moment, biting the bottom corner of his lip when that smug smile returned, right before he lifted a fist and planted it on her face, knocking her out cold.

"Grab the girl. She goes with us," he spewed while shaking out the pain in his hand.

* * *

WHEN THE LINE REMAINED SILENT, WITH THE EXCEPTION OF A few howls and barks in the distance, Blake feared the worst – they all did. Esteban would have a good ten plus minutes on them in any direction. He had Megan, but where was Colton? What had they done to him?

They heard his intentions with Megan, and it made his skin crawl. They would find Colton and Megan and bring Esteban to justice, once and for all, at any cost. This ended tonight. This shit didn't happen in McKenzie, not in his circle!

Colton's body could be seen, lying before the steps, from the road. Each of the friends mumbled something under their breaths that sounded of prayer. The fear they carried all the way there had been realized as they raced to their seemingly lifeless friend's side.

Jumping into action, Carigan went into EMT mode, using the large kit Dawson kept in his truck, with the help of her nurse friends, Sam and Everly. Morgan stayed with Colton and the ladies as protection, should Valdez or his men still be on site.

Dawson and Blake slowly crept around the perimeter of the house in hopes of finding Megan, or even better, Valdez.

"You better not fucking shoot me," Blake warned, nodding to the gun Dawson had drawn. "You don't have a badge – it better be clean if you discharge your weapon."

"You taught me how to use it…we're all good."

"Will you two shut up?" came a slight voice from behind them. They each turned to find Jessie taking up the rear with a small handgun front and center. Blake dropped his arms and gave her an eye roll, but before he could protest, she chimed in, "Don't even, Blake. You taught me, too. The girls got Sparks – I'm with you," she said.

She cut him off again. "You told me I shoot better than this asshole…I'm going!" she bargained, referring to Dawson.

Dawson's jaw dropped, and he glanced at Blake with a questioning look. Blake looked between the two before nodding his head in agreement with Jessie. Now it was Dawson's turn to give an eye roll.

"Okay," Blake said. "I'll tell you the same thing I told…"

Jessie threw her arms in the air and said, "Christ! Do you always talk this much? Only shoot the bad guys – don't screw up. Got it! Now, let's find Fancy Pants before it's too late," she concluded while nudging the two men ahead.

Their training in Search and Rescue together paid off for them as they worked as a team, clearing the scene all of the way down to the lake and back around. They didn't find Esteban…or Megan.

31

———

"WE HAVE A STRONG PULSE, O2 RATE IS GOOD, HE'S breathing on his own, and he's just out. Nasty hit to the head," Carigan updated when the three returned to the scene.

"He's stirring. We think he's waking up," Sam offered as she finished wrapping his head to protect the large gash across his forehead.

As if on cue, Colton opened his eyes and looked at the faces hovering around. A flash of confusion was followed by fear shortly after as he wrestled his way up, yanking the neck collar off that had been put on as a precaution.

"Megan" was the only thing he got out as he stood and fell again, holding his head, making a strained face.

"Whoa, handsome!" Everly said, helping him sit again. "You had the snot knocked outta ya. Take it easy."

"Where's Meg?" More straining, head obviously in pain, he asked the question he already knew the answer to.

"Take it easy, lover boy," Blake charged, walking up with a black box in his hand. "Is this what I think it is?"

All eyes were on the small ring box as he dropped his head and slumped his shoulders in a defeated nod.

"Oh, Colton, love…" Carigan choked. "We're getting her back. You hear me, boy?" she said, her Irish dialect imposing as it always was when she was emotional.

Declan returned to the group, a sour scowl on his face, anger radiating. Blake read him like a book, knowing full well where his anger rooted from—he found his men.

"There isn't much here, small blood splatter there." Blake pointed to the porch steps behind him. "May have a small trail that direction but only goes a few feet."

"Christ," Declan spat.

"What happened, Dec? You said she was safe, eyes on her at all times!" Colton accused, his voice seething with anger. "Where were those eyes? Why did Valdez himself walk right up to us? How did half a dozen or more assholes get this close? They fucking have her, man…" His voice cracked, choking on his last words at barely a whisper. "They have her."

He spun the little black box in his hands, clearing his throat as if his emotion was nothing more than an irritation that could be resolved so easily.

"I'm sorry, Sparks. We'll get her," Dec said, his words sympathetic. "It looks like they had the spin on us, three men dead. No struggle at all, from what we can tell. That only means one thing."

"Inside job," Blake delivered firmly rather than as a question.

"Shit. Any idea who?" Morgan asked.

"Three men dead on a four man team…pretty good idea that it's the missing fourth man," Dec reconciled.

"So we've had a traitor trailing us, on my property, in my home, this whole time. Fucking great. Now, they're one step ahead. How do we catch up?" Colton asked, ready to move on to what was really important.

Dec excused himself when one of his teams arrived back from a preliminary search. Voices were out of range, but body language and hand gestures indicated their interest was in the trees surrounding the lake. Saying they took her through the woods was like saying a bar has alcohol.

"I don't think I've heard your animals this loud before!" Sam said. "They must be worried."

"Boss! The gunfire – I think he was hit!" Colton tried to get up, but his world spun beneath his feet.

"Hold up, big guy. Get your bearings. I got you," Dawson said, grabbing Colton's arm to steady him.

"I'll go check on him. Help me, Cari? Might need your EMT skills," Morgan offered. Having an operating ranch, Morgan was pretty well versed in animals, just not gunshot wounds.

As soon as the door opened, Duke shot out, making his way to Colton. He nudged Colton with his nose several times while whimpering and eventually began barking. Colton scratched his ears, comforting his spooked dog. His behavior intensified. He would growl and violently bark, run several feet, do it again, then run back to Colton's side, each time becoming more aggravated. Duke finally resorted to biting at Colton's pant leg and pulling with every lap, back and forth.

"Has he ever done this before?" Morgan asked, walking out of the house.

"No, actually, never. He must really be spooked. He has become attached to Meg. Maybe he *is* worried," he replied. "How is Boss? Everything okay?"

Morgan looked to Blake, giving him a nod, each remembering a time when they noticed Duke acting exactly this way, not too long ago.

"Boss took a hit to his ear. He'll be fine, just looks a little lop sided on top. Say, Duke might be trying to…tell us something," she hesitated to share.

"The night of the fire…he took off toward the woods, wouldn't listen or stop. Got a ways in and lost whatever he was chasing," Blake shared.

"What, like Lassie or some shit?" Sarcasm slid from Colton's words.

"No, well…sort of. What if he saw or has a scent?" Morgan questioned. "What else have we got at the moment?"

"He does have it bad for Meg, follows her everywhere." Colton crouched down, holding his dog's head in his hands, scratching his ears and asked him, "Do you know something, boy?"

After a quick deliberation between man and his dog, Colton rushed inside the house, ever so briefly returning with a loaded gun, sliding an extra magazine in his waist band. He called for Duke, who led the way down to the lake shore, headed toward the flock of trees resting behind Megan's house.

"Sparks, what are you doing?" Blake scolded.

"Getting my girl back."

Dawson kissed his wife before running after his friend, slapping Blake's arm as he went by as if inviting him along.

"Let's go, Coop," Jessie said as she passed, following Dawson and checking her weapon, having changed into a pair of pants and sweatshirt at some point.

"You're not going!" Blake insisted.

"I am. That's my partner, just like Morgan is yours. You'd have *her* back – I have *his*. I'm just as trained as Tayler is!" She took off after Colton and Dawson at a fast run, not looking back for approval.

"Shit!" Blake quickly followed, keeping Jessie close, protecting more than just his friend.

Duke led them deep into the dark woods, moonlight the only light to chase. The dog paused at the same clearing as he had the frightful night of the fire. With everyone gathered, Dec and his men on their heels, they waited for Duke's next move. Just as he did before, he shifted from left to right, this time going right.

Dec talked quietly into his wrist, giving orders to his team. The McKenzie Ridge team went right with a portion of Dec's team while the rest disbursed in the various directions, assuming the dog's hesitation was because he was picking up the scent from Valdez and his men from both directions. That suggested that they were everywhere.

Light came into view, just ahead of them. Duke sat and stared at what appeared to be an old hunting or forest service cabin. The team crouched low while Dec delivered coordinates and orders into his wrist again. Movement from inside cast shadows through the dark, dirt-stained windows. This had to be where they were, where Meg was, given the short head start. They had probably been here all along, watching and plotting. A loud rumble in the distance caught their attention – cars, several, headed their way.

"He's *leaving*. We've got to go in *now*!" Colton exclaimed in a panic.

"Not yet. My men are nearly in pòsition. We'll have them surrounded," Dec replied.

"They get her in a car, and we won't see her again. We need to go now. There can't be but a dozen or so in there," Colton negotiated, determined to get inside and get Megan back.

"Stand down, Sparks! You'll get her killed! You hear me? Do I need to place you under arrest?" Declan threatened. "We do this the right way – no one who matters gets hurt. You got me?"

Fury filled Colton, knowing she was in there, and there wasn't a damn thing he could do. Dec was a good guy, seemed good at his job, whatever it was, but Megan was his life, and it was getting harder and harder to put that in someone else's hands. He understood there was a procedure to follow, a protocol, but he had promises to keep, and he intended to make good on them. He would get her out of there or die trying.

Four SUV's in various dark colors rolled to a stop in front of the cabin, blocking half from the team's view. The door, still visible, opened, and three men walked out, each heavily armed, taking their post, securing the area. One stood at the rear of the small convoy, one at the front, and one centered himself between the vehicles and the cabin. Declan continued to rattle off information to his team, in some sort of code, while the rest watched, keeping track of what and who was in front of them.

Each driver remained in the vehicle with it running, confirming the idea that they were taking off with Megan, their bargaining chip, along for the torturous ride. Colton's anxiety and anticipation reached new heights, remaining patient becoming increasingly difficult. A few brief moments passed before more activity approached the doorway.

Four men disbursed, one to each vehicle, opening the rear doors. Finally, the major players found their way out of the cabin. Dec's suspicions were confirmed when his missing man, Tom Boyd, exited first, Megan bound, blindfolded and gagged in his tight grip. Valdez was the last to make his way out. There they all stood, only yards away, and Colton was still sitting in the fucking bushes, watching his life stand in peril.

"My team has a clear path from the back. They swept six men, giving them access from the rear. I have eyes out here."

He pointed to his left. "Snipers, ready to disable the vehicles…tires first, then driver if need be. They aren't leaving."

"How do we get her? When do I grab her?" Colton inquired.

"*You* don't, bro. *You* stay right here. *We* bring her to you." Dec put his hand on Colton's shoulder, giving it a squeeze, trying to assure him they had this under control.

"We have the element of surprise – less than a minute and we're done," Blake offered. "Jessie, Morgan, you stay here with Colton. Morgie, you got eyes in the background here, got it? Dawson, you follow me in. We're only support. We let them do their job, and I leave with all of my people in one piece."

A branch snapped behind them, putting everyone on alert, and setting the plan into motion before they knew what happened. On instinct, Blake tossed Jessie and Morgan's heads to the ground, weapon drawn on whoever was behind them. Word must've made it to Valdez just as quickly because his people scattered, taking defensive positions.

Gun fire rang out like a fireworks display in July. The man behind them eliminated, Blake began to move in, Dawson at his side. Shots whizzed by, so close, Blake shoved Dawson down, yelling for him to stay low and fall back. Their organized plan quickly shifted to chaos, and he wouldn't be responsible for Sam becoming a widow, or their children fatherless.

With vehicles out of commission and his men falling at his feet, Esteban grabbed Megan, using her as a shield as he went for cover behind the SUV's. Tom Boyd stayed close, offering protection, shooting at his own team like the traitor he was. Shots rang from behind, turning Blake's attention to his own team. Jessie had fired at another of Valdez's men, apparently wounding him in the groin. She smiled and winked at Blake, gun aimed at her prize, while Dawson zip-tied the hands and feet of her target.

Shocked and impressed, he moved in, watching Dec's back as they got closer to Megan. Several shot to death, most wounded and zip-tied, it appeared that Valdez was down to a barely-there army. Creeping from behind the vehicle, Valdez used Megan as their armor. Declan and Blake had a clean shot on Tom. Esteban, being the coward he was, had himself pinned between Meg and the SUV, gun placed at Meg's temple as insurance.

Blake circled back around to meet Esteban at the front of the vehicle while Dec used traitor Tom as a distraction. With Blake in place, Dec discharged his weapon, nailing his target in the right thigh, clean shot, straight through, and likely a nice break as well. Tom lay on the ground in the throes of pain, screaming like the bitch that he was, doing exactly as the shot was intended to do…distract. Dec smiled, thoroughly satisfied with his shot, even if it didn't make up for the lives lost at Tom's hands.

"You're done, Valdez. Let her go!" Blake said, weapon locked on Esteban. "It's over!"

32

———————

Colton approached, kicking the weapon out of Tom's reach before flipping him over, enjoying the pain it was causing him. He zip-tied his wrists, flipped him back over, tying his ankles next. Dawson moved in, assisting Colton. They moved Tom to a nearby tree where they left him for the moment. Medical help would arrive…eventually.

Meg's blindfold was now draped around her neck, having fallen in the scuffle. Eyes locked on Megan, he gave her an endearing grin and said, "It's going to be okay, baby. You're okay. We're going home. Just a few more minutes." She grinned back, the best she could, through her puffy face and fat lip, her left eye swollen nearly shut.

Colton maintained eye contact, trying to comfort her from afar. His positive affirmation and smile was a performance of a lifetime. On the inside, he was reeling. The sight of her bruised and swollen face, blood mixed with tears staining her cheeks, body bruised, dress torn…she was roughed up nearly beyond recognition. It took everything Colton had to follow orders rather than tear that beast who held her limb from limb.

Esteban was completely surrounded with nowhere to go, the worst kind of desperate there was, the most dangerous, too…he had nothing to lose at this point.

"You shoot me, she dies. So, this is how it goes. I'm getting in that car, and she comes with me. You give me a driver, unarmed," he reasoned, as if he thought he still had a chance. "When we are far enough away, I let them go – nobody follows. Do I make myself clear?"

Declan laughed at Esteban's desperate attempt to portray he was still in charge with two dozen weapons casting a red dot on various parts of his body. The man was already as good as dead. All they needed, for that clear shot, was his weapon pulled away from Meg's head. She wouldn't be amongst the final casualties, not while he was calling this game.

Colton knew as well as anyone that the success and failure of the night rested on getting that gun away from Megan's head. He also knew that anyone who got in that vehicle was as good as dead, too. It was time to save his woman.

"I'll drive," Colton said, tossing the weapon from his waist band to the ground and kicking it away. He lifted his shirt and turned in a circle, showing that he wasn't carrying another weapon. He raised his arms in a surrender position and walked toward his target.

"Sparks, stand down," Blake yelled. He moved in, trying to intercept him. "I mean it Colton. *Back off*…back the fuck off!"

"Colton, listen to Blake, please…don't do this," Megan cried.

"I'm going where she's going. Not negotiable," he said, staring down Valdez, showing his lack of fear and full confidence. "We all know how *this* ends, Valdez. When you are far enough away, you kill her, right? Well, I can't live with that, so I'm going where she's going. However this ends for her is how it ends for me!" Colton was now an arm's length from Esteban, not showing a single sign of his anger or loathing.

"Sparks…" Declan demanded.

"It's not up to you, any of you," Colton said, eyes still locked on his enemy.

"Fine, this pathetic man goes. You can live together or die together, entirely your choice. No one follows, Mr. O'Reilly, and you know I will know." A smug smile and leering eyes gave a knowing wink. He was toying with them, reminding them that his reach was far and pockets deep. Anyone could be bought.

"Let's go, Mr…Sparks," Valdez ordered.

Colton moved toward Megan first, catching Esteban off guard.

"You drive, you buffoon," Esteban said, strengthening his grip on Megan, causing her to cry out.

"She's hurt, asshole. I'm helping her into the rig. I'm guessing she can't entirely see where she's going, given what you did to her face!" Colton shot back, standing firm, face to face with evil. So close he could smell the cigar and expensive scotch on his breath, smug bastard.

"Fine. Quickly!" Esteban backed down, enhancing Colton's confidence.

Colton looked to Blake first, sharing a knowing look to which Blake gave a subtle nod. He turned to Megan, resting his hands at her waist, making eye contact with Morgan and Dawson at the rear of the vehicle, both giving a similar slight nod. Completely in sync with his friends, his family, he took this mission into his own hands, bringing on the grand finale.

He whispered, "Hang on. I love you," to Meg, who fell right into Morgan and Dawson's waiting hands with a vigorous push from Colton. They swept her around the vehicle and into the shadowy tree line, guarded by Dec's people and even Jessie. As quickly as he turned her over to safety, his left elbow made contact with Esteban's face, stunning him with the unforeseen action taking place around him.

Stunned and disoriented, he was easy to overtake. Colton slammed Valdez against the vehicle behind him, pinning him with his own body. One arm across his enemy's neck, one holding his arm with the weapon above his head, slamming it repeatedly against the car until the gun fell to the ground. The upper hand his, Colton continued to beat the holy, living hell out of his adversary.

While the crowd around him looked on, letting the extra punches to the root of his rage slide, Declan signaled for his guys to step in and pull Colton off of a bloodied Esteban Valdez. Dawson stepped in and talked his friend down, pulling him out of Valdez's reach.

Esteban slid down the vehicle like a rag doll, landing hard at their feet, only semi-conscious. Colton sunk to his knees, cradling his head in his hands while he caught his breath, and the reality surrounding him sunk in.

His awareness shifted when Megan slumped down in front of him, wrapping herself tightly in his comforting embrace. Her body shook, overcome with sobs. He held her face in his hands and gave her gentle kisses anywhere he could that wouldn't cause her pain.

"God, I thought I lost you," he said, voice shrinking to a whisper. "I thought you were gone."

She replied with shaky words while gently tracing the bandage across his swollen forehead, bringing on more tears and a hint of a smile. "I'm fine. I'm here. We're both okay!"

Distracted by their reunion, the reach Valdez made to his

ankle was missed. He pulled out a small weapon and aimed it directly at Megan and Colton.

Tom, still propped against the tree where he was left, shouted, "Gun!" Causing a whirlwind of actions to follow.

Esteban slurred his final words before getting a shot off. "Fuck you!"

The activity felt as if it was transpiring in slow motion. Another gun shot rang out, causing everyone to take defensive positions and to aim their weapons at their villain. Colton rolled himself over Megan, in an attempt to shield her from tragedy, when a loud growl pierced the silence, followed by a sharp yelp...Duke.

Scanning the scene, shock came over everyone at what would be the dramatic end to it all. Blake stood, frozen with his smoking gun in hand, facing a dead Esteban Ricardo Valdez.

Mere feet from Meg and Colton lay Duke, shaking and whimpering in pain, having taken the bullet meant for his family. Colton rushed to his dog, checking him over, yelling to Morgan for help. The rancher was the closest thing they had to a vet on scene. Now an active crime scene, Declan and his people began to gather evidence and prepare to close their case.

Emergency medical from all branches and surrounding counties were called in to assist. A stretcher was brought in, at Dawson's request, for Duke, their hero, the only part of their immediate team injured. They quickly moved him to the waiting ambulance after Meg crawled up on the gurney to hold him and comfort him.

The tears fell fast and hard, watching her dog fight his injury, fight for his life. She whispered loving thoughts and sweet nothings in his ear, making sure he knew how much he was loved and what a good boy he was.

How quickly, she thought, that this animal became more than her fiancé's pet. She loved this furry guy as if he were family. She hadn't realized that was possible until now.

"Please fight, buddy. You can't die. Please, don't die. I have so many treats at home for you. You're a hero, Duke," she whispered

"We have Dr. Bain on standby at the emergency clinic at Sugar Pine Equestrian. They already have Boss there, waiting for Duke," Carigan updated.

"Boss?" Megan grasped her chest as if to protect her heart from more bad news.

Suddenly, her own injuries felt so insignificant, such an odd thought, she realized. It was a testament to how far she had come, how much her life had changed, and where her priorities had shifted.

33

THEY PULLED UP TO THE PET CLINIC, MET BY DR. BAIN AND his staff at the entrance. He quickly looked at Duke's injury before a sullen look dropped across his face. He turned to the couple, patted Duke's head and said, "We'll do everything we can for our hero, here…everything, okay?"

Not a *he'll be fine,* or *we can fix this*. A vague promise to help without a guaranteed outcome.

Evie called in a favor, asking Doc Charles to meet them at the animal clinic. Megan and Colton needed to be seen but refused to leave Duke and go to the hospital. He was happy to oblige, having just finished closing down the Gala and dismantling his band's equipment.

Using a free exam room – sterile is sterile – he dressed the wounds needing attention. Plenty of stitches, bruising, and cracked ribs later, they were back in the waiting area, hoping for good news. Declan arrived hours later to find everyone there, including Doc Charles, who insisted on waiting in the event he was needed for anything.

Tom Boyd sang like a bird, giving up more info than they had expected. Turned out, he was in need of a fast payday…

sick kid. Valdez swooped in with the dangling carrot that Tom needed to save his child. Understandable to some degree…a desperate parent will sacrifice anything for their ailing child. Unfortunately, this sacrifice was going to cost him life in federal prison.

Dr. Bain interrupted the random chatter that had erupted when the heaviness of conversation had become too heavy and they needed a change of subject to maintain sanity.

"Well, we never found the bullet. He was a mess…"

EPILOGUE

THE FIRST SNOW OF THE SEASON FINALLY FELL. LATE, BUT beautiful. The tragedies of the past few weeks were fading, although they would never be forgotten. Routines were resuming, and life was finally feeling a sense of normalcy settle in. Lydia had been staying with Colton and Megan, getting reacquainted with her son.

Megan's house was nearly done with repairs from the fire. Lydia and Jax would stay there, wanting to remain in McKenzie Ridge. She had fallen in love with McKenzie, just as Meg had, and quickly became part of the tight-knit group.

Everyone had gathered at Colton and Megan's to celebrate their engagement, something that had been overlooked, given the events that immediately followed the proposal. Declan arrived but only for a quick goodbye. He had wrapped up in McKenzie and was off to his next adventure, whatever that meant.

"Are you sure you have to leave, Dec boy? It's nearly Christmas!" Cari pleaded, sounding just like their Irish mother.

He wrapped an arm around her while she wiped a lone tear. "Sorry, Cari, duty calls. I've a lot to follow up on. Valdez is out of the picture but not his operation. I'll be back," he said, making eye contact with Lydia, whose cheeks blushed. "It may be time I start to slow down a bit, find some roots. We'll see."

Of course, the women in the room didn't miss her shyness and the desire-laced look Declan passed her. "Interesting!" Evie said, sipping her drink. Sam nudged her, causing her to spill.

Jessie leaned in to Everly and whispered. "Don't worry. We'll get that out of Princess 2.0 later." She motioned between Lydia and Declan.

Granny had pulled together quite the feast and called them all to the table for grace and their hearty meal, insisting on a plate for Declan to take with him since he couldn't stay.

Finding his way through the small crowd of kids and animals littering the floor, Colton made it to the front porch where Megan was sitting on the swing, Duke's head in her lap and a blanket over him, covering the bandages that wrapped his shoulders. Boss sat at her feet, his head still bandaged to protect his wounded ear, or what was left of it.

"Are you okay?" Colton asked.

She smiled. "I am…just taking a breather." Her bruises had faded to yellow, cuts and scrapes healed, swelling gone. It seemed healing physically was easier than emotionally.

The door opened, Dec crossing through, offering a hand shake and a "bro hug" to Colton.

"Taking off, bro?"

"Yeah, duty calls, man."

Dec reached down and patted Duke and then Boss good-bye. Megan stood to bid him farewell, her eyes full. He hugged her tight and said, "Take care of yourself and that sister of yours. She's a handful – good luck!"

She laughed at the humor he used to break up the overwhelming emotion surrounding them. "Seriously, if you guys need anything, anything at all, you call me!"

"Okay," she said with a nod, wiping the tears that insisted on falling. His leaving was the final chapter of her old life and the beginning of her freedom to be who she was meant to be.

Colton held Meg close while they waved their friend goodbye.

"He'll be back. Did you notice how he looks at Lydee?" Colton laughed.

A bewildered look crossed her face, "Really?"

"Really. So tell me what's dancing around in that pretty head of yours?"

"It's all good things. I promise. Just so many changes the past few weeks. I'm so glad to have Lydee back. Glad Jax has his mama, but I'm going to miss being his temporary mama," she admitted. "Who knew, I'd want to be a mom!" she laughed at herself, as if her admission was an odd desire.

"Oh, baby. They'll be next door. He'll be here all the time. Maybe we need to think babies…" Colton wiggled his eyebrows and gave her a naughty grin and wink.

"Maybe." She laughed. "Let's start with those animals you promised."

He kissed her sweetly and said, "I love you, Meg, with everything that I am."

"I love you, too, forever."

He turned her around, hands on her shoulders and led her to the door.

"Now, let's get in there, eat, and get rid of everyone so we can start practicing for those babies!" He smacked her ass, earning a joyful laugh that settled in his heart.

"There you are!" someone called out, and the room erupted in cheers.

He finally had his Hallmark moment. Colton just began his happily ever after…

* * *

I hope you loved Colton and Meg's story!
If you thought the suspense was edge of your seat in Hidden,
*you're in for a wild ride with **Forgotten**!*
Three words: Epic plot twist!
An unconscious man is found on Morgan Jameson's property
and she may be falling for him despite his mysterious identity.
Danger ensues, but is it at the hands of one of their own, or
does it have something to do with the new guy?
It's not just Morgan's heart on the line, it's lives too.
Make sure you download Forgotten next!

ABOUT STEPHANIE ST. KLAIRE

USA Today Best-Selling Author & Screenwriter, Stephanie St. Klaire is a multifaceted romance writer who has found her calling making readers bite their nails in suspense and hang on the edge of their seats with bated breath, as they wait for the next startling mystery to be unveiled.

Whether she's off the grid hunting her diabolical killer's next victim or plotting gritty crime thrillers that will leave you questioning her sanity, she always brings the chaos and the heat. (Watch yourself or you just might end up a character in one of her stories!)

Equal parts Hallmark and Criminal Minds, SSK balances her dark side by writing rom-com as her alter ego Stephie Klaire.

The Pacific Northwest native currently resides in Portland, Oregon with her husband, five children, and two ferocious lap dogs— where every day is Taco Tuesday and Christmas isn't just a season... it's a state of mind.

*Get a **FREE** ebook when you sign up for SSK's non-spammy newsletter...*

www.stephaniestklaire.com/newsletter

Join Stephanie's private Facebook Group & Other Places to Find SSK:

www.stephaniestklaire.com/findssk

WHAT TO READ NEXT BY SSK

McKenzie Ridge Series

Rescued

Hidden

Forgotten

Fearless

Redemption

Brother's Keeper Series

The Fall of Declan

The Rise of Declan

Reclaiming Liam

Redeeming Luke

Pursuing Dace

Hunting Wylie

Love, Cass (a series companion novel)

The Keeper's Series

Final Deception

Familiar Threat

Deadly Pursuit

Fatal Diversion

Royal Reckoning

Forced Enemy

Trivial Deceit

Lethal Jeopardy

Dangerous Chaos

Corrupt Justice

Stand Alone

Chameleon Effect

FREE BOOKS & SALES

Stephanie always has FREE books and sales running and
they're constantly changing…
For current Freebies and Deals, go to:
www.stephaniestklaire.com/freeandsales

FORGOTTEN CHAPTER 1 - FREE SAMPLE

"C'mon…you can do it! Push!" Morgan said, excitement rolling off of her encouraging words. "C'mon, mama!"

"Oh my gosh, this is too much! I can't…" Megan, so nervous, and exhausted, couldn't finish her thought.

Holding Meg's hand, Colton became her rock, giving her strength when she thought she had none. "Breathe, baby, you *can* do this! Hang in there, almost done!"

"Alright, this is it guys! Here comes another contraction," Morgan warned, getting ready to receive the little bundle about to be delivered, "here come's baby!"

"Colton! Oh my God, here comes the baby! Oh my…"

Morgan looked Meg in the eye, "Breathe, Meg, breathe! I need you to focus, honey, you got this!"

"She fainted! She fainted again, do something, Morgie!" Staying calm was becoming increasingly difficult for Colton; he was becoming desperate, ready for this part to be over.

"It's okay. It never lasts long…" Although rare, Morgan had seen this before, and wasn't alarmed. "She's just excited."

Colton chuckled, "and she's back! Phew, it didn't last as long this time!"

"Here it comes! I see the baby!" Excitement rolled off Morgan as she had the privilege of seeing the baby first, standing at the delivery end of the event. This part never got old. "Look at that face!"

"Colton!" Megan shouted, tears streaking her cheeks in an endless stream. "Look at our baby!"

The joy on Morgan's face was short lived, quickly turning to a focused stare. "Hold on, here come's number two!"

Megan and Colton looked to one another, Meg reeling in fear, Colton shocked. "Two?!" they questioned in unison.

"Yep! Twins." Surprised by the couple's response to more than one baby, Morgan prepared them for what could come, "we may get a third, even a fourth! There's no telling how many are in there!

Hyperventilating, and fanning herself with her hand, Meg tried to keep it together, summing up what Morgan had just said and coming to terms with it. "More than two…"

"Honey, there can be as many as a dozen in there! Didn't you guys google this or anything?!" Now Morgan was the surprised one, concerned for her friend's lack of preparedness.

Meg looked to Colton, waterworks fully engaged. "A dozen? How will I take care of twelve babies?! Is this really happening? I change my mind, I can't… I can't do this!"

"A little late for that, here comes…" Morgan said.

With his hands holding her face, Colton looked in her eyes, and comforted Megan. "Baby, We'll do it together, it'll all work out. I promise."

Just what she needed to hear, Meg smiled and nodded, ready to take on whatever challenge they were presented with.

"I really thought you guys did your research before committing to this… Oh, here it comes! You have another little girl!"

Colton wiped his forehead. "Wow, more females! The boys and I are almost outnumbered here!"

Toweling off the newest member of their family, Morgan swaddled both babies together and handed them to Meg to see for the first time. "I think that's it! Just two this time!"

"I can't believe they're here, after all these weeks! Look at them!" Megan beamed with pride, as her heart filled with a sense of joy she had yet to experience before.

"You've been through your first birth, you're a pro now, darlin'" Colton prided.

"No… Priscilla here did all the work – I'm just her really bad frantic coach!" Megan admitted, not taking an ounce of credit. "Can you believe it, babe? We have three pigs, now!"

When Morgan Jameson wasn't protecting the peace as a Police Officer in the small mountain town of McKenzie Ridge, she was playing the role of town livestock Birth Doula. Having grown up on a ranch, and now owning it, afforded her that talent. Today was all about pigs, special pigs.

Priscilla the fainting pig was the latest addition to Colton and Megan's menagerie of special needs animals. When Priscilla got too big to fit in her previous owner's pocket, she landed on Colton and Megan's door step with a note attached to the collar around her neck that said, *she faints and eats a lot – we think she's pregnant.* Sure enough, she was, and Megan hadn't let Priscilla out of her sight since.

McKenzie Ridge rested in the Pacific Cascade Mountains of Oregon. It was a small town but had its own variety of hustle and bustle as a popular tourist destination. Morgan had lived in McKenzie Ridge her entire life, and couldn't imagine living anywhere else – ever. If not for her century long family roots, then because of the people.

Her friends were dear to her, more like family. She sat back, wiping her hands on a nearby towel, over flowing with joy as she watched Colton and Megan introduce their newest additions to the rest of their perfectly imperfect furry family. The rest of the gang – the walking upright human kind – began to file into the small barn they all had helped Colton build to house their growing brood of lovable beasts.

In this group of friends, it didn't matter who you were, where you were from, they loved you and loved you hard. It didn't matter if it was Dawson and Sam's kids meeting a milestone or pigs being born – they were there for each other through everything. Including chasing down bad guys, like they had the previous fall when Meg came to town and brought the past she was running from with her.

"My pig, my Meg?" questioned Lydia's son, Meg's toddler nephew, Jax, who was opening and closing his hands as he reached for a baby pig.

"Oh no you don't," Lydia intercepted, sweeping the tot off his feet, "you can come visit *your Meg*, and *her* pigs all you want, but *that* will never be *your* pig, son."

Colton ruffled Jax's hair, "Don't worry about it bud, we'll work on her. Maybe start with a fish." Colton finished with a wink, earning a dirty faced smile from the cookie eating toddler.

"Just what this town needs," Jessie interrupted, tossing in a dramatic eye roll aimed at Blake, "more pigs."

"Darlin', I'm not sure how to take that. Is that a cop jab, or pegged at my *manhood*?" Blake chimed, in response to Jessie with a mischievous grin and waggling eyebrow.

"Trust me, you'll know when I'm interested in your… *manhood*, darlin'," she rebutted in a breathy tone, running a finger down his chest, stopping at his belt buckle. "But, I wouldn't wait around for *that*."

Jessie left the barn, middle finger in the air, "Cover their eyes," she said, referring to the kids present. "If I can't say the words in front of them, gestures are happening."

Anticipating a vulgar verbal attack, Sam and Lydia had placed their hands over the kid's ears, and quickly moved them to their eyes, shielding them from what was simply known as *being Jessie*. The more crude, the better, if you asked Jessie. To her, a sweet loving hug and the middle finger meant the same exact thing and insults were compliments.

"Seriously Blake, when are you two going to get past the hate part of your *love hate* relationship?" Morgan asked her partner.

The group snicker earned her a go to hell look from Blake, to which she winked – he clearly wasn't fooling anyone when it came to his feelings for Jessie.

The air shifted and light mood grew heavy when Duncan Haines, the foreman from Morgan's ranch, Pinecrest, briskly landed in the large barn doorway.

"Morgan, we gotta go!" he said with his cell phone to his ear. "There's a problem at Pinecrest…it's a body, Morgie."

The silence was deafening as the wave of shock from his words quaked through the space. They each looked from person to person until clarity set in and each jumped into action as they always did. This group of family-like friends each made up the town's various sectors of law and order, spanning from Law Enforcent, to Fire, Emergency Medical, and even Emergency Room Personnel. They were there for each other and they were there to fulfill their civic duty.

Blake Cooper pulled his ringing cellphone from his hip, certain the call was regarding the very thing that brought a chill over the room they all stood in. "Cooper, what do you got?" he said, answering a call from dispatch. A long pause ensued, before he nodded his head as if the person on the other end of the phone could see. "Got it, thanks."

"Just got called out to your place, Morgan. Rescue is needed, Dawson and Carigan – that's you. It's your property, and a possible crime scene, Morgan, you're not working this one. That means I'm going to need some extra hands, we're spread thin today. Colton? Everly?" Blake resorting to his friends, some on and some off duty, wasn't questioned or second guessed. This is what they did, helped each other.

"Dawson, you drive?" Carigan O'Reilly chimed, breaking the silence.

"You got it, partner – let's go," Dawson replied, assuming they would be called out as the on duty EMT team anyway. Sure enough, both his and Carigan's phones began to chirp.

"I'll ride with you," Colton said, nodding to Blake, before kissing Megan's forehead as he handed her the baby pig he had been holding. "Jessie's already gone, but I'm here to help any way I can."

Duncan, or Dunny as they called him, nodded, appreciating the quick response, and said, "He has a pulse – he's alive."

A sigh of relief escaped Morgan. At least this stranger, a man it seemed, was alive.

Everly Shaw, ER and Life Flight Nurse for McKenzie Ridge and its surrounding area, quickly intercepted. "Don't move him! I'll call Doc Charles on my way, he's working ER tonight. I'll have him meet us there, he lives close by." She was already on the phone, summonsing help before she finished her thought and made her way to the door.

Dunny rode with Evie, so he could relay information from the scene to Evie and she could assess and instruct throughout the ten minute drive up the ridge, to the ranch where their victim lay. The scene could best be described as organized chaos, everyone having a role and knowing what they could contribute.

With everyone out the door, as quickly as they'd come, headed to *her* property, Morgan looked to a wide eyed Megan who was staring blankly at her new little additions, not sure what to think with everyone leaving so quickly.

Sam stepped up and said, "Go, Morgie. The babies and Priscilla are fine. I'll stay and help Meg and Lydia. Call me if you need me, though. I can be there in no time."

Without hesitation, Morgan gave Meg a quick hug, and headed out the door with Blake after saying a few final encouraging words, "Priscilla knows what to do, honey, you just watch and enjoy! Congrats."

And they were gone.

FORGOTTEN CHAPTER 2 - FREE SAMPLE

The fifteen minute trip to Pinecrest felt much more like hours. The small caravan of vehicles quickly found its way up the winding ridge to a place that may never feel the same. A man, Dunny had said. A body. That must've meant lifeless at first glance, hence the excitement when a pulse was detected.

Pinecrest had its fair share of accidents – it was a fully functioning ranch with livestock and equipment – plenty to get a person injured from time to time. This felt different. What was a man, a stranger no less, doing on her property? How *did* he get there?

A rancher on a horse met them at the end of the main drive that ended at the main house. He led them through the property. Passing the various barns and out buildings, the Dude Ranch Dinner Gazebo, beyond the gardens and her small vineyard to the open pasture, they traveled the bumpy terrain that never seemed to end.

Pinecrest was the largest operating ranch for miles. They primarily ranched cattle, but had their hands in other crops and livestock that served the surrounding area markets with everything from spring fruits and veggies to pumpkins and apples in the fall. With 200 plus acres that sat at the ridge above the town that McKenzie Ridge was named for, Morgan's property also provided a lucrative tourist attraction as a fully operating Dude Ranch, about six months out of the year, and a fun dinner destination where guests could experience a real cowboy dinner over the coals and cowboy traditions. A truly one-of-a-kind experience, Pinecrest was every kind of wonder, it was home, and now it was marked with something potentially devastating.

The small convoy approached the furthest part of the property, deep within the pasture, just before the flurry of tree's and trails that lined its outer edge. There sat two ranch hands, their horses tied to a nearby fence post, while they hovered over an unresponsive body that lay between them.

"What happened? Who is he?" Morgan asked, studying the man's face, while Carigan and Dawson went to work with Evie's help.

Dunny replied, "Not sure who he is, doesn't appear to have any I.D. on him." He paused and looked around with a puzzled look on his face. "How the hell did he get clear out here?"

With a few hands too many, Blake and Colton began to roam the area, looking for clues, and other potential victims since the scene didn't give a clear idea of what happened. That was something they kept to themselves as anxieties were already running high.

"He's stable – head trauma, possible rib fracture and that left knee looks suspicious considering how it's laying. We need to get him to the ER and figure out how hard he hit his head, he isn't wanting to wake up. I'm headed in now, meet you there," Doc Charles announced.

"Let's get him on the board and ready for transport, then,

O'Reilly," Dawson said to Carigan. He turned to Everly with his final instruction, "Fifteen minute ETA, Ev. Call it in?"

The team moved quickly, to secure their patient and stabilize any potential injuries for travel. "Shaw, you can follow us," Dawson announced, calling Everly by her last name as they often did in their professional roles.

He finished rattling instructions to Carigan O'Reilly as they loaded the man in the back of the ambulance, headed for McKenzie General Hospital, but not before the handsome stranger opened his eyes, looked at Morgan with a bright icy blue stare locked on hers, and reached for her with one hand. As quickly as he came to, he was gone again. A sharp gasp escaped Morgan as a response to the overwhelming emotion that washed over her. Climbing into the ambulance herself, Morgan held his lifeless, albeit warm, hand the rest of their short trip while trying to reconcile the feeling his stare blanketed her with. "Who are you?" she whispered.

* * *

As day became night, Morgan found herself on the road, headed back to the hospital, while the day's events played back in her mind. She was given a quick update by Everly, who had been charged with the stranger's care. Severe concussion, a few cracked ribs, and a sprained knee – nothing too serious – not even a coma, but a deep sleep that was simply a symptom of a concussion of this magnitude.

Sleep eluded her, after such a long afternoon full of excitement of every kind. After her handsome stranger was in the safe and capable hands of Doc Charles, he had been admitted in serious condition and stable, so she had returned to Pinecrest to assist in the investigation. She was a cop, she had been involved in many investigations over the past several years, some very close and personal. This one, however, ate at her.

The term *close to home*, as literal as it was, didn't begin to describe its relevance and the severity of it. Blake had called in a small team – all the manpower that their small town police force could spare – to scour the grounds surrounding the accident scene. Their group of friends banded together, as they always did, to assist them. They had come up empty, not a single clue as to who the stranger was or where he had come from.

"This is it, Morgie," Blake had said, calling her by her nickname.

"Horse tracks? There's a whole mess of them. Look at the pattern," she replied, while pointing out several scattered track patterns in a small area.

"More than one rider?" Colton asked. "Are we looking at foul play here? Where's the other rider?"

Morgan paused as she approached the area that revealed the majority of the impressions and knelt down, touching the soft ground. "No, I don't think so," she said, eyes closed as she took in a deep breath. "One horse, one rider."

She stood and looked to the tree line, scanning it as if the answers rested amongst the brush lined forest beyond.

"She's doing it again – that Indian voodoo shit," Jessie interrupted, earning her an eye roll that ended in a side-eye scowl.

"First, we don't do voodoo, and I prefer Native American. It's just intuition. If you look to the earth for the answers, sometimes she'll lead you to them." Morgan turned her back to the group and looked back to the tracks and beyond.

"Oookay. Should we buy *her* a drink first or something?" Jessie joked, referring to the earth as *her*.

"He came from that direction," Morgan said, pointing

beyond the scene, opposite the populated side of the property. "He was riding, the horse was spooked, that's why there are so many tracks in this general area. It was frightened. The rider was likely trying to regain control and was tossed," she finished and turned back to her friends.

"Wow, she told you all of that? The earth is quite a story-teller," Jessie mused.

"That she is, you should hear what *she* says about you… I'd watch your step. That wasn't Indian ways, she didn't tell me about the rider. It was just good old fashion police work!" Morgan snarked.

"And I thought we weren't allowed to say *Indian,*" Jessie snorted, appreciating her friend's clean jab.

"No, just you. Only you aren't allowed to say *Indian,*" Morgan retorted with a wink, earning her a prompt middle finger salute in reply.

"I agree with you, Jameson, it adds up – I think we can rule this as an accident unless the vic has something else to share that would change that," Blake concluded, scanning the area as if piecing together the account himself to confirm the theory. Colton followed Blake's gaze while standing with one hand on his hip and scratching his chin with the other. "Looks like we have a missing horse, then."

FORGOTTEN CHAPTER 3 - FREE SAMPLE

Morgan's thoughts were drawn back to present as she sat bedside, staring at the man found on her property, not entirely sure how she got there or how long she had been sitting in his room. He was clean-shaven, revealing a firm chiseled jaw and prominent cheekbones. His dark raven hair was well kept in a clean close cut style that was slightly longer on top.

She couldn't help but notice his hands. They were big, strong even, but what stood out more so was how clean and smooth they were. Even his nails were nicely trimmed and even.

He lay in a hospital gown now, but she recalled his attire when they found him. He wore crisp new looking jeans, a white V-neck t-shirt under a blue flannel that matched the eyes she was able to see briefly, and a soft leather jacket. He looked the part of a common town folk, or even a rancher at first glance, but she saw through the designer duds and man salon grooming. This guy wasn't used to working with his well-manicured hands, and although she couldn't help but notice the fine outline of a well-defined physique, under that gown, she imagined it was the result of a high paid trainer, rather than a hard day's work.

He screamed pricey suit and tie, expensive lifestyle, and high rise city folk. Not that there was anything wrong with that. In fact, she imagined he probably looked mouthwatering in a good suit. This imagined life she'd manufactured while sitting there could explain why he ended up in the predicament that he did – inexperienced city boy. Perhaps. It didn't explain why he was in McKenzie, on her property, or where he came from though.

As if question cued his awareness, the sound of a gravely throat clearing and restlessness in the bed had her on her feet. Her stranger was tossing and turning in agitation as awareness sunk in. The pull in his arm, from the IV that had been placed, caught his attention quickly and had him upright scanning the room.

Obvious confusion washed over him, as his hands rose to his head as if to steady the dizziness his sudden movement caused. His breath caught on what must've been pain, given the grimace he wore across his face. He began to cough a dry cough, holding his right side as he did.

"Whoa, easy there," Morgan said, in a gentle tone as she lifted a cup of water with straw to his mouth, "drink this, it's just water. Small sips – it'll help."

The man complied, and began to relax with each sip of water, quenching his thirst and hydrating his scratchy throat. Morgan lifted the head of his bed and fluffed his pillows before helping him lay back. "There ya go, is that better?"

"Yes," came a deep husky voice. "Where am I? What's all this?" he finished, motioning to the IV before finding the gauze on his head that he discovered moments prior when his head had protested his rapid movement.

"You were hurt. Thrown from a horse, we believe," she answered gently.

"Who-who are you?" he asked, clearly still confused.

"Morgan Jameson. You were found on my property. You hit your head pretty good," she said, motioning to his gauze wrapped head, "you also have a few bad ribs, and sprained knee. Doc said you'll be sore for a while, but should heal just fine."

"That explains the headache, geez," he replied in a pained tone, letting out a deep sigh. "I can't believe they told you all of that, so much for privacy."

"Well, like I said, you were on my property and I also happen to be the investigating officer on the case." She winked, trying to keep the mood light. "So, my turn. Who are you? Who should we call for you?"

His stare froze, and his face paled as his eyes grew large and his body tensed. Something was wrong.

"What's your name?" Morgan clarified, remembering his concussion and possible confusion it could cause.

He turned his head away, ever so briefly, "I…I," his startled gaze returned to Morgan with a furrowed brow and expression of concern, or maybe fear, etched on his face. "I don't know."

* * *

"We haven't had a single missing person's report, Doc," Blake said, catching up Doc Charles on the stranger's case. "We've expanded nationally…nothing."

"Surely someone's missing him? How can that be?" Doc questioned.

Blake shook his head, baffled himself. "No clue. Ran prints and everything – not a single hit."

"We're in a tough spot then. I should've released him yesterday, at the latest, but..." Doc Charles crossed his arms across his chest and shook his head. "He's all there, smart guy, just doesn't know who *he* is."

"I made some calls, cashed in favors, nothing," Blake offered, referring to his *connections* that nobody really knew anything about other than they were somehow connected to his secret suspected undercover special ops military past. Nobody asked questions about it because they would just go unanswered.

"Look, there's no reason for me to keep him, medically. My assumption is that he has subconsciously forgotten for some reason and it will all come back. I just don't know when," Doc replied.

"Pfft," Morgan guffawed, "assumption? How *science-y* of you, Doc."

"We've run the tests, done the scans – no medical reason other than a hit to the head that's healing nicely. We've seen stuff like this before; I think there is a psychological factor weighing on the physiological aspect, complicating his overall circumstance," Doc recited, matter of factly.

"So...you're saying this guy doesn't *want* to remember?" Blake questioned.

"Perhaps. What I can confirm without a doubt – it's not entirely from the injury, and I need to release him...but to whom or where?"

Morgan's stare met that of the stranger's through the hospital room door window that stood between them. Doc's words raced through her head while she took in the timid smile he cast her way. Something about this man had her attention. Something more than his polished good looks.

There was something genuine, wholesome, and maybe even a bit lost, dancing in his eyes. She believed Doc, there was something more. His wounds were more than skin deep; she could see it – something that made him want to forget his own name and where he belonged. Whatever it was, it was pulling her in, and she hoped she wouldn't regret what she was about to do.

"He can stay with me – release him to me," she said with urgency while shifting from foot to foot as her fingers rubbed together in an anxious manner.

"Pffft…have you lost *your* mind, Jameson? No, won't allow it," Blake scolded with crossed arms and what felt like a fatherly tone.

"Excuse me?" She gasped, completely offended by his audacity. "I'm your partner, not your child, Blake Cooper."

Blake tossed his head back and released a deep sigh. "Morgie, we don't know anything about this guy. If Doc's right…"

"I'm right," Doc interrupted with a sly grin, amused by the banter before him.

Blake gave him a side eye warning before finishing. "If Doc's *right*," he paused, daring Doc to interrupt with another cocky claim, "then this guy may not be – all together, if you catch my drift? It may not be safe…at all."

With her hands now firmly placed on her halfcocked hips, Morgan questioned, "So are you going to take him in? Offer him a place to stay while we sort all of this out and find out where he belongs?"

"Hell no!" he quickly retorted. "I live alone and like it that way."

"Then that settles it!" With a quick shrug of her shoulders and a sassy grin that read challenge accepted, she made a brisk pivot to her left and entered her mysterious stranger's hospital room.

"Aww, shit," Blake conceded with a dramatic eye roll.

"Well, that went well," Doc chuckled. "If you'll excuse me, I have a John Doe to release to Jameson there."

* * *

"I can't accept your offer Morgan, it's too much," the stranger admitted. "It wouldn't feel right."

"It's no trouble, you fell on my property. It's only fitting I offer you a place to stay until we figure out...who you are and where you belong," she insisted.

The stranger sat, speechless, fully aware that if he did have somewhere to go, though he hadn't a clue where that was at the moment. Morgan's offer sounded more of a done deal than an option. He felt like a burden, though her offer didn't feel like one of obligation, but more one of genuine concern.

"You know I don't hold you responsible, right? I may not know how I got there, but it certainly wasn't your fault. You aren't responsible for me," he gently said, hoping his message was understood.

"I know," Morgan retorted. "Where will you go instead? Doc here is giving you the boot."

"I...I don't know."

"See, it's settled. Granny Lou has your clothes; she's washing them for you. I'll be back later this afternoon with them when I pick you up. "Gentlemen..." She offered a nod to each as she left the room, not leaving opportunity for anymore resistance from any of the men who were quickly becoming a pain in her ass.

"Is she always like that?"

Blake and Doc both laughed and said, "Yep!" in unison.

Blake's smile quickly transitioned to an intimidating frown, zeroing in on the town's new anonymous guest. "I want you to know I am not a fan of this plan," he began in a dark tone, full of promises, not threats. "Jameson is a hardass. She can hold her own, but she's my friend. You're not, and I'll be watching."

Appreciating the moment for what it was and feeling a deep connection to the situation himself, Doc stepped forward, crossed his arms and chimed in, announcing his agreement. "Yeah, me too…" he began, losing his tough guy presence just as quickly as he found it, "besides, you're my patient so I really will be lookin' in on you from…time…to time."

Blake's stern head shake and disappointed expression in Doc's quick to soften attitude knocked the wind from Doc's tough guy sail.

"What?! I'm not as good at this as you! I'm a doctor, I fix people. I leave the ass kicking and bone breaking to you – you keep me in business."

"Hey, I understand," the stranger said with both hands up in front of him, surrendering to their strong arm declarations. "I'm not a threat, you have nothing to worry about. I'll be gone just as soon as…I can."

FORGOTTEN CHAPTER 4 - FREE SAMPLE

Morgan parked in front of the hen house, otherwise known as Granny Lou's house. The scattered vehicles strewn about were a good indication that she was really preparing to enter the hornets' nest. Or, the ladies weekly *girl time* that included Gran's famous snickerdoodles and some sort of doctored up beverage.

Their group had grown over recent months with Meg and Lydia being added to the mix. Their conversation ranged from planning and organizing the latest town event, to who was caught sneaking out of what house at what hour. The small town gossip grapevine tended to run strong through Granny as the town's geriatric mafia leader.

Given the smirks and knowing looks Morgan received as she entered the sunroom that hosted the gathering, the gossip grapevine was in full force and the news of Morgan's house guest beat her to the party. "You can all drop the scandalous grins; you're making this something it's not," she said, standing tall with confident shoulders back, ready for the inevitable meddling she had just stepped smack dab in the middle of.

"Why, Morgan, we haven't a clue what you mean, dear," Evie replied with batting eyelashes and a sickening sweet tone.

"Can't say I blame ya – hear he's a hot piece of…" Jessie added, before being cut off by a not so amused Morgan.

"Right – *not a clue* – just like none of us has a *clue* about you and Doc Charles, Ev? Or, maybe you and Blake, Jess?" Morgan deflected all attention back to the two most likely to sling shit with a confidant grin and raised brow. She was a *no shit zone* kind of girl – and she could play dirty right back.

"Now girls, that's enough of that," Granny intervened. "How is *Guy* doing today, honey?"

Her stare was pointed at Morgan, but the whole group began to look back and forth, not sure who Granny was talking about, and suddenly concerned with her current mental state.

"Who…Gran?" Sam asked first, her medical background raising red flags.

"Guy!" she responded, scanning the room, taking in the looks of confusion. "You know, *Guy*! Morgan's *Guy*!"

"Uh, I don't have a…guy, Gran," Morgan gently delivered, not wanting to further upset Gran who already seemed confused.

Granny Lou's eye's launched in a dramatic eye roll, followed by a deep exhale and a few choice muffled words said under her breath. "GUY! Morgie's Guy? The Guy? Guy from her property? Guy, in the hospital? The mystery Guy? The Guy that doesn't know who he is – God bless'em – thee *Guy*!" she said in utter frustration.

"You done thought I lost my marbles again, didn't ya? I may be of vintage age, but I'm as sharp as a spring chicken and I know a Guy when I see one. Everyone's going around calling him some sorta *Guy* – so I named him somethin' proper…and appropriate." She chuckled, quite pleased with her own reasoning.

"Oh – Guy. That Guy," Evie chuckled, shaking her head.

"I don't think it's appropriate to really name him – I mean, he already has a name," Morgan said softly, considering what Gran had just said.

"Oh does he now? And what would that name be, dear?" Gran questioned.

Morgan looked at the faces around the room, noting that each of the women was looking down, some biting their lip, and trying not to laugh.

"Well…" she began.

"Well, what dear? You plan on hollerin' *hey you* every time you want the boy's attention? Well that's about as polite as a snake bite at midnight in the middle of winter, dear," Gran added with a wink and smile. "Guy."

"Guy?" Morgan continued to question, rolling the name around.

"Guy!" Granny said over her shoulder as she left the room with a wave.

"She has spoken," Carigan chuckled. "So, how is *Guy*?"

"Seriously? Is this going to be a *thing* now?" Morgan asked. "Everyone calling him Guy?"

A resounding *yes* was said in unison, including a small distant voice from the kitchen – Granny Lou.

"Who cares, it's not like we know what else to call the guy – see, she was right! Guy makes sense," Jessie agreed. "So dish, why the sleep over?"

Morgan sat in an empty chair, closing the circle around the table. "It's not a *sleep over*; I'm just putting him up until we know who he is. I mean, where else is the guy gonna go?" Morgan closed her eyes and shook her head at the last few words she shared.

On cue and with her finger always on the pulse, Granny chimed in from the kitchen, yet again, "See? I told you! Guy!"

"How does she do that?" Carigan's question was more than a loud whisper.

"I may be old, but I'm not deaf!" came the voice from the kitchen again.

Carigan's eyes widened and jaw dropped, prompting Evie to chime in about her bewildering grandmother. "Don't bother, I gave up trying to figure her out a decade ago – she probably has the house bugged or something."

Granny walked back into the room with a fresh plate of her famous snickerdoodles in hand. "Oh, don't be foolish girl; I wouldn't know a thing about that. It's just this house – good acoustics – sound flows through these halls like a babbling brook."

"Acoustics?" Evie said under her breath to Jessie beside her, who responded with a baffled shrug.

"So, back to Guy," Jessie added. "What's the story – sleepover – spill!"

"I said it's not a sleepover. He is being released from the hospital and doesn't have anywhere to go, and I happen to have plenty of room on the ranch with all of the bunkhouses and the carriage house," Morgan defended.

Carigan found a hole in the story and took the opportunity to clarify in an *it's none of my business but* tone, in between bites of her cookie. "Hey, I thought you said you were at capacity with the season opening last weekend."

"Oh, guess I didn't really think about that – well, I'll figure something out. Plenty of room in the main house too, it's just me," Morgan reasoned.

"I knew it! Morgie's planning a *sleepover* with her sexy

stranger! Go Morgie!" Jessie cheered with a cat call whistle and fist pump.

Evie wouldn't be left out of the campaign to make their friend blush, and leave all of the fun to Jessie. "You're at least going to let those busted ribs heal a bit before you – ya know…" She let the rest of the words trail off to the imaginations of those giggling along with the taunting, but before she tossed in her own slow low whistle and a single brow waggle.

"Seriously? Okay, you guys have your smutty fun. I'm just picking up his clothes so he has something to wear out of the hospital. I'll figure out what he's going to wear the rest of the week, later." Morgan stood to leave, annoyed by her good intentioned, irritating friends.

"Isn't that the point, Morgie? Nothing to wear makes it a lot easier to…"

"For the love of beer and whiskey, Everly Louise Shaw, leave the poor girl alone. What she's doin' is a kind gesture. Besides, I'd guess it to be a few weeks before anything starts to stir." Granny's attempt to defend quickly diverted to rib poking of her own. "A bit of a prude, our Morgie."

Morgan's head fell back in a dramatic collaboration with her loud exasperated sigh. "Later! Thanks for washing these! Get back to planning the Spring Fling, and stop worrying about what's *not* going on at my house!"

"Wait! Morgan?"

She stopped and slowly turned, disgust and irritation on full display as she responded, "Yes, Sam?"

Hand in front of her, palms out demonstrating she comes in peace, Sam said, "I can grab a few things of Dawson's for…Guy. We'll be out for Ellie's riding lesson tomorrow anyway – I can drop them by then?"

Megan chimed in with a delighted expression, clearly thrilled with the idea. "Me too! I mean, I'll bring some of

Colton's things. That should tide him over. I'll come for… Ellie's lesson too!"

"Me too," Jessie hollered. "But I'm not bringing clothes, or coming there for the kid's lesson. I just want to go for the show."

"Of course you do!" She turned to leave, tossing a wave in the air as she went, knowing full well that she would have a full cast of looky-loos in the coming days. "See you *all* tomorrow."

FORGOTTEN CHAPTER 5 - FREE SAMPLE

The sun was high, drifting west across the clear blue sky to settle for the day in a few short hours. Morgan let herself into her stranger, Guy's, room where he appeared to be resting. Doc said to expect a lot of that, rest was good for him, truly the best medicine. She gently placed his neatly folded and clearly ironed, clothes on the chair to the left of his bed, by the window. She paused to study him while he slept. It was much easier to stare when he wasn't staring back.

His body was relaxed and his face peaceful with the exception of his furrowed brow that suggested unease or concern. Perhaps a bad dream. His dark hair was combed back as if being styled and tidy and perfectly kept was just its natural way. Tracing his strong, chiseled jaw with her gaze, she noticed the stubble that had filled in over the past few days. It looked good on him.

She didn't hate his previous clean-shaven style by any means. In fact, it was quite handsome and made her sweat a little. But, the light dusting of dark shadow provided a rugged look with an ounce of edge that didn't make her sweat – it made her hum. Hum in places that she had put to bed years ago. Hello, libido.

Her curiosity took her eye further down from his broad shoulders to his narrow waist, where his strong hands rested. His position pulled the generic hospital gown in such a way that what couldn't be seen was easily imagined. Especially as her view managed to wander further down where the thin sheet covering him had a certain rise to it that made her lick her lips as her powers of invention were deeply inspired. Good Lord, it was getting warm in here.

"Like what you see?" A deep husky voice startled her from her near dirty thoughts, causing her to jump and return her wide eyed attention to the Caribbean blue eyes watching her. His head was tilted, and his raised brow matched the amusement of the smirk he was wearing.

"Huh? Oh, sorry. I was…" Heat flooded her blushing cheeks, making it harder to find her words. Fully aware of the hole she was quickly digging for herself.

She grabbed the pile of clothes she had brought with her and finished her thought. "I uh, was just thinking. I have your clothes, but noticed you…" She paused again when her gaze aimed for his day or two scruff but landed on his sexy mouth.

"Uh huh?" His smirk was a full grin and a chuckle escaped as he slowly sat up. His eyes bore into her so deep she could feel him everywhere.

She swayed from foot to foot, trying to relieve the embarrassing tingle he was creating. Why her nearly extinct sexual desires came out of hibernation at this moment and with this man was more than she could negotiate in the moment. She would work that out later. For now, her goal was to wrangle her hormones and stop making an ass of herself.

She was pulled from her miserable sense of embarrassment when a sharp sigh followed by a hissing groan broke free from her handsome stranger. He grabbed his right ribs with his left hand while trying to balance on his right hand in a half sitting position.

Morgan quickly moved to his bed side and placed an extra pillow, from the chair, behind him before propping her hand there to help hold him up. Using the button control on the bed's railing, she raised the head of the bed before carefully leaning him back against the pillows. His pain was evident by the subtle groans, but also the sweat beading across his forehead. His eyes were closed while he took slow calming breaths, trying to collect himself.

"There we go. Are you okay? Should I grab Doc Charles?" Her concern was for his physical pain; her heart break was for what he must be going through emotionally. The pain he wore in his expression was more than damaged ribs and a bum leg, or even a bump on the head. The ribs were just a sharp reminder of where he was and why. Clearly an unwelcome reminder.

"No, no… I'm okay. I guess it's a sign I'm healing." He offered.

"Healing? How's that? I'd say it's more a sign you still have some healing to do." She fussed while dabbing his forehead with a tissue.

"Trust me, it's healing. I was feeling so good, I forgot about those ribs until I moved – progress." The playful wink he tossed her warmed her heart.

"Progress," she agreed with an amused chuckle. "What I was going to say before your ribs so rudely interrupted is that I have your clothes, but hadn't thought about…" She waved at his face, fanning her hands around, "This."

He raised his right hand and held it to his left cheek, sliding it down to his chin where he stroked the layer of scruff.

"You hadn't thought of my…face?" he finished with a confused tone that matched his expression.

Waving her hands again, flustered, she reasoned, "Shaving, I hadn't thought about…shaving. That's what I was – staring at. I need to stop at the drug store for some toiletries on the way home, that's all."

"Toiletries?" His mischievous grin made an encore appearance; his amusement in her excuse became obvious. "I'm pretty sure that wasn't my face that you were staring at, but I appreciate the thought all the same, Officer Jameson."

"Morgie – err, Morgan." Hard to rile Morgan Jameson was trying on shades of red again, embarrassed not only by her inability to keep her cool around her mystery man, but also because she had been caught. Caught staring at something far more personal than, his face. "You can call me Morgan, Guy."

"Morgan Guy?"

"No, Morgan – just Morgan. You're…Guy."

"Guy? That's my name? You found out who I am?"

It wasn't lost on Morgan that his tone was more disappointed than anxious at the idea of finding out who he was. She believed him when he said he hadn't a clue who he was, call it cop's intuition. But, she also believed that for some reason, he subconsciously didn't want to remember. There may not be a mystery as to what happened to him – accidents happen – the question was why was he okay with it, even if he didn't realize he was?

"No, sorry. We still don't have anything on your identity yet. I can assure you, we have all of our resources on it – we will figure it out." Morgan laid a sympathetic hand on his, reassuring him that he was a priority, and to comfort him. She didn't mean to rile his hopes or concerns, whichever he might have been feeling.

She quickly pulled her hand when his expression softened and his smile warmed at her touch. He must've felt it too. What, she wasn't sure, but she saw in his eyes the very emotion that coursed through her. He was a stranger even to himself. She would chalk that up to gratitude on his part, and compassion on hers.

"Guy – it's what Gran calls you."

"Gran?"

"Sorry – Granny Lou – Louise Shaw." Morgan fumbled her way around her words, trying to get herself together. It wasn't like her to be so frazzled and out of sorts. "She thought *hey you* and *that guy* might be impolite. So, Guy it was, err…is." She chuckled, hoping he would see it that way too.

"Guy…" he paused, staring off into nothing as if tossing it around or trying it on for a good fit. "Makes sense, I guess. It's a bit of an unusual situation and it beats the hell out of *John Doe*, I'm not exactly dead. It's a good name – nice to meet you Morgan, Guy." He extended his hand to shake hers and tossed her a million dollar, panty melting smile with a wink to seal the deal. She had to reel in that deep belly twinge and remind herself that he was just a grateful stranger, and not confuse kindness with dirty desires.

She smiled a sweet smile while returning the handshake. *Get it together, Jameson.* "Nice to meet you, Guy."

Grab your copy of, Forgotten! Available on all major retailers!